"Someone in Sandburg might very well be pregnant."

"Ugh," Margaret said. "How could a grown woman, even an Abnormal, want to endure such a condition, and for what, an imperfect child? Where's the logic? It has to be some imbecile," she concluded.

"An imbecile wouldn't be thinking about prenatal care, Margaret," BertRam pointed out. "Let's hope they find her quickly and get her out of your town without any attention being brought to the incident. Someone from your own little community is defying the accepted mode of behavior and risking everyone else's health and welfare."

"And I repeat, for what purpose? To give birth to an imperfect offspring?"

"If there is such a woman in Sandburg, she has to be an Aberration. Let's hope there is no such woman after all."

Natalie stared right through her, actually turning her eyes inward to look at the darkness that clouded her own mind and filled her with fear.

ANDREW NEIDERMAN

THE BABY SQUAD

POCKET STAR BOOKS

New York London Toronto Sydney Singapore

An *Original* Publication of POCKET BOOKS

A Pocket Star Book published by
POCKET BOOKS, a division of Simon & Schuster, Inc.
1230 Avenue of the Americas, New York, NY 10020

ISBN: 0-7434-1270-2

First Pocket Books printing August 2003

10 9 8 7 6 5 4 3 2 1

POCKET STAR BOOKS and colophon are registered
trademarks of Simon & Schuster, Inc.

Interior design by Davina Mock
Front cover photo illustration by John Vairo, Jr.; photo credits:
Pictor International/PictureQuest, Vector Verso/PictureQuest,
Image Network/PictureQuest, Christopher Wadsworth/Photonica

Manufactured in the United States of America

For information regarding special discounts for bulk
purchases, please contact Simon & Schuster Special Sales
at 1-800-456-6798 or business@simonandschuster.com.

For my wife, Diane,
the wind beneath my wings . . .

THE
BABY SQUAD

Prologue

●●●●●●●●●●●●
::::::::::::

Hattie Scranton lumbered up the sidewalk toward the Sandburg Food Mart. Her long legs kept her a good foot or so ahead of the five other women clumped just behind her. They were all so much of one face that it appeared they were wearing identical masks highlighted with blazing, angry eyes, lips white with rage and stretched like rubber bands making their chins so taut they threatened to tear. Their neck muscles strained with each step they pounded into the concrete sidewalk.

Hattie had her long arms extended straight down the sides of her six-foot-one-inch body, her hands clenched into sizable fists for a woman. They looked like small sledgehammers growing out of her wrists which kept her ankle-length light blue dress from flapping. A thin layer of shimmering perspiration pasted her thin, dull brown hair against her forehead.

The beautiful spring upstate New York afternoon had already brought people out of their homes and

businesses in this restored, quaint country community, but the sight of the women drew more ob-
servers. Those passing by in their automobiles
slowed down when they saw Hattie and her group
parade down the mauve cement sidewalk along
Main Street. All of the residents knew something
very significant was happening. Some pulled over
and got out of their cars to follow, gathering like
children behind the fabled Pied Piper. Others continued to watch from a safe distance, their faces
mixed with fear and curiosity. They held themselves as if they expected to hear an explosion at
any moment, their bodies tight, poised.

Hattie and her women were heading directly for
the Sandburg Food Mart. Their gaze was so fixed
on those large glass front doors that there was no
doubt about their destination. Shoppers stepping
out of their cars to go into the supermarket
paused, and women and men loading their trunks
with groceries froze the moment they saw Hattie.
It was as though anyone looking at them became
like Lot's wife in the Bible, a pillar of salt.

All eyes were on what had become known as
Sandburg's own baby squad.

Hattie stepped up to the doors that opened automatically, and then they all entered the immacu-
late, brightly lit supermarket. Once inside, it was as
if Hattie could part the air the way Moses had
parted the Red Sea. Some shoppers who saw her
entrance even imagined they heard the swish and

later would swear they had felt the resulting breeze whip past their faces.

Employees in their crisp white uniforms at the registers became paralyzed, hands holding produce in midair. Conversations at the registers ended. A wave of silence washed over the grand food and produce market. A few shoppers toward the rear by the meat counter didn't realize it and soon found their voices echoing. That brought them to attention. They gazed at one another in surprise and then looked toward the front, where Hattie slowly turned her head, her long neck as stiff as a pole holding a flag of battle, straight, firm, determined. Her eyes panned the market and finally settled on the target: Jennie Marlowe and her pretty seventeen-year-old daughter, Lois.

Hattie's face bloomed into a satisfied smile, the smile of a hunter who had cornered her prey. She lifted her shoulders slowly, priming herself like a cannon being adjusted for the proper trajectory, and then, without any further hesitation, she made a beeline for her targets. The women beside her moved in unison, their heels clicking on the tiles. They remained a respectful few feet to Hattie's rear.

Jennie Marlowe retreated a yard or so, and Lois moved completely behind her, using her mother as a shield.

"What?" Jennie cried out, grimacing and leaning back as if she anticipated being struck. Hattie continued to march right up to her, stopping inches away. Her women formed a wall around them, flanking Jennie and Lois on both sides. Hattie opened her right hand, and Jennie gazed down. In Hattie's palm were two pills.

"These," she said, "were found in your daughter's locker at the school this afternoon after a routine search. Ted Sullivan called us immediately."

Routine searches of student lockers had long been a procedure at Sandburg Central, as well as at most schools throughout the nation. The courts had decided that the lockers weren't student property, and no privacy law applied, no civil rights, no warrants required. This applied to anything on the student's person or anything the student carried once that student had entered the premises of the school.

It was no surprise that Ted Sullivan would discover any illegal drug or weapon. The Sandburg high school principal ran his school with military efficiency. When the bell sounded for class, the hallways cleared so quickly the air itself seemed sucked into the rooms.

Jennie stared at the pills. "What are they?" she asked, and glanced at Lois, who quickly looked down at the floor.

"Prenatal vitamins," Hattie said, her lips contorting to express her distaste even for pronouncing the words. "*PNV* is clearly stamped on the tablets."

Those standing nearby gave audible gasps. A woman loading groceries onto the cashier's table lost her grip of a large can of tomato juice. Its clang echoed like a gunshot through the market. Someone in the rear released a shrill cry.

"Prenatal vitamins? That's ridiculous," Jennie said, smiling on the verge of a defensive laugh. Her lips quivered with her effort to keep cool. She gazed at the pills as if they could leap out of Hattie's hand and sting her. "They don't look like anything. In fact, they look like candy."

"Hardly candy," Hattie said through her teeth. "Ted Sullivan suspected it, and Bob Katz confirmed it at the drugstore not ten minutes ago."

Hattie's words were driven like nails into Jennie's soft twist of lips, which then looked glued against her teeth.

"We called your home as soon as we were told, and Chester told us where you were."

Jennie shook her head vigorously as Hattie continued to speak.

"Of course, she must have gotten them on the black market or from someone else who had," Hattie continued. "Bob is certain of that. He has seen them before and will so testify, even in a court of law, if necessary," she added, directing her cold, steely gray eyes at Lois.

"No," Jennie insisted, still shaking her head. "She has no reason, no call to get that on the black market or otherwise. Lois? Were these in your locker?"

"We know they were," Hattie said before Lois could reply. "She can't deny it."

"Yes," her daughter admitted.

Hattie's eyes grew small, her back and her head arching like a cobra. The tip of her tongue between her nearly clenched teeth moved with nervous excitement, resembling a snake's that could already taste the prey it had cornered.

"How did you get them?" Jennie asked, breathless.

"I traded for them," Lois revealed, looking at her mother but consciously avoiding Hattie's eyes.

"Traded for them? Why? What is this sick fascination you have for everything to do with natural pregnancy?" Jennie practically screamed at her, her lips trembling with both fear and anger now.

Lois was silent.

Jennie turned to Hattie and forced a smile.

"She's not pregnant, Hattie. It's not that. Believe me. It's just this stupid little new fad some of the young people her age are getting into these days. Take my word for it. There's nothing else to it."

"No," Hattie said firmly. "I can't take your word for that."

"What are you saying, Hattie?" Jennie asked, the smile leaping from her face like a frightened bird.

"She will have to come with us to Dr. Morris. Now," she added, punching the word at them.

"This is silly, Hattie. Wouldn't I know if my own daughter was pregnant? Of course, she can't get pregnant. I can show you her NB1 certificate," she said, reaching for her bag. "It's properly stamped and dated at her birth. I . . ."

"She has to come with us this instant," Hattie insisted. "You and I both know," she added, her face so close to Jennie's now that their noses practically touched at the tips, "that there have been plenty of NB1 forgeries."

"Not hers!"

"As well as an occasional aberration caused by an impurity," Hattie added.

Since the middle of the twenty-first century, all females at birth were vaccinated with a substance that prevented their eggs from being fertilized through sexual intercourse. The walls of the egg simply rejected semen and could be penetrated only in a natal laboratory. It was, as Hattie had declared, 99.99 percent effective, but there was always the fear of a female falling into that 0.01 percent.

No one had yet moved in the supermarket. No one wanted to make a sound and miss a word. The people who had followed Hattie and her group gathered outside the door as well.

Hattie stepped back, a cold smile on her face. "What will happen to Chester's insurance business if you refuse?" she asked.

The crimson in Jennie's face began to recede, only to be replaced with a milk-white complexion that looked practically devoid of blood. "It's just wasting everyone's time," she warned, her voice weakening, her lips trembling. One could almost see her bones softening. "It is! It really is!" she cried with desperation.

"It's never a waste of time to protect the image and reputation of this community, not to mention the government subsidies we all depend upon," Hattie countered. "Chester included, because if the people and the businesses he insures go down, where do you think he will go?" she asked with a smug smile.

Jennie nodded, bit on her lip, and then looked at Lois. The inevitable outcome of this confrontation was written into her face now.

"No, Mommy," Lois said. She shook her head vigorously and took a step back.

"You brought this on yourself, Lois. You and that obsession." She turned back to Hattie. "Can we at least finish our shopping?" she asked. "We'll go to the doctor's office right afterward. I swear."

"No. You'll come back and finish your shopping later. Dr. Morris has been alerted, and he is waiting. If you'll notice," Hattie added with authority and confidence, nodding toward the entrance of the supermarket, "a number of concerned citizens are waiting to know the results as well. It's not just what I want. We all take great pride in what we have accomplished, and no one wants to see it lost or damaged. I would hope you would have the same attitude, the same sense of loyalty to your community, Jennie."

Jennie looked at the crowd and turned back to Lois.

"Mommy, no!" Lois cried a bit louder, her eyes like two broken egg yolks seeming to spread into her temples.

"We'll drag you out of here if we have to," Hattie warned, stepping between her and Jennie. "It's up to you," she added. She looked as if she wished it would happen that way.

Lois felt heat in her chest. She glanced at the onlookers. She liked being looked at, liked being popular, but this was already far too embarrassing to take and far more frightening than anything she could remember. She tried to swallow but couldn't and nearly fainted with the effort.

Jennie pushed the cart aside, gazing after it as if it were filled with the family jewels. Instantly, a shelf stocker moved forward to take it.

"I'll keep it to the side," he said, obviously looking for a sign of approval from Hattie. She simply nodded, but it was enough to make him feel important and pump his bloating chest with pride.

"Lois?" Jennie said.

Lois Marlowe stepped forward reluctantly, her head lowered in defeat. As she started toward the supermarket entrance, the baby squad drew around her. People cleared out of their path. Jennie tried to smile. She raised her hands and called to some friends.

"It's nothing, just a false alarm. You'll see. You'll all see," she insisted.

No one smiled.

She sucked in her breath, pulled back her shoulders, and caught up with her daughter.

As they left the supermarket, she began to chant a prayer under her breath.

"Let it not be so. Oh, dear Lord, let it not be so."

One

::::::::::::::

Natalie Ross stood completely naked before the full-length, light walnut, oval mirror in her bedroom and pressed her palms to her abdomen. How much longer did she have before it would show? The home test had been positive. She had bought it on the black market and taken it the moment she had suspected. Of course, there was the strong possibility that the test was inaccurate. Once you went to the underground for something like this, you had no guarantees, but her body was rife with the symptoms: no period for months now, morning sickness, and very sensitive nipples during the onset of her condition. She was even experiencing food cravings, like Jell-O pudding on top of corn flakes. If she figured correctly, she was easily entering her sixth month!

Preston had accepted her explanation for her nausea and vomiting the first time he had witnessed it. She went through a convincing performance, throwing out the leftover chili and warning him not to so much as taste it. She even claimed to have gone to the doctor. Fortunately, Preston had seen this happen only once. The three subsequent times, he had already dressed and gone to work, and she no longer suffered any morning sickness.

Nor had he witnessed any of the food cravings. Sometimes she wondered if he would notice anything dramatically different about her. He was like an absent-minded college professor these days, working harder than ever and often bringing it home either in his briefcase or in his head.

Natalie closed her eyes and concentrated. Her best friend, Judy Norman, told her if you placed your hands on someone and put all your concentration into the effort, you could feel their energy and sense what truly lived within them. She was talking about something far different, of course. She was speaking of honesty, intention, good and evil. Lately, Judy was into all that spiritual stuff. Natalie didn't reject it all. She was skeptical but not resistant. The truth was, she wished it were all true. She wished there were something beyond, some spiritual force that understood her, applauded her, and certainly did not condemn her.

Yes, there's a child forming inside me, Natalie thought, *a true marriage of Preston and me. I can feel it in my heart. It is already part of my very being. I am pregnant. It's not some fantasy. I shouldn't have to concentrate or meditate to search for any sense of her or him within me.*

As a preadolescent, she had always suspected she was not a natal laboratory baby, known as an NL1. The prophylactic material used to make the egg invincible became known simply as NL1. Sometimes she had dreams about inoculations. Where they were given remained vague, even in the dreams. NL1 babies had no need for any inoculations against any of the childhood illnesses, of course, nor did they need flu shots or any of a slew of vaccinations that prevented a long list of maladies, from anemia to any of a number of zoonoses, diseases caught from animals.

If those dreams weren't nightmares, they were memories she was eventually taught to suppress. Suddenly, they were all coming back.

Her parents had done a good job of hiding the truth from her as well as everyone else as long as they could, and afterward, she had performed well herself, knowing that if she weren't convincing, she would be an outcast and certainly not what she was today: the wife of a prominent lawyer with a very promising career as part of a very influential firm.

Naturally born children, now called Abnormals, generally were fortunate if they were able to get menial jobs these days. Certainly, no one with any class or status would even think of marrying such a person.

Her problem, of course, was preventing herself from becoming pregnant. Ever since her menstruation had begun, she'd been on birth control pills, another black market product, this one disguised well as vitamins or sometimes common aspirin. They were even stamped. Who could tell except a pharmacist or a chemist? Certainly not Preston, she thought.

And then it happened.

She bought either a placebo or a pill so old it had lost its effectiveness. Her mother had warned her. Never depend on them. Do what you can to prevent pregnancy. Watch your cycle. Don't make love at the prime times, if you can at all prevent it.

Easier said than done, of course, and now she was paying the price. Or was it a price? Lately, she had been feeling . . . good. The morning sickness had passed, and, if anything, she felt healthier. And then there was the dream, the vision of a child who was completely and actually her own, with no tampering; nothing that was a part of her, a part of who and what she was, had been removed. She believed what the Naturals believed: there was a greater, closer, more symbiotic tie between mother and child. Wasn't that wonderful?

"What the hell are you doing?" Preston asked from the doorway.

She nearly leaped across the room. Rushing for her turquoise velvet robe, she tripped over a slipper and caught herself before she hit the bedpost. Then she put on her robe and flipped her long, thick, reddish brown hair back over her shoulders.

Preston called it her mane. He kidded her about it, but he was quietly proud of her beauty.

"I was trying to see if I've gained any weight, if you must know. Did you have to sneak up on me like that?"

"Who snuck up on you?" Preston asked. He shrugged and crossed to his closet. "Hell, I was making so much noise coming up the stairway, you would have to be in one helluva trance not to have heard. I called to you when I came in, too, Nat. What's up? Why the concern about your weight? You look terrific, as beautiful as ever."

"I felt bloated," she said, and sat at her vanity table. "The doctor says I'm eating too much salt. Why are you home so early, anyway, Preston?"

"Why am I home so early?"

He stared at her. In her mirror, she saw the strange smile on his face, and then she remembered.

"Oh," she said.

"Oh? Is that all you can say? It's just the most important dinner of the year for me. Mr. Cauthers and his wife are taking us out, and everyone at the firm knows when Mr. Cauthers takes you out to dinner with just his wife and himself, it's to tell you that he and the other partners have decided to give you a partnership. I think after seven hard years of proving myself, I deserve it, of course, but I won't take anything for granted these days."

He squinted at her.

"I thought you were just as excited about this as I was. At least, you indicated that when I first told you about the invitation. Hell, you were the one who suggested the restaurant, Nat. How could it slip your mind?"

He looked frustrated, disappointed. Preston was such a good-looking man, with his dazzling dark eyes, Roman nose, and strong mouth. All of his features were perfect, in fact, and he had the self-confidence of someone who knew he was good-looking and impressive. That demeanor had served him well.

"It didn't slip my mind, exactly. I am excited. I just lost track of time, Preston."

"Doing what? Living in one of your fantasy stories?"

She spun on her seat and glared at him. "Just because I spend most of my day writing romance novels, it doesn't mean I'm not involved in other things, too. Besides, I make good money for us, don't I? I thought you respected what I do. I thought you believed there was a role for entertainment, too. Or was that just hot air, Preston? Have you been humoring me all this time?"

Put him on the defensive, she thought. It always worked.

"No, of course not. I just . . . oh, forget it," he said. "I'm taking a shower. Which do you think is better tonight, the blue suit or the brown?"

"I like the three-piece for a dinner like this, especially with the Cautherses."

"Gray, but . . . all right, I'll wear that one," he said, and went into the bathroom.

She stared at herself in the mirror.

She was gaining more and more weight. She could see it in her chin. Soon she would have to resort to the same type of girdle her mother had worn. Like her mother, she wasn't really going to show until she was well into the sixth month, probably, but that was well along. People had premature babies in the sixth month, babies that survived. She could give birth without Preston even knowing she had been pregnant!

What would she do?

She could still go underground and find an abortion doctor. She'd go far enough away and remain anonymous, of course. Preston would never find out if she did it soon.

Or she could do what she had finally discovered her mother had done.

With her husband's blessing, she could go into hiding and have it.

Visions of the baby inside her returned. She could have her very own child, a child who was truly hers and Preston's. Wouldn't he be happy? Couldn't she make him see how wonderful it would be?

A baby who was really all that they were.

The thought made her heart beat faster. She saw a flush come into her cheeks.

She had really begun to make the decision by getting those prenatal vitamins, even though she had told herself she was just keeping the option open.

She gazed at herself in the mirror again, a different, sterner, and more sensible Natalie Ross looking back at her.

Be careful, the image in the mirror warned. *You're tiptoeing over very thin ice.*

You could ruin everything.

Just as in most communities, there was always a nagging rumor in Sandburg that there was a young woman capable of becoming pregnant. Perhaps because of Sandburg's perfect record, its standing in the nation, and its subsequent fame, residents were more paranoid. Stories about Hattie and her squad were infamous. They actually checked a suspect's garbage, looking for evidence of black market products. There was even the story about a young woman they followed for days until they finally planted a pregnancy test in her toilet. Some of the stories were exaggerated, but it was enough to keep most women a little nervous, because even those who knew they couldn't get pregnant feared the fallout of a false accusation. People would always look at them with some distrust even if they were exonerated.

Critical students of history made comparisons to the witch hunts of colonial times or to the red-baiting paranoia about Communists during the 1950s, more than a century ago. An accusation was as damaging as a conviction in all cases. From time to time, such a strong rumor about a woman stirred the day-to-day commerce of the small upstate New York village and disrupted the even flow of courteous intercourse among the inhabitants. The turmoil and the rage wouldn't stop until it was proven beyond a doubt that the alleged suspect was indeed innocent.

However, just about everyone was grateful for Hattie and her baby squad, as they had come to be known. Every businessman and woman working and living in Sandburg applauded their vigilant enforcement of the national decree that had been established once perfect progeny could be created in the nation's maternity laboratories and once the human genome had been perfected. It wasn't simply a law so much as a proclamation, a national desire, its enforcement left up to the local communities, but its encouragement came from rewards in the way of grants and subsidies to those communities with perfect or near-perfect records. Everyone in Sandburg was quite aware of what had happened in Centerville, the next village to the north, when three pregnant teenage girls were discovered.

Three! How could such a thing happen in this

day and age and right under the eyes and noses of the adults and parents around them? The town became a pariah, the stores and businesspeople either had to move or simply had to close, and every citizen and business lost the special government subsidy.

Enforcement of the decrees actually had become a national obsession, and most felt rightly so. Gone forever were all the old childhood diseases, deformed and retarded infants, inherited physical and mental illnesses, cancers, diabetes, multiple sclerosis, Parkinson's, nearly every known malady tied to defective DNA.

But what was even more valued now was the government licensing of all potential parents. One no longer simply got married and had a family. Parenting was recognized as an art, a skill, work that required intelligence and a real understanding of childhood mental and physical development. No one got married because the woman was pregnant anymore. No one resented the children they had and failed therefore to give them the proper care and upbringing. Consequently, teenage crime as it once had been known and feared was practically nonexistent.

The last violent incident of any national note in a public school involving a young person occurred twenty years after the passage of the laws requiring all females to be inoculated against pregnancy. They were given the dosage of NL1 just after

birth. Natural childbirth was quickly becoming an-
cient history, at least for the middle and upper
classes of society.

Literally everywhere, in every public place, were
posters depicting pregnant women in the most un-
attractive ways possible: their faces distorted, their
bellies exaggerated, their lips writhing in pain and
agony, and often one could find a graphic poster
of a deformed child with the words: "Born Naturally. Who wants it?"

Oddly enough, young people such as Lois Marlowe had what Hattie Scranton called "a sick fascination" for natural childbirth despite all the propa-
ganda and enforcement against it. At the moment,
having gone through an embarrassing examination administered by Dr. Morris, Lois wasn't feeling fascinated with anything remotely associated
with the condition. Part of the physical exam was
really unnecessary, such as the vaginal and breast
examination conducted with the entire baby
squad watching, but Hattie wanted Lois to feel as
uncomfortable as possible. Let it be a lesson to
her.

Lois was sitting in the waiting room while her
mother, the doctor, and Hattie Scranton's baby
squad conferred in the office. Her face was still
stinging from the blush of embarrassment and
fear.

The door opened, and she looked up sharply.

"Come in here, Lois," her mother ordered.

She rose slowly, her heart thumping.

"I'm not pregnant, Mama." She was terrified of some mistaken diagnosis. There were all sorts of horror stories about something like that. Even after months and months went by and the woman showed no signs of pregnancy, people still believed she could have been and could have had an abortion. Go and try to live in the community after something like that was spread.

"I know. Come on," Jennie Marlowe said. She looked emotionally exhausted, her hair falling, her face still pale.

Lois stepped through the doorway and gazed at the women who glared at her with such rage she couldn't keep her eyes from sinking to the floor and lowering her head.

"We want to know where you got those pills, Lois," Hattie said.

"I traded for them," she replied in little more than a whisper.

"We heard that. With whom?" Hattie said.

Lois raised her gaze. They wanted her to turn someone in. How would she face the others?

"Why?"

"It's illegal drugs," Dr. Morris said. "You know better than that, Lois."

"It was just for fun, a curiosity. No one did anything with them or had any reason to want them other than that," she argued.

The women simply stared.

"Someone is usually pregnant when she has such a pill in her possession," Hattie said.

"No, no one's pregnant."

"Who gave you the pills?" Hattie repeated, a word at a time, each one pronounced with venom.

"You'll have to tell them, dear," Jennie said.

Lois shook her head. "I can't. It wouldn't be right. Everyone will hate me."

Hattie and the others wouldn't be satisfied with just knowing that. They'd want to know why she traded for the pills, what they were doing with them, and all the other things. The other girls would be afraid that she would name those who had participated in the pregnancy games, for sure. Hattie would want to know who they were. She would have to name names.

"Please, Lois. I'd like to get out of here and go finish my shopping. Just tell them," she added firmly.

Lois shook her head, tears streaming down her face now, each one a little drop of fire.

"If you don't tell us, we'll turn this over to Chief McCalester, and he'll give it to the district attorney, who will get an indictment and have you arrested for possession of an illegal drug. You'll go to jail," Hattie threatened.

Lois's heart was pounding so hard she thought she would faint, but she just shook her head and through her clenched teeth muttered, "I can't. They'll hate me."

"Very well. You had your chance," Hattie Scranton said.

"Give me some time with her," Jennie pleaded.

Hattie glared and then softened a little. "You have twenty-four hours," she said. She stepped toward Lois. "I don't know what's wrong with you young people today. What can possibly be fascinating about something as painful and disgusting as natural pregnancy and birth? Do you know what happens to our bodies, how distorted we get, our faces and legs swollen, our breasts with the sensitive nipples, the morning sickness, all of it, all of that horror?"

Lois nodded.

Of course she knew. Besides the posters, she had seen the illegal photographs and had seen an old medical book with illustrations. She didn't feel it was as disgusting as they all did. What would they do if they learned about those pregnancy parties where she and some of her girlfriends pretended to be pregnant, stuffed their skirts, and paraded about as if they were six, seven, eight, and nine months pregnant?

"You're simply an ungrateful, spoiled bunch, and you'll all be punished for it, believe me," Hattie vowed, convincing Lois that once she told she would be opening the floodgates. She imagined all of them being marched down to Mr. Sullivan's office, all the disgrace and all the anger her friends would rain down upon her.

Hattie spun on Jennie. "Twenty-four hours and no more," she fired at her.

Jennie nodded, reached out to turn Lois toward the door, and marched her out ahead of herself. She didn't speak until they stepped into the street.

"Your father is going to be inconsolable, Lois. You haven't begun to see the full brunt of what's about to fall on your head. Turn around, go back there, and tell them who gave you the pills," she pleaded.

Lois shook her head.

I'll be like Joan of Arc, she thought. *I'll be burned at the stake and become a saint.*

Her mother had no idea how courageous she could be.

She would never tell.

Never.

Kasey-Lady growled and barked and lifted herself up, practically garroting herself with the choke collar and chain. Percy sat arrogantly on a rock just a few feet beyond Kasey-Lady's run, sunning himself. The stray cat was a fighter, strutting with a chip on his shoulder. The truth was, if Kasey-Lady, a purebred golden retriever, did break loose, she would be the worse for it, not Percy.

Stocker Robinson watched from the pantry screen door and smiled to herself. Ever since her mother had found Percy down at the lake and brought him home, Kasey-Lady had been out of sorts. She wanted to be at that cat so much, she cried and whimpered. What filled her with so much hate and aggression? Stocker wondered. She wished she had some of it. Being the chubbiest girl in her senior class at school made her the object of ridicule almost daily. The others spread rumors about her, claiming she wasn't a Natal, that her mother had given birth to her in the garage or some such ridiculous place, grunting and squeezing her out like a tumor, bathing her in blood. They even drew nasty pictures and wrote things on the toilet stall walls about her.

Most of the time, she didn't have the courage to stand up to them. Instead, she looked for ways to ingratiate herself, ways to buy friends.

"I'm going to town, Stocker," her mother called from the kitchen. "You wanna come along?"

"No," she called back. What was she, five years old and supposed to be excited about a ride to town with her mother?

"If Daddy calls while I'm gone, tell him I'm making the pot roast tonight."

"Okay," she called back.

She continued to stand there and watch Kasey-Lady rage. When her mother came out, she chastised the dog, who then lowered her head and retreated until her mother got into the car and drove away. As soon as she had, the dog went back to its barking. Percy yawned and spread out on the rock.

Stocker was suddenly taken with an impish impulse. She went out and knelt down beside Kasey-Lady, who stopped barking and waited patiently for her to pet her and talk to her. She licked Stocker's hand and then glared at Percy, who didn't even show a bit of interest.

"What are you going to do to him, Kasey-Lady? Eat him up?"

The dog seemed to nod.

Stocker smiled.

Then she undid the dog's collar and chain. Once the animal felt her freedom, she charged ahead. Percy stood up quickly, arching his back. The dog growled and circled, snapping at the cat, who lifted his paw and held it poised. Kasey-Lady moved her snoot in and out, snapping, each time just escaping Percy's claws. Then, without warning, the cat leaped from the rock and landed on the dog's back. He tore and tore, and the dog spun and yelped, throwing the cat off. He landed on his feet, hissed, and ran into the brush.

Kasey-Lady whined in pain.

"You a wuss," Stocker cried at her. "Get back here," she ordered. The dog did so and lowered her head as Stocker reattached the chain to her collar. She saw streaks of blood on the dog's coat.

The thing of it was that despite this outcome, the dog would bark and threaten again, and if she were turned loose, she'd do the same thing until she got lucky or maybe lost an eye. Her innate hate either blinded her to reason or filled her with extraordinary courage. It was all how you looked at it, Stocker thought.

The ringing of the phone pulled her attention to the house. Was that Daddy?

She hurried in and picked up the receiver in the kitchen.

"Hello."

"Stocker, it's Betsy."

"What?" she asked. Betsy never called her. She was the only other girl in the class who was as desperate for friends, and it was like admitting she was one rung lower than Stocker if she was the one to call all the time.

"Did you hear about Lois Marlowe?"

"No."

"They found prenatal vitamin pills in her locker and took her to the doctor for a checkup. Now they want to know how she got them."

Stocker felt her throat tighten. "Did she tell?"

"I don't know. Do you know how she got them?" Besty asked with an underlying note of suspicion.

"No. How the hell would I know?" Stocker replied quickly.

"There's going to be an investigation, I bet. Everyone will be called down to Mr. Sullivan's office. I bet whoever knows is going to tell."

"Who cares?" Stocker said.

"I don't know. Somebody," she sang.

"Well, not me," Stocker said, and slapped the phone back onto its cradle.

She sat there a moment, fuming. Kasey-Lady started barking again.

"Shut up!" she screamed, charging back to the screen door. "Shut up, shut up, shut up!"

She felt her throat scratch.

Betsy's words echoed. *Whoever knows is going to tell.* The words rang like an alarm bell in her head.

The tears of pure red rage came on the heels of her marching fear.

Natalie loved the Cherry Hill. First, it was off on its own on a side road no one would normally take, Porter Road. There were very few homes between Sandburg and Route 52 via Porter Road, so the county highway department did little to maintain it. Occasionally, when a pothole grew deep enough to present a potential of car damage, the road superintendent would bring out a crew and patch it. Otherwise, it was as bumpy and cracked as the surface of Mars. After a particularly heavy rain, part of the road would wash away and often flood in low areas.

Yet, ironically, it was this inaccessibility, this special effort it took to get to the Cherry Hill, that made it a successful restaurant and lounge, especially for the well-to-do. The owner-chef, Joachim Walter, was a forty-year-old *cordon bleu* chef who created wonderful German, French, and Hungarian dishes.

The main room looked like the set of Rick's café in *Casablanca*. Along with the famous ceiling fans, there were higher levels for some tables, little nooks for privacy, and a special room for catered affairs. On weekends, the Cherry Hill featured Connie and Tino Planta. He was on the piano, and she sang sultry songs reminiscent of the 1940s and early 1950s, songs filled with romantic lines and promises of love.

Actually, Natalie was surprised the Cautherses had taken her suggestion and chosen the Cherry Hill for this dinner meeting. She couldn't imagine a stuffier couple. At sixty, Bertram Cauthers looked like a man nudging seventy-five, with tufts of yellowed white hair along the crest of his head and larger puffs around his temple and behind his ears. He had birthmarks over his wrinkled bald skull and a complexion that made her think of tissue paper. With a rim of red at the base of his eyelids, his dull brown eyes were always somewhat watery. Tiny veins crisscrossed his bulbous nose. They looked as if they had been scribbled down the sides with a pen. His thick, pale lips were always turned up when he finished his sentences, and there seemed always to be a small bubble of sputum at the corners, something that nauseated and disgusted her.

His wife, Margaret, was almost the same height

at five feet ten, but she was broader shouldered and wider in the hips. She had a small bosom, which made her stomach more prominent. Despite her wealth, she never seemed to get the right hairdresser, because her dyed hair always looked metallic, the strands harsh and thin like metal threads cut and trimmed under her ears. They were swept around too sharply to emulate the latest New York or Paris model. She wore too much makeup, too. Somehow, however, she did still have nice facial features, a small nose, a soft, sexy mouth, and wonderful green eyes.

They were already at the bar when she and Preston arrived. Margaret had a heavy drinking hand. She loved her martinis. The drinking didn't make her belligerent; it made her talkative. She had an opinion about everything, even the newest driveway materials, since her brother-in-law had just redone his.

"Driving up here made me think of it," she told Natalie. "Those bumps and cracks in the road. I swear, I was afraid I'd lose my appetite the way Bertram drives, even with the sensitizing shocks in the Astro Car he's always bragging about. I can't imagine driving up here in a less expensive automobile. Your teeth could be shaken loose."

"I know," Natalie said, laughing, "but I always think it's worth it after I get here."

"Do you? I suppose it is," Margaret said, but not with any real enthusiasm or agreement.

Bertram had reserved one of the tables off to the right, where they could have more privacy. Natalie thought it was too far away from Connie and Tino. She was hoping to get involved in the music and ignore the business conversation.

After they sat and she and Preston were able to order their cocktails, Margaret pounced. It was her usual topic. "When are you two going to break down and order a child? I know you've got the highest approval rating possible, and for God's sake, you work for the firm that has the most influence when it comes to that, Preston."

Natalie glanced at Preston, who fit a smile on his lips like a mold of wax.

"We're getting close," he replied.

"Close? You two have been getting close for as long as I have known you. How long has that been? Bertram?"

"Preston has been with the firm nearly eight years now," he dutifully recited.

"You shouldn't be afraid you won't be able to do your love books," Margaret continued, sipping her martini. Natalie hated that terminology, *love books*. They were romantic novels, not love books. "You shouldn't worry, anyway. Babies are nothing like what they were to take care of," Margaret continued. "And besides, you can afford to have a mother's helper. I did when we were making much less than you two are now."

"Margaret, maybe you ought to let them come

to these decisions themselves," Bertram said softly.

"Oh, they don't mind my putting in my two cents, do you, Natalie?" she asked.

"Well . . ." Natalie looked at Bertram, and his eyes widened. "It seems more like fifty cents."

Both Bertram and Preston roared. Margaret's mouth dropped, and then she, too, laughed.

"That's the nicest way I've been told to shut my mouth in decades."

Connie and Tino Planta began their second set with "The Very Thought of You."

"Oh, I love this song," Natalie moaned.

Margaret glanced back at the singers and nodded. "Sweet," she said.

The waiter brought Natalie and Preston their cocktails.

"I've been waiting for you two to get your drinks," Bertram said. "I want to make a toast."

"Oh, wait!" Margaret cried with a grimace of panic. "I don't have anything left in my glass."

"Well, just use your water for now until you do," Bertram ordered sternly.

"That's no toast," she muttered, but picked up the glass. "Well? What is this toast that can't wait another second, Bertram?"

"To our newest partner, Preston Ross, and his beautiful wife. Congratulations."

Preston beamed, and they tapped glasses.

"Oh, well, that *is* special. We'll have to do it again," Margaret insisted, "as soon as I get a refill."

"Let's do it all night," Preston said, and everyone laughed.

Natalie turned to pick up the last few bars of
the song. It amused her that she was more interested in it than she was in her husband getting
this great promotion. Maybe that was because
they had anticipated and expected it. There was
no spontaneity anymore. Everything was planned,
contrived, designed.

Even Margaret Cauthers overdoing the martinis
was anticipated.

There were no more surprises.

Except the one inside her.

Except that.

Two

∷∷∷∷∷∷

Lois cowered on the bed. Her father seemed to swell to twice his size in the doorway of her bedroom. Anger and rage filled his face like fire pumped into a steel-skin balloon, turning his light complexion crimson and threatening to explode in spontaneous combustion.

"Are you crazy? Don't you know what this could mean? I'll be ruined. We'll have to move. We'll lose everything we have, everything I've spent years and years building for this family, Lois."

He stepped farther into the room and closed the door softly behind him. Her normally even-tempered father suddenly looked like a maddened killer. Her heart wasn't merely pounding. It was raging in her chest, throwing itself against the walls of flesh, a petrified, terrorized organ anticipating its demise.

Chester Marlowe was only five feet nine and barely one hundred sixty-five pounds. He had a shock of straw-yellow hair that, along with his freckles, made him look ten years younger. His boyish charm was what made him so successful as an insurance salesman. How could anyone distrust so innocent a face, with those two soft blue orbs and that bright, sparkling smile with its snow-white set of perfect teeth? Whatever promises this man made were surely done deals.

He held out his hands as if he were begging Lois to be sensible.

"You refuse to tell them? You refuse to give them what they want? You risk being arrested? Who is so much more important than your parents that you would sacrifice our well-being to protect him or her? Who?" he cried.

"I don't want to be a rat, Daddy. No one will speak to me anymore."

"You don't want to be a rat? What do you think you're going to be in twenty-four hours? An angel? A hero? What?" he demanded, now only inches away.

They had just finished reading *Gulliver's Travels* in English literature class, and she was impressed with the section about the land of the giants, "Part Two: The Voyage to Brobdingnag," where Gulliver was the tiny one and ordinary people were gigantic. Every feature of human beings was exaggerated. Their nostrils looked like deep caverns; the skin pores, their smelly breath, all of it was seen in a different light. Exaggeration made them ugly, terrifying. Her father seemed that way to her at this moment. He looked as if he could breathe fire down at her.

"Where did you get those pills?"

"In school," she said.

"I know that. Who gave them to you?"

She hesitated.

His face seemed to liquefy, turn plastic, his mouth stretching, his eyes bulging.

"*Lois!*" he screamed.

She covered her head, expecting a storm of blows, but nothing happened. He stood over her, a black cloud ready to burst.

"I . . ."

"What?"

"I'll get her to confess herself," she countered.

He seemed to deflate a little. "When?"

"First thing in the morning. She'll go with me to Mr. Sullivan's office. I promise. That way, I won't look like a rat."

The reasonableness of her suggestion calmed him further. His face softened. His eyes cooled, and his shoulders relaxed. "You must do this, Lois. You must bring this to an end tomorrow, and you must apologize to the authorities for being so uncooperative, understand?"

She nodded.

"Good. Good," he said, nodding. He started for the door. "There's nothing wrong with having loyalties, but you have to get your priorities straight. Your first loyalty should be to your family, Lois. I'm still a little disappointed in you," he added.

"I don't like being a rat," she repeated.

He shook his head, opened the door, hesitated, and then just walked out, closing it behind him.

Lois waited a moment and then reached for her telephone.

"By the way," Bertram Cauthers said as their soufflés were served, "I understand there was some commotion in your village earlier today."

"Oh?" Preston said, holding his spoon over the chocolate crust. He looked at Natalie.

"I haven't spoken to anyone today except Judy Norman," she said, "and Judy didn't mention anything unusual. After that, I was in Middletown doing some shopping, and by the time I got home, it was time to get ready to go out. I didn't even check my answering machine," she added with a light laugh.

The truth was, she had become immediately involved in her condition.

"We've got one of those annoying, pestering ones," Margaret complained. "You know that digital thing that announces, 'You have messages,' every twenty seconds until you turn them on. Imagine being nagged by a machine," she muttered.

"It's very helpful," Bertram insisted. "When you have a lot on your mind, you can miss important things."

Margaret laughed at him, which annoyed him. "If someone has something important to tell you, Bertram, he or she will do it regardless of your calling them back, I'm sure. Everyone is so worried about their careers and their businesses these days."

"Getting back to what I was saying," Bertram continued, his eyes lingering like two branding irons on his wife's grin and then shifting to Preston and Natalie, "it appears the baby squad discovered a teenage girl hoarding prenatal vitamins in her school locker. They hunted down her and her mother in the supermarket and immediately escorted them out to have her checked for pregnancy. Full physical exam," he emphasized.

"How degrading," Natalie muttered, but no one heard her.

"Really? Who was that?" Preston asked.

"Lois Marlowe, Chester Marlowe's daughter," Bertram replied.

"No kidding. He has most of my insurance. What happened?"

"She isn't pregnant, but there is a good deal of suspicion now. Someone in Sandburg might very well be pregnant."

"Ugh," Margaret said. "How could a grown woman, even an Abnormal, want to endure such a condition, and for what, an imperfect child? Where's the logic? It has to be some imbecile," she concluded.

"An imbecile wouldn't be thinking about prena-

tal care, Margaret," Bertram pointed out. "And besides, I don't think there are many women like
that around anymore, even in a small community
upstate. What do you think, Preston?"

He swallowed his spoonful of soufflé and nodded. "There are a few domestic servants I might
suspect."

"Let's hope they find her quickly and get her
out of your town without any attention being
brought to the incident. Here we are holding a
government contract to review and bring forward
parental applications for licensing, and someone
from your own little community is defying the accepted mode of behavior and risking everyone
else's health and welfare."

"Maybe whoever it is has permission to have a
child," Natalie suggested. "I've heard of variances
granted to some Abnormals under the right circumstances. Right?" she asked Preston with some
obvious hope in her eyes.

"The baby squad would know about that," Cauthers said. "It's so rare, you could count on your
fingers how often that was done in this state over
the last two years," he quickly countered before
Preston could respond.

"And I repeat, for what purpose? To give birth
to an imperfect offspring?" Margaret added. "There
simply are no right circumstances. Wouldn't you
look twice at such an individual requesting such a
variance and wonder if she was all there?"

Natalie glanced again at Preston, who was nodding. "I agree. If there is such a woman in Sandburg, she has to be an aberration or probably an illegal child to begin with, the parents not properly licensed," he said. "Or, as you suggest, Margaret, she is the child of some unbalanced woman."

"If she is married, you have to wonder if her husband even knows," Margaret said prophetically.

"If he does, he should be strung up," Bertram said fiercely. He looked as if he could personally execute the man. "You're going to head up our parental licensing division now, Preston. Stay on top of this situation, and let me know if there is anything we can do. It's your hometown, for crissakes.

"I'm close friends with Chief McCalester. I know we can depend upon him to be discreet if need be. I wouldn't want any bad onus on your village. The fact is, if such a thing did occur, you might very well have to consider selling your home and moving out of there."

"Selling?" Natalie practically screamed. "But, we just built, and . . ."

"Now, now, don't jump the gun, Natalie," Bertram said calmly. "I'm not saying it's all going to turn out that badly. As I said, even if there is some validity to the rumor, we'll do our best to keep it quiet. But I just want you guys to be in on the beginning, so if you should have to sell, you won't be as damaged by the events. You know how quickly real estate values fall when something like this happens in a community these days. Who wants to pay the added taxes and lose the development funds, not to mention the diminished business, the empty stores, and the vacant commercial buildings?

"It just happened in a community in Orange County, Goshen. MicroVenture canceled its plans to build that plant and bring in four hundred employees. You know about that, Preston."

"Yes," he said.

"Think of the developers, the businesses, the investment money already committed and now lost and all because of what was, in this case, four women who defied their baby squad."

He shook his head.

"What the hell is this society coming to? People are never satisfied." He looked up at Preston. "Don't let it happen in Sandburg."

Preston nodded. "I'll be on it. Let's hope there is no such woman after all."

"Whether there is or not, as far as the general public is concerned, there isn't. Get the picture?"

"Absolutely," Preston replied.

To Natalie, he was like some lower officer taking orders like a toy solder.

"Good." Bertram smiled, took a deep breath, and gazed around. "You were right, Natalie, this place is worth the trip."

Connie and Tino Planta announced they were taking a break.

"Oh, poop," Margaret cried, "just when I finished my soufflé and wanted to hear them."

Natalie stared right through her, actually turning her eyes inward to look at the darkness that clouded her own mind and filled her with fear.

Chester Marlowe wore earphones when he watched sports, especially prize fights. Jennie sat reading Natalie Ross's newest romantic tome, *A Sudden Kiss.* She was so entrenched in the story, she could have been wearing earphones as well. Lois easily tiptoed down the stairs and out the rear door of their home undetected. She decided to take her bike and rolled it out of the shed. Then, as soon as she was on the street, she got on and pedaled in computerized high gear all the way to Highland Road before turning off to meet Stocker Robinson at the Lakehouse, for many years a favorite rendezvous for high-school lovers.

Lois half hoped to catch her current boyfriend, Miles Parker, in the throes of lovemaking with Selma Prince as well. She was very suspicious of her boyfriend these days. He had good excuses for not being able to see her too often, and she caught him talking with and looking at Selma frequently. She expected him to break it off with her any time now, and she certainly didn't want to be the one dumped. She could kill two birds with one stone here tonight. It was almost that

more than her father's rage that motivated her to
meet Stocker at the Lakehouse.

Spring in the Catskills was rarely as warm as it
was this year. There were summers without nights
as humid and tepid as it was tonight. By the time
Lois reached the clearing where most of the young
couples parked their cars, she was drenched, her
blouse sticking to her arms and between her
breasts, the sweat trickling down to her navel. She
had her midriff exposed and wore a pair of knee-
length khaki shorts, a pair of pink sneakers, and
no socks. Her light brown hair was loose, some
strands falling over her eyes.

It's time to trim my bangs, she thought as she
pedaled down the hard gravel drive. Now that it
had taken so much effort to get up here, she wondered why she had even bothered.

I'm so stubborn, she told herself. *I do things
even I don't really want to do, but I do them because someone tells me not to, or I don't do them
because someone tells me I have to do them.* She
had already admitted this weakness to Ms. Letter-
man, the school psychologist, recently, but it was
one thing to recognize it was true, another to do
something about it.

She had certainly been terrified when Hattie
Scranton and her coven of witches came tearing
across the supermarket toward her and her
mother, but she couldn't believe she was going to
be forced to take a pregnancy test. How degrad-

ing, and yet the way everyone was looking at her made her feel important. To be sure, her name was on everyone's lips tonight, and tomorrow she would be the center of attention at school.

She had considered simply giving them Stocker's name. Who cared about Stocker Robinson? But it would just make her look as if she had been frightened, and then, despite the person she was betraying, she would still be considered untrustworthy. Who would take a chance confiding in her? She was seriously worried about the other girls who had been fantasizing about natural birth. Surely they would all be afraid she was going to turn them in, too. Then they would stop inviting her to their homes and to their parties. Why, Miles could even use this as a good excuse to dump her, and everyone would congratulate and console him for it. *See if you could get a new boyfriend so easily then,* she told herself.

No, this was easier, better. Let Stocker take the fall. Who cared about Stocker Robinson?

Surprisingly, there were no automobiles here. The lake looked deserted. Even the frogs were in hiding, she thought, until she drew close enough to hear the water pop where they jumped in after bugs. Over to the right in the deeper woods, she could hear an owl. It sounded more mournful than usual. Unfortunately, there was no moonlight tonight, even though the sky was almost cloudless.

The light of the stars was enough to silhouette the old Lakehouse hotel, a shell of a structure closed down so long ago, when the Catskills resort world had died, it was practically a historical site. The wood was gray and moldy with age, and every piece of metal on it was rusted. All the windows had been blown out by boys practicing their pitching. The front door hung on one set of hinges like a wounded soldier leaning against the wall. Persistent and determined weeds grew up through the portico floorboards, and shutters dangled like loose black teeth. The hollowed-out building gave her the shivers.

She stopped and lowered her feet to the ground, the bike between her legs. Where the hell was she? *The quicker I get this over with,* she thought, *the better.*

"Stocker!" she called.

"Yeah," she heard, and spun to her right to see her stepping out of a dark shadow cast by the large old oak tree.

"What the hell are you doing? How did you get here?" Lois asked quickly. She didn't see her bike or any vehicles.

"Walked," Stocker said, approaching.

"Walked?" Lois looked at the thick bushes and forest between Stocker's house and the lake.

Stocker held up a long, black flashlight. "I got a path." She jerked the flashlight toward the bushes. "Been here lots of times," she added. "I've even been here when you were here with Miles a few times."

"What do you mean?" Lois asked, the answer coming even before she finished her question. "You spy on people? That's disgusting."

Stocker shrugged. "It's better than my daddy's X-rated sensorama DVDs." She smiled. "Go on and ask me."

"Ask you what?"

"You know, about Miles and Selma Prince."

Lois tightened her grip on her bike handlebar. "What about them?"

"They were here." She turned on the flashlight and directed the beam to a corner of the clearing. "Right there. She started by giving him a blow job. I couldn't miss seeing it. He sat on top of the front seat, and she got between his legs . . ."

"Shut up. You're lying."

"I don't care if you believe me or not. What the hell is so important that I had to meet you here? I had to, you said," she added, spitting the *t* in *to*. "Well?"

"I got caught with the pills you gave me for the digital video of Open Heart."

"They stink. I thought they were better than Anal Causes, but they don't come close. You can have it back."

"I don't want it back, stupid. I came here because I was caught with the pills. Didn't you hear anything about it? Are you so far out in the boondocks?"

"I didn't give you those pills," Stocker said coldly.

"What?"

"I don't know what you're talking about, Lois."

"You can't say that now, you idiot. Suki, Clair, Shirley, all of them know you traded them for Open Heart."

"They didn't see the trade. It's their word against mine, and they're all your friends, not mine. Of course, they would lie for you. Who wouldn't believe that?"

"Stop it, Stocker. I protected you today. I could have been arrested!"

"There are no pills in my locker," Stocker said. She felt like Percy teasing Kasey-Lady. Lois looked so frustrated, flabbergasted, chafing at the bit. She laid down her bike carefully and turned to her, assuming the demeanor of Mrs. Rosner, their stern English teacher, her chin tilted upward, her eyes looking down her nose.

"I want you to go to Mr. Sullivan tomorrow morning and tell him you gave me the pills." She took a breath and continued. "That way, I don't have to turn you in, and everyone will respect you for coming to my aide. You'll be heroic, and everyone will go to bat for you," Lois said in the tone of a negotiator.

Stocker stared at her. "I don't think so," she replied after a moment. "Is that it?"

"You don't think so?" Lois dropped her hands

to her waist. "If you don't do it, I'll turn you in. I swear."

"Like I said, it's your word against mine. We're not even close friends, Lois. Who is going to believe such a story? I'll just say you're using me to protect someone else, one of your close friends. I know what some of you do at your precious secret parties. Everyone will believe you're all ganging up on me, trying to make me responsible for something I had nothing to do with. I'll cry, and I'll swear, and I'll invite them to come to my house and search my room.

"You never invited me to any of your parties, did you? I wasn't part of the PYPC, Pretend You're Pregnant Club, was I? Isn't it more logical that one of them, one of your own, gave you those pills?"

Lois started to speak, but there were no good and powerful words to challenge Stocker. The frustration exploded when Stocker turned and started toward the bushes.

"Thanks for wasting my time," she muttered.

"Hey!" Lois ran forward, reached out, and grabbed her shoulder, spinning her around. "Don't be an idiot. I'll tell them you got the pills from your mother, who found them in someone's house," Lois said, coming remarkably close to just how Stocker had gotten them.

The truth was, she had gone with her mother to clean the Rosses' house, and she had been the one to find them along with those articles on natural pregnancy. Her mother didn't even know, or, if she did, she kept it secret. Being an Abnormal herself, it was understandable her mother might be sympathetic, but Stocker couldn't care less. It was just the excitement of finding it all and then using what she had found to help make herself a little more popular at school.

"So?" she bluffed.

"So? So no one will want to hire your mother to wipe a glass dry. That's so."

Stocker stared at Lois. Finally, she had said something that rang an alarm bell.

"Just go into Mr. Sullivan's office before homeroom tomorrow, and tell him the truth. I'll say you told me you found them in a paper bag someone dropped on the street. Yes, that's a good story. They'll believe that, and they'll leave us both alone."

"That's so ridiculous. Only an idiot would believe that."

"They'll believe it."

"How do I know you would even say such a stupid thing? How do I know?"

"You don't know," Lois said confidently. "But you better do what I say, and I better not hear that story about Miles and Selma from anyone. After homeroom," she repeated, and turned to go back to her bike.

"Lois," Stocker said.

Lois turned into the downward motion of the

swinging heavy black flashlight. Stocker struck her right across the left temple. The blow was so hard it spun her head around, which twisted her at the waist. She stumbled, blood already starting to drip.

"Wha . . ."

The thought flashed through her head that she had been struck, but the rest of her battled to deny it. How could Stocker have had the nerve? *This can't be happening to me. She wouldn't dare, and besides, I have homework to finish.*

She turned back, and the flashlight came down with even more force, cracking her skull. There was a very bright light and then an instant darkness. This time, when she spun, she sank as well, her legs folding. Her body slammed against the gravel, shuddered, and then grew still.

Stocker stared down at her a moment and then kicked her in the stomach. Lois's body didn't even twitch.

I'm like Percy the cat, Stocker thought. *Go on, come at me. I'll show you.*

The stream of blood trickled out of the deep gash on Lois's forehead and drew a line over her once beautiful cheek. Her mouth was open enough to remind Stocker of a dead fish, just like the dead fish she occasionally found on the shore of the lake.

She knelt down and looked into Lois's glassy eyes.

"I'll tell anyone I want about Selma and Miles. It just so happens, I don't want to tell, but I would if I wanted to. You hear me?"

She slapped Lois's shoulder with the flashlight, and then she stood up and looked out at the lake.

Someday, she thought, she would be in a car parked here with some boy, too. Maybe with Miles, even.

Someday.

But not tonight and not tomorrow.

She started away, her head down until she reached the bush, and then, without so much as glancing back, she disappeared down the path she had long ago beaten from her house to lovers' lane, where she got the best sexual education.

The water popped with the sound of frogs, oblivious to anything but the struggle to feed and be satisfied before the morning's sunlight.

Three

::::::::::::

"**W**here is that girl?" Chester Marlowe demanded. He looked up impatiently from his newspaper. Jennie turned from the electric range, where she was preparing his scrambled eggs, and looked toward the kitchen doorway. She glanced at the clock.

"I don't know," she said.

"Well, get her down here. Before I go to the office, I want to be sure she's going to do what she promised."

Jennie sighed deeply and turned down the flame under the pan. "I thought teenagers today were supposed to be easier on parents," she moaned.

"Most are!" Chester exclaimed.

She glanced at him as if he were crazy and started out and up the stairs.

"Lois," she called. "Lois, it's time to come down to breakfast."

She reached her daughter's bedroom door and listened. The stillness triggered a small alarm that quickened her heartbeat. She reached for the door-knob.

"Lois?"

She opened the door and faced the still unmade canopy bed. Lois knew that making her bed and straightening her room was the first order of business after she woke in the morning. The room looked as messy as it had been in the afternoon yesterday.

"Lois?"

She walked to Lois's bathroom. No shower was going, no water running, no lights were on, and Lois was not in there, either.

"Lois?" she asked, turning in a circle. She hurried out of the room and checked every other room on the floor, even her and Chester's bedroom to see if Lois had gone in there for some reason, the bathroom as well. She was nowhere. Her heart wasn't beating quickly now; it was thumping with a slow, heavy downward beat, pounding her chest like a sledgehammer. She hurried to the top of the stairway. For a moment, she couldn't get up enough breath to shout.

"Chester!"

He stepped into the doorway of the kitchen and looked up at her. She was shaking her head.

"What?"

"She's not here."

"Not here? You mean, she already left for school?"

"I don't think so," Jennie said. "The room's un-made, and the bathroom looks unused."

"Unused? I don't get it," he said, refusing to un-derstand. He charged up the stairway, rushed past her, and looked into his daughter's bedroom.

Jennie came up beside him. "I think she ran away last night," Jennie said meekly, anticipating the thunder and lightning to follow.

"Ran away? Christ almighty," Chester moaned. "We'll be absolutely destroyed."

He turned and hurried back down the stairway to the wall phone in the kitchen.

Chief Henry McCalester had just walked into his office when Chester called. The sentry moni-tors were all going full blast. His deputy chief, Charlie Krammer, was at the console looking very attentive. Henry wasn't fooled. He knew the twenty-seven-year-old ex-army soldier often dozed off at the controls, but he was otherwise efficient and still in excellent physical shape. He had served with the military police for the last few years of his army stint and had a very good police-man's demeanor.

McCalester himself was a big man, well over six feet four and nearly two hundred fifty pounds. His upper body was muscular, his neck thick, but he had a pouch and rather poor posture. His shoul-ders turned in and down as if he were always carry-ing a backpack full of bricks. He had dark eyes and heavy eyebrows. His lips were thick, with a distinct turn downward in the corners when he was in thought. He shaved every morning, but his beard was so heavy he had a shadow over his chin by midday. Despite his poor posture, he could be very intimidating, especially to high-school students.

With the crime rate appreciably down in most regions of the state, the county executives had cut the police force nearly in half and depended upon the state for most of the more involved investigations. Each small community had a police chief and two deputy chiefs to help maintain a semblance of twenty-four-hour surveillance and enforcement. Henry McCalester, at fifty-one, was one of the senior members of the department and almost as well known as the county's chief supervisor.

"Quiet night," Charlie remarked. He looked at the phone when it rang. Henry answered it.

"McCalester," he said.

"My daughter's missing, Henry," Chester blurted.

"Who is this?"

"Chester Marlowe."

There was a deep, long pause.

"Missing? How do you know that, Chester?"

"She didn't use her bathroom this morning. She always takes a shower after she wakes up, and she hasn't been downstairs for breakfast. I feel it in my gut, Henry. She must have snuck out last night. We went looking for her this morning, and she's gone!"

"Sure she's not on her way to school?"

"Pretty sure," Chester said. "You heard about the trouble yesterday?"

"Yes, yes, I did," McCalester said. "I was hoping it would all be over today."

"Me, too."

"All right," McCalester said, sounding tired already. "I'll take a ride over to the school, Chester. You going to be at home?"

"I guess I have to wait for your call," Chester said. "Jennie is beside herself." He was even more so, but he didn't want to admit it.

"I'll be as quick about it as I can," McCalester promised. "Don't panic yet," he added. *But if she did run away*, he thought, *you couldn't panic enough*.

Chester cradled the receiver and turned to Jennie.

"He's going over to the school to see if she's gone there."

"She hasn't," Jennie said firmly.

"Where has she gone?"

Jennie shook her head and bit her lower lip. Her eyes were like lights on an old-fashioned pinball machine. "I don't know. I just don't know that girl these days."

"I should have taken her by the back of her neck and marched her out of the house to the police station last night," he said. "I shouldn't have believed her. I should . . ." He paused and looked at Jennie. "They make our kids invulnerable to disease and all sorts of physical imperfections. Why don't they make them obedient?"

"I have a feeling they never will," Jennie replied.

She sank into a chair, then realized the scrambled eggs were exploding in the pan, and jumped up.

"Oh, the eggs!"

"Who cares about eating now?" Chester mumbled. He circled his hands around his cold mug of coffee and stared down at the black, syrupy liquid.

All they could do was wait and watch the clock as it ticked toward their future, each movement of the second hand chipping away everything he had accomplished and built.

The students in Mark Downing's senior homeroom sat quietly and looked up at Chief McCalester, who stood next to Mr. Downing and whispered occasionally.

The bell had rung, and the halls were now empty. McCalester turned to the students. "Anyone here know anything about the whereabouts of Lois Marlowe this morning?" he asked.

No one spoke. He panned the room slowly, lingering on every face for a split second.

"Anyone here speak to Lois Marlowe last night?" he followed.

Again, he was met with silence.

"This is rapidly becoming a very, very serious police matter," he continued. "If anyone has any information about Lois and is not forthcoming, he or she could be in big trouble for withholding that information. Well?"

The only thing that broke the silence was the scraping of Stocker Robinson's chair as she pulled herself closer to her desk.

"Okay," he said, and turned to Mr. Downing. "Thank you." He glared at the students one more time and then walked out of the room, the back of his neck tanned with a blush of frustration and rage. One or more of those little bastards knew something, he was thinking.

He went directly to Ted Sullivan's office. The principal's inner office door was open, and the moment McCalester appeared in the outer office, Ted Sullivan was up from his desk, beckoning to him to come right in. He did so and closed the door behind him.

"She didn't show?" Ted asked.

He had his hands on his waist. He was a former basketball star for the Sandburg Comets and had served for five years as head coach after graduating from college and becoming a physical education teacher. He then returned to college, achieved his administration degrees, got married, and was lucky enough to have it all achieved just as the former principal, Ward Young, was about to retire. That was nearly fifteen years ago.

Ted and his wife, Marian, didn't apply for a parenting license until they had been married five years. They had a daughter, Sophie, in the fifth grade, and they were thinking of applying for a second child, a boy they wanted to name after his father, Eugene. Henry McCalester had been a policeman in Sandburg when Ted was in high school, so despite his status in the community, he still showed Henry deep respect.

"Nope."

"Any of the other students know anything?"

"If they do, they're not saying."

Ted nodded, his eyes growing small. "I'll keep on it."

"Good. I have to call Chester Marlowe."

"Go on. Use my phone," Ted said, stepping aside.

"Thanks."

Neither Chester nor Jennie moved when the phone rang. They looked at it and then at each other first. Chester rose slowly, took a deep breath, and lifted the receiver. He listened after saying hello.

"I understand," he finally said. "Thank you."

He hung up and turned to Jennie, shaking his head.

"Where would she go?" he pondered.

Both their sets of parents were thousands of miles away, his in Europe and hers in California.

"As far as I know, she didn't have much money," Jennie said.

"Makes no sense."

She nodded. "What are you going to do, Chester?"

"Go to work, I guess, and wait there. I'll just go out of my mind here." He went to the garage door. "I'll call you if I hear anything and you do the same."

"Right," she said. She thought they should kiss, they should hug, but he walked out too quickly. She heard the garage door go up, and she heard him start the car and back out. She waited to hear the garage door come down, but she didn't. After a few more moments, curious, she went to the door to the garage and looked in. The garage door was indeed still up, and Chester's car was idling, but he wasn't in it.

"Chester?"

She stepped into the garage and walked toward the car. Just as she reached it, he came around the corner of the house.

"What?" she demanded, holding her breath.

"The shed door was open. Her bike is gone!"

They stared at each other for a moment, and then he hurried back into the house to call Mc-Calester. He felt almost as if he were betraying his own daughter, but this wasn't even slightly humorous anymore. In a matter of a few hours, the whole community was going to know. His only hope was to bring it to an end as quickly as he could.

Natalie hadn't been able to close her eyes until nearly three in the morning. The debate that raged inside her had her turning like a roast on a spit.

She forced herself to remain still when Preston groaned and asked her what was wrong.

"Maybe the food I ate was too rich," she suggested.

"Take something," he advised, and she rose with the opportunity to get away from him for a while and think. She went into the kitchen and did get a glass of milk. Ever since she had concluded she was pregnant, she took great care about what she was going to eat or drink. No one even noticed how little alcohol she had consumed at the dinner. They were all too involved in their conversation, and Margaret was only concerned with what she had to drink, not Natalie.

It would be horrible to go through with this and have a child who was somehow deformed or undeveloped because of something she had done. No, the child would have to look and act as perfectly as one of those mass-produced in the Natal Production Laboratories.

After hearing that conversation at dinner, how could she even still be considering it? Such a revelation about herself would end Preston's career in a New York minute and send her reeling into a maelstrom of disgrace from which she would never return. What would she have accomplished except their destruction?

On the other hand, if Preston saw it the way she saw it, he could become very excited about it and supportive. Together, they could find a way to accomplish it, couldn't they? Preston was so resourceful and brilliant. Look at what he had accomplished with his life already. It was not out of the question to envision him as a statewide political candidate in a matter of a few years.

She had always felt he loved her more than most husbands loved their wives these days. He was passionate, gentle, and, most of all, really a romantic. He loved her candlelight dinners, the music, all the things she would do to make their lovemaking cozy and special. He enjoyed watching old movies with her and actually had tears in his eyes when Humphrey Bogart and Ingrid Bergman said their goodbyes on that airstrip in Casablanca. Wasn't he always kidding her with "Here's looking at you, kid"? Why, if anything, he would probably bawl her out for keeping it from him all this time. There was no need to sneak around. How could she even think he would give her up because she fell into some unfair and distorted terminology such as an Abnormal? Was there anything abnormal about her? How many women in this community, in this whole county, were as attractive and as intelligent as she was?

She should go right back into that bedroom, wake him, and confess it all, she thought. For a few moments, she was actually on her way, and then she paused and thought. He would be too groggy and too confused to understand and be supportive. It was something that she had to prepare. She had to set up a nice dinner, his favorite wine, the candles lit, some music, and then she would tell him, and he would reassure her. They would never be more in love than they would be at that moment.

Was she a foolish romantic to think so?

She refused to believe it. She knew her man, knew how hard and how long he had courted her and how important it was for him to win her love. When he finally had proposed, he had looked as if he would shatter like brittle china if she refused. How could she have been such a trophy, so sought after, and not hold on to that endearing love?

We're special, she thought. *Everyone envies us. They see the magic between us, how it's not only lasted but grown stronger and stronger. All eyes are on us when we enter a party or a banquet. It's easy to see the adoration and the jealousy in their faces and feel like celebrities. We are celebrities. We star in our own movie every day of every week, every week of every month.* That, too, she was sure, was what brought Cauthers and his partners to the realization that they had better make Preston an offer now, before it was too late, before another firm appropriated him and all that came along with him, which surely meant her and their marriage.

Confidence brought her back to the bed, and finally, after a little more thought, she closed her eyes and got some restful repose. She overslept, however, and by the time she woke and turned to

look for Preston, she realized he was having breakfast. She could hear the monitor in the kitchen
nook rattling off the Wall Street report. She rose,
washed her face with cold water, and put on her
robe. He was nearly to the door when she entered.

"Good morning. Sorry I overslept," she said.

"It's all right. I've got a lot to do today. You
must have been dead to the world. You didn't even
wake when the phone rang."

"The phone rang?"

"Uh-huh. Bertram. That man gets the news a
few seconds before it happens, I think."

"What news?"

"That girl he was talking about last night, the
Marlowe girl."

"Yes?"

"Her parents reported her missing this morning.
She was supposed to turn in the person who gave
her the prenatal vitamins."

"That was definite? They were prenatal?"

"Absolutely the real thing. There's a police
search under way. Bertram's worried about it exploding the story. He said he feels like the little
boy with his finger in the dyke. I'll call you later,"
he added, gave her a quick peck on the lips, and
scooped up his briefcase as he reached for his
sports jacket. "Oh, I guess you should call Judy
Norman and set up our celebration dinner with
them."

She nodded.

"Looks like another unusually hot day," he called back.

She heard the door to the garage open and close. She still had not moved from the kitchen doorway.

Something was tickling the back of her mind. It was like having an itch in your skull. There was no way to scratch it off.

She finally turned and went back to their bedroom. A cold sensation began at the base of her spine. This fear that was building was surely unfounded. It was simply part of the paranoia anyone in her condition in this society today would have to feel. Ridiculous, she told herself, but nevertheless, she went to her walk-in closet and located the key to her jewelry case, which was not well hidden. She always left it on the dresser top. Once she opened the case, she lifted the top tray and looked at her pamphlets about natural birth and her two pill bottles. One was her now useless birth control pills, and the other was her prenatal vitamins. She plucked the bottle and opened it, turning it to spill the pills onto her palm. Only three came out.

A sharp sting shot through her heart with electric speed and nearly took her breath away. She shook the bottle and turned it over, and then she put her forefinger in and felt around. That was it? Only three? At minimum, a half dozen or so were missing. When she was down to six, she would always get more.

What did this mean?

Who could have taken them? Who would come into my closet and look through my jewelry?

It can't be.

I'm mistaken, she told herself, even though she couldn't see how she was. She had to believe that.

The alternative was terrifying.

It was hard to swallow and catch her breath just thinking about it.

She put it all away quickly and went to the phone to call her source.

I just need more, that's all. I just didn't keep good track of it.

That's all.

Please.

That's all.

Without any confidence, she accepted the theory and went forward with all her hopes and plans as if none of this even mattered.

Am I a foolish romantic? she wondered.

So what? I have to be to write what I write. It's not a fault.

Four

Butch Decker sat in his New York Power and Electric bubble-cab truck and reached for his lunch pail. He had gotten the order to check the line on Wildwood Drive twenty minutes ago and had driven up to pole 7001 as he was directed to do, but it was his lunch hour, and the thirty-eight-year-old lineman treated his lunch hour with a religious sanctity. They'd have him working straight through the day without a break if they could.

The antiquated lines on this side of the community should have long since been buried, especially when the Internet, digitals, video phones, and health options with blood-pressure checks and blood and urine analysis through sensiphone chips had been added, but the loss of real estate value, the decline of the resort community, and the desertion of buildings and even some homes put the region pretty low on the totem pole.

His grandad used to love to say, "The squeaky wheel gets the oil."

Well, that was still a very accurate adage, especially when it applied to work done on people's utilities. The more complaint calls they received at the central office, the farther up the ladder the complaint rose. Practically no one complained about this zone, Butch thought. If the central office had anything else for him to do, even a routine signal check, he would not be here today. That was for sure. As Grandad would say, "You can bet the bank on it."

He unwrapped his sandwich and stared at it a moment. Wasn't Vikki supposed to make him a sandwich out of that meat loaf they had last night? He was looking forward to it. It had been delicious. This looked like . . . damn, another liverwurst, and just because she had found that great buy on the sandwich meat at the supermarket last week. Great buys meant whatever it was would be coming out of his ears as well as his rear for days and days.

He unscrewed his thermos and took a long gulp of the cold, fresh lemonade. He had made that himself with the lemons his sister had brought back from California. A little too tart, he thought, and shook the thermos to stir up the sugar. He sipped it again, smiled to himself, and went to bite his sandwich. Liverwurst or not, he was hungry. After he took the first bite, he sat back and stared ahead at what he knew to be the old Lakehouse. It wasn't much different from the way it was when he was just a boy throwing rocks through the windows with his buddies.

I'm surprised no one's come up here and burned it down, he thought, but then he thought no one had it insured anymore, so what would be the point? The fire department would take its damn time coming up to put it out, thinking it would be easy because they could pump water from the lake and . . .

He stopped thinking and sat up. The bubble cab had tinted windows but provided a nearly three-hundred-sixty-degree view of everything. It was set higher up than most vehicles, too.

Was that a bike on the grass? He gazed harder. Yes, it was a bike, and not some old rusty thing, either. It looked like one of those very expensive ones with the computerized shifting. Who would leave a bike like that just lying there? Suddenly, his mind reeled around a possibility. He knew people saw this clearing and this view of the lake as some sort of lovers' lane. It was that when he was a teenager himself. *Someone's probably at it in the grass,* he thought, *humping away in the weeds.* They were so high, thick, and wild here, even with his perspective from the cab, he couldn't see over them or through them.

But young people should be in school now, he realized. Was it two kids playing hooky and then playing nooky? He laughed at the possibility. Maybe someone's mother borrowed the bike. Might be even a better sight, he thought, and laid down his sandwich. Slowly, as quietly as he could, he opened the door of the cab and stepped out.

Billy Prater would be jealous as hell. Butch had just recently told him about the Cornfield woman up at Devine Corners basking naked in the sun. All he did then was look down from the pole, and there she was as plain as day, nude, sprawled, her legs bent at the knees. He nearly dropped his tools.

"You oughta take a camera out with you," Chuck Stackhouse had said. "Never saw anyone as lucky as you when it comes to stumbling on things like that."

Billy grunted. "Maybe he's lying," he said.

"Maybe, but even so, it's a good one. I like hearing lies like that," Chuck replied with a laugh that originated somewhere in his belly and came up like a rolling tin can because of his smoker's cough.

Butch moved with the grace of an Indian through the brush, pausing to listen and then walking forward as if he were walking on air. Years of hunting rabbit gave him that skill. He was about to catch two human rabbits at it, he assumed, and parted some tall weeds to peer ahead.

When he saw her, her back was to him, and for a moment, he thought a young girl had just decided to take a nap. He stared and realized there was something not right. She was far too still for a nap. He cleared his throat loudly, but she didn't turn or lift her head, so he kicked a stone in her direction. It rolled inches from her head, but still she did not move.

Troubled now, he walked toward her.

"Hey," he called. "Are you all right, miss?"

Her immobility filled the caverns in his chest with ice water. When he stood beside her, he saw the bloodied temple and the glassy look in her eyes. A line of ants had begun to invade her open mouth, most likely harvesting any remnants of any food in her teeth. A few were coming out of her nostrils, the brown marching line so thick it looked more like a shoe lace.

The sight turned his stomach. The little liver-wurst he had eaten rose like an angry beast and filled the back of his throat with an acid that made him cough and choke until he started to heave. He turned away, ran down to the lakeside, and knelt by the water, dipping his hands in to scoop the cold, clear liquid over his face.

He caught his breath.

"Christ almighty," he moaned. "Poor kid fell off her bike and got killed."

He rose slowly and made his way back toward his truck, avoiding the corpse. When he got into the cab, he reached for his intercom and raised the dispatcher. It was Selby Davis, Tommy's wife. Tommy was another lineman, but they worked different shifts so one or the other could take care of

their six-month-old. After nearly nine years of trying, they had finally been licensed to become parents. She had just taken her shift.

"Call Chief McCalester for me, Selby," Butch
began.

"Why?"

Selby had to know everything, he thought. She
might as well work for the county newspaper.

"I'm up at the Lakehouse at pole 7001. There's
a dead girl here, lying beside her bike. Looks like
she's been dead awhile."

"Oh, my God."

"I'll wait for him."

"Okay. Oh, my God."

He sat back, glanced at his sandwich, and then,
remembering how sharply it had risen in his
throat, reached down, plucked it off the seat, and
tossed it like a Frisbee as far and as hard as he
could into the weeds.

Lucky she didn't make the meat loaf, he thought.

It would have been a waste.

The applause resounded in the lobby of Cauthers,
Myerson, and Boswell. All of the secretaries and
paralegals had come out the moment the elevator
opened and Preston stepped into the offices. There
was a monitor over the elevator door that showed
who was in the elevator coming up to their plush
offices in the new Towers Building in Monticello,
New York, the county seat. It was actually the

tallest building in southeastern upstate New York, rising to forty stories with a restaurant atop called Sky Porch. Cauthers, Myerson, and Boswell had their own lunch table reserved at the south-side window with an expansive, breathtaking view of what were known as the foothills of the Catskills.

From the expressions on the faces of the personnel, it was as though they had all been greeted that morning by a marquee that announced Preston's promotion to partner or even as though they had advance notice before he himself had been told. His secretary, Rose Walters, stepped forward and presented him with the first gold-bordered business card that read "Cauthers, Myerson, Boswell, and Ross."

"Congratulations, Mr. Ross," she said, her eyes beaming like candlelit crystals, "from all of us."

He gazed at the card and smiled at Rose, who at fifty-four was often like a mother to him. His own parents had died four years ago in a tragic train wreck, one of the nation's worst in twenty years since the advent of the bullet train. They were on their way back from their Florida residence when the laser guidance system went down. His mother had always been terrified of air travel, no matter what the safety records. How ironic, he often thought. Maybe it was true that when the clock ran out, it didn't matter where you were or what you did about it.

"Thank you, Rose. Thank you, everyone."

They surged forward to shake his hand, embrace him, and pat him on the back.

He felt as if he had just won the New York City Marathon. It took him nearly ten full minutes to get to his office. For a while, he just sat there staring out at the view of the expanding community. Northwest of the city was the new airport with the most modern controller equipment and four landing strips capable of handling international flights, the state-of-the-art heliport, and the terminal that took passengers on the bullet train into Manhattan. Around the airport, business had bloomed, including restaurants, hotels, and one of the three licensed Las Vegas–style casinos. Even in bright daylight, its never-ending neon stream of enticements could be seen.

The whole picture reminded him of a documentary he had seen about the inside of a beehive with its queen being serviced by lines and lines of drones. Everything that had been constructed around that airport depended on it for its life.

Off to the right were the fifteen thousand acres of the hydroponic farm, producing enough vegetables for the entire Hudson Valley, as well as exporting to the north and west of the state, New York City, and Long Island. The community was a bed of activity, with its environmentally acceptable automobiles moving in a constant metallic stream over the new double-level highways and wide state roads.

I'm a partner, he told himself. *I'm a full partner.*

He felt gigantic, growing, exploding with new power and promise. This was the most prestigious and influential law firm in the tricounty area. They had taken over the entire thirty-eighth floor, and Bertram was negotiating to seize space on the thirty-seventh as well. To be part of all that expansion and development, to be a major player in it, was quite an accomplishment in so short a time. He was truly the wunderkind of the local legal community.

There was a knock on his door, and a moment later, Ross entered carrying a basket of fruits, nuts, and candies the secretarial staff had bought him.

"Everyone is just so proud of you, Mr. Ross," Rose said when he displayed his surprise. "If I heard it once, I heard it twenty times. They all feel like they're moving up the ladder with you."

"Thank everyone for me, Rose. Really. This is very nice. But," he said, turning to his desk, "I'd better get my nose in my work before I let my head get too big."

She nodded. "Mr. Cauthers sent over the files for the parentals and asked you to give it priority."

"Oh?"

She nodded at the table at his left. He hadn't even noticed the pile of folders when he entered. His mind was still in the clouds.

Parentals were submitted by couples to apply for children. Cauthers, Myerson, Boswell, and now Ross was a firm that specialized in representing such applicants before the review boards. They had become so well known and trusted that once they accepted a case, it was almost sure to be approved. He had assisted in at least forty by now and knew the drill. What it amounted to was sticking your nose into the most private aspects of a married couple's lives and going over every detail of their existence with a fine-tooth comb so there would be no surprises at the hearing. By the time he or one of his partners went before the review board, they could practically recite their clients' DNA.

There were a number of instances where a red flag would raise a concern and result in them rejecting the case. The couple either had to try another firm, which didn't hold much hope, reapply when the problem was fixed, or give up. That often led to a divorce, and then the family relations division of Cauthers, Myerson, Boswell, and now Ross would be involved on a different level.

He knew of at least two instances of this that had resulted in violence, one spouse murdering another because of a rejection. Juries were reluctant to sentence the perpetrator to death and even balked at life without parole, especially female jurors if the defendant was a woman. It was almost an unwritten justification for homicide or, at least, quite understandable. In the eyes of many, when a married adult was unfit for one substantial reason or another to be a parent, he or she was unfit to live. Once again, Cauthers, Myerson, Boswell, and now Ross were involved in their criminal division. They had never lost a client to either the death penalty or life without parole. A number were already out of prison and remarried, some even reapplying for children.

Preston moved the pile to his desk after clearing it off and opened the first case. Someone else who was just promoted to a partnership would revel in it all day, go to lunch early, drink and celebrate and get less than zilch done, but not him, not the wunderkind. He'd work harder today than he had worked yesterday, and tomorrow he would work harder yet.

He was well into his third hour when he heard a soft knock and looked up to see Bertram Cauthers entering his office.

"How are you doing, Preston?"

"Good. I think I have four positives already," he said, patting the pile. Positives resulted in a larger fee for the firm.

"Fine. I'm afraid I have some terrible news. It's going to bring a great deal of scandalous attention to your little community, Preston."

"What?" He sat back in anticipation.

"That girl, Lois Marlowe, the one with the prenatal vitamins . . ."

"Yes?"

"Dead."

"What?"

"It looks like a homicide. McCalester called me ten minutes ago. A detective from the state CID is coming down."

"Oh, no."

"Looks bad. There'll be a great deal of attention on Sandburg with everyone conjecturing that there is an Abnormal who might just have done the dark deed. Hattie Scranton is calling her squad together. Everything is going to be accelerated. The general consensus is it's some aberration or clandestine Abnormal. More motive to cover up disclosure, perhaps."

Preston shook his head. "I can't imagine who," he said.

"Maybe you should talk to Natalie about some of your friends to see if she has any suspicions. I wouldn't want either of you associating with such a person. All we need is to have something like that picked up. Imagine what it would do to our credibility as the premier legal analyzers of parentals."

"Yes, I understand," Preston said, shaking his head. "McCalester had no leads?"

"He's not equipped to run a murder investigation, but with the state boys swooping in, I don't expect it will be long. Anyway, I'm sure it will pass in time. It's just a bad black mark on your town. I know how fond Natalie is of your home, but I wouldn't look down on a move. In due time, of course. You don't want to do anything to draw any more attention to the situation."

"Absolutely," Preston said.

Bertram smiled. "Damn sorry to have something unpleasant occur on your special day, Preston. Why couldn't the murderer have waited one more day, huh? Don't let it put a damper on your celebrations. Take your wife out, enjoy, and celebrate."

He nodded at Preston's files.

"Sorry to interrupt. Talk to you at lunch," he added, and left the office.

Preston turned the next page of the file he was reading, but his eyes slid off the page, and he stared for a moment at the closed door. Then he called Natalie on the video phone. It rang and rang, and then the machine voice answered and gave directions to forward the call to a cellular. He pushed the numbers and listened as the cellular answering machine came on.

"Where are you? Why aren't you working on your new novel this morning?" he asked first, unable to hide his annoyance. He was always annoyed when he couldn't reach her with all these methods of communication tying people together. "There's been a terrible incident in town. If you haven't heard yet, call me."

He thought about the Normans and remembered they were scheduled to go to dinner to celebrate with them. Bertram Cauthers had made him paranoid, however, and suspicious of everyone. Judy and Bob Norman were into their parental years. They, too, hadn't yet applied.

Why not?

What if it were Judy?

Natalie's best friend.

"Damn it, Natalie," he muttered after the phone clicked off. "Where the hell are you?"

Natalie had permitted Judy Norman to pull her away from her Wordsmith and her new novel for an early lunch at the Cliff House in Spring Glen. The cozy little restaurant had a patio under glass that was built on a promontory overlooking the Sandburg Creek. Today it would be absolutely breathtaking, Judy had said.

"Besides, who wants to celebrate with our husbands only? Let's have our own celebration, just the two of us. They'll just get into talking politics and bore the panties off us."

Natalie couldn't help but smile. Judy made her feel good. She was always so bubbly and up, eschewing depression, ducking and bobbing around and under people who were "containers of negative energy." She assured Natalie that these people only brought you down, ruined your own karma.

Her husband, Bob, wasn't as outgoing, but he was generally a very calm, centered man who rarely complained. What she liked about the Nor-

mans was that they never argued in public, never
brought their personal problems to a dinner date
or any other event, and were always very consider-
ate of each other and the people they were with.
Contentiousness, dark moods, little annoyances
didn't dominate. They had a sweet, youthful aura
about them.

Bob Norman was a good-looking six-foot-one-
inch man with a trim build and a graceful manner.
He had inherited his father's very successful furniture business, but he had brought his own creativ-
ity and energy to it and expanded it threefold.
They had one of the nicest homes in the community, built on a knoll with a lake on the property.

Judy was thinner and smaller than Natalie. At
times she looked almost childlike, but she had
beautiful almond eyes, rich dark brown hair that
she kept trimmed at her collarbone, and a smile
that simply made everyone feel better about themselves. It flashed on and off like a digital camera
light. Before she and Bob married, she had
worked for an accounting firm and was getting
her own CPA license, but after they courted and
married, she went to work at Norman's Elegant
Furnishings and ran the accounting department
there instead. Natalie always felt they resembled a
team more than she and Preston did.

On at least two different occasions over the
past month or so, Natalie was on the verge of revealing her condition to Judy. She was, after all,

her best friend and probably, next to Preston, the only other living soul she trusted in this community.

Judy never seemed as fanatical as most of her other female acquaintances when it came to Abnormals and natural birth. The worst she had ever said about it was she couldn't imagine herself carrying a nine-pound infant in her small frame.

"I'd be bent over like an old lady," she claimed, and laughed.

They had other topics that interested them, anyway. Judy was a good reader, and Natalie used her as a proofreader, looking for her reaction first when she had completed one of her novels.

"Sometimes, often," she said, her eyes twinkling like Christmas lights and that little dimple flashing in her left cheek, "I wish I lived back in the 1950s. You make it sound so wonderful in your stories, Natalie. It's like that old movie we rented, *A Summer Place*, remember? There's a palpable sense of the passion we don't get in our films today. Everything's so . . . perfect. Understand?"

"Exactly," Natalie had said, happy someone else could feel what she often felt about romance and love and marriage. Maybe that was why she had come so close to revealing her condition to Judy. Today, she thought, she would.

"You look so thoughtful," Judy said, reading her instantly when they had sat at the table in the Cliff House. "Almost as if you're worried sick about something, Natalie. Why would anyone whose husband just got the promotion yours got be worried about anything?"

The waiter interrupted them with a rendition of the specials. As soon as he left, Natalie turned back to Judy.

"I'm not worried about Preston's promotion as such," she began. "You're right. It's wonderful, everything he's ever wanted."

"You both wanted," Judy corrected.

"Yes, that's true. Both of us."

"You once told me, Natalie, and you wrote it in *Heart Strings*, that for a marriage to work, the husband cannot be happy unless his wife is happy, and vice versa, right?"

"You're right. Of course, yes. I really believe that," Natalie said. Why shouldn't she? In general, wasn't her marriage really predicated on that premise?

She had met Preston in what she considered an old-fashioned, romantic way. Having a dull time at a mixer that involved her school, NYU, and Preston's school, Columbia Law. She had been bored from the get-go and detoured herself onto a patio. She had a great view of the New York City skyline with airplane lights blinking against the stars and a magnificent full moon.

Most of the young women her age had opted for the Matchmaker, a computer system that analyzed thousands and thousands of people and spit out the perfect match-ups. Whether it was just good public relations or what, the statistical results supported a nearly 98 percent success ratio and, more important perhaps, bragged about a 100 percent success record when it came to the couples applying for parental licenses and children.

Once, many, many years ago, parents actually matched up their children and arranged marriages. Supposedly, that had a significant success ratio, too, but nothing like The Cupid computer. Slipping through the rather large cracks was anything that even remotely suggested what she would characterize as romance. If you were told the person who had been scheduled to meet you was your best chance for a perfect and successful relationship, why worry about candlelight and music? It was a fait accompli almost before the first words had even been spoken.

This had always bothered her more than it did her girlfriends. Divorce had become such a fear because it had dramatic ramifications on chances to have a second marriage and children. Wasn't it better to have the best possible setup? Love was really a fantasy, anyway, right?

Wrong, Natalie thought with every part of her being. She actually was sickened by all the devices used soon after the beginning of the twenty-first century to bring young people together: dating games, television shows, restaurants that had special singles evenings putting eligibles at the same tables, Internet companies that promised compatibility—all of it contrived, plotted, moving people about as if they were all . . . predictable.

That was it, she thought. That was what made romance possible—spontaneity, unpredictability, surprise. She had always been an excellent English student, a good writer, and a rabid reader, especially of old books now treated as curiosities, as if America were practically primitive only twenty-five years ago.

"They say that when the moon is full, people are more passionate," she had heard a man say from behind her. She turned and looked into Preston's face for the first time, the glow of moonlight electrifying his eyes. "Think that's so?" he asked with that wry smile of his that teased and taunted. He was truly a flirt from the start, and she loved every minute of it.

"So do I," Natalie heard Judy say. It interrupted her musing.

"What?"

"I believe what you wrote about marriage, what makes it successful."

"Oh. Yes."

"You're in such deep thought, Natalie. I just know . . . oh, isn't that Carol Saxon?"

Natalie turned as a dark brunette entered the restaurant accompanied by a rather officious-looking bald man in a blue suit. The waiter led

them to the table next to theirs, which deflated
Natalie instantly. Carol Saxon was one of Hattie
Scranton's baby squad members, a busybody who
enjoyed invading other people's privacy. She had
the facial features to fit such a personality: a long,
pointed nose; two large, protruding eyes; and a
harsh, sharp chin that looked like something she
could use to open gift boxes. Like some of the
other women in the squad, she had a manly demeanor about her, too, Natalie thought. She
walked with her shoulders back, strutting, glaring,
always looking angry.

"Hi, Carol," Judy said as they drew closer. Judy
could be friends with a cockroach, Natalie
thought, or at least be pleasant to one.

Carol nodded. The bald gentleman pulled out
her chair for her and then sat.

Judy turned and twitched her nose as if to ask,
What's that terrible stink? Natalie stifled a laugh.

"This is Martin Borrick," they heard Carol announce, and both turned back surprised. "Mr. Borrick is a deputy reviewer on the county's baby acquisition board and a state investigator for subsidy
assignments."

"Oh, how busy you must be," Judy said with a
smile.

He nodded, pressing his rather feminine lips together.

"Especially today," Carol said, "as you must
know."

"Today?" Judy turned to Natalie, who couldn't help but look away. "Oh. You mean that business with the Marlowe girl and the pills?"

"That and what happened, yes," Carol said.

"What happened?" Judy asked, her eyes wide. Natalie turned back to them, her heart beginning to pound.

"They found the girl this morning. She was murdered, her head bashed in. Up at the Lake-house."

"Oh, my God!" Judy cried. "Murdered?"

"You can imagine what that means for our little community. Mr. Borrick is here to help us salvage the situation. We can thank Hattie Scranton for that."

"Yes," Martin Borrick said, his voice betraying a slight lisp, "You are all indeed fortunate to have someone as dedicated as she is. We would hate to see her community besmirched by some pregnant Abnormal and a criminal one at that."

"You mean you think the killer is a woman?"

"Of course," Carol said. "Who else could it be but someone who was trying not to be revealed? And last I heard, men don't get pregnant."

"How terrible," Judy said, ignoring her caustic tone. She turned back to Natalie and shook her head.

The waiter brought their mineral waters and lemon. "Have you decided what you'd like for lunch?" he asked them after he served the drinks.

"Oh. I'll have shrimp salad," Judy said quickly. "Leave out the anchovies."

Natalie stared at the table. Her appetite was completely gone, but she didn't want to reveal that. "Me, too," she said.

"You love anchovies," Judy said, smiling.

"What? Oh, yes, with the anchovies."

"Very good, ladies." He took back the menus and left.

Natalie sipped her drink.

"So," Judy said, leaning in toward her, "why are you so worried, so distracted, Natalie?"

Natalie shot a glance at Carol Saxon. The woman looked as if she were listening in on their conversation, but she always looked as if she were eavesdropping on other people's discussions. Nevertheless, it made Natalie nervous, very nervous.

"I . . ."

"Yes?"

"I don't know what to get Preston. As a celebration gift. I thought we could maybe go to Saks after lunch," she quickly replied.

"Oh. Oh!" Judy cried. "I have a great idea for you. Did you see that new briefcase with the built-in cellular, computer, and Web screen?"

Natalie shook her head.

"You can get it engraved, too. The date and everything. How's that sound?"

"Perfect," Natalie said.

"Good. You had me worried for a moment. I

thought you were going to tell me something absolutely dreadful. Like," she said, nodding toward Carol, "we haven't heard enough dreadful news for one day. Who needs any more?"

Natalie nodded and smiled. "Yes," she said. "Who needs any more?"

Five

:::::::::::::

Ryan Lee stepped out of the CID jet and stood for a moment on the tarmac, gazing at the small but plush mountains that surrounded the Monticello airport. In his right hand he carried his investigator's bag of goodies. It looked like an old-fashioned doctor's medical bag, but his military-style haircut, his department-issue sunglasses, and simply his official-looking demeanor told even the most dull perceiver that this was no doctor, not in any medical sense.

Although Ryan had never been in this specific community before, he had been in the southeastern New York region twice on an assignment for the state's criminal investigative division, but only to assist a senior officer and to do what he categorized as gofer work: "Go for this, go for that."

Finally, he had been given his own assignment, handed something with real responsibility to do. It had taken him almost a year more than any other candidate and trainee, but he was well aware of the reason. He was, after all, the naturally born child of an Abnormal and thus considered inferior. It was the primary reason, despite his test scores and his achievements in preliminary training, that the Federal Bureau of Investigation still rejected him, and there was no way to employ an antidiscrimination law. The Supreme Court had ruled fifteen years ago that taking the method of birth into consideration was not discrimination in any pejorative sense. It was the right of any employer to choose the best-qualified personnel, and that applied to government employers as well. Natals were by definition superior to what were now derogatorily referred to as Abnormals.

Ryan's father was Chinese, and his mother was French. He had the classic Eurasian face, with striking dark eyes and the sort of high cheekbones models coveted. Asians were the most resilient group when it came to fighting for natural childbirth. His father had inherited that determination. Ryan liked to believe it was because he had a greater sense of heritage, a greater need to keep himself tied to his ancestors, but even most Asians had fallen in line after a while. He was truly an exception now, and he had to pay a price for that.

For Ryan Lee, becoming part of the state CID wasn't a terrible degradation, however. It was still a highly regarded police entity. The division of criminal investigations provided local police departments throughout the state with expert detectives. In some circles, it actually had as impressive a reputation as the FBI.

Just after the beginning of the second decade of the twenty-first century, the burden for investigating murders and other serious felonies was taken off county and town police departments and shifted to the state police. It was logical to assume that no county or small city, could finance the education and development of a detective division sophisticated enough to practice modern crime-solving techniques.

The NYSCID, as it was known, was educated and trained in a special facility resembling the FBI school at Quantico. Preliminary testing to qualify for the vigorous training quickly culled those who would have little or no chance at success. Ryan had scored at the top of his group and, at the CID school, always remained in the top 10 percent. However, once his background was revealed, his superiors always had the same reaction: they anticipated a breakdown, failure, the inability to contend with pressure whether it be physical or mental. He never failed them, and slowly, over time, he emerged as what they grudgingly called an anomaly.

He proved just as effective and as efficient in the field as any Natal. Finally, he was called into the command office and handed this case: the apparent murder of a teenage girl in a small Catskills community. For him, more than any other officer in the

CID, failure probably meant the glass ceiling. He would go not a step further in his career, and he would even be encouraged to back up and look for a lower-level police position. He had nightmares in which he saw himself directing traffic.

At six feet two, firm, muscular, and athletic, Ryan had an impressive presence the moment he stepped onto a crime scene. He had a dark complexion with a strong, masculine mouth to complement his strikingly piercing eyes and high cheekbones. At school, he was affectionately called Captain Abnormal. In short, no one looked more the part, even the young men who had been born in the Natal laboratories with high IQs and genetically created physiques that rejected too many fat cells and were as easy to mold as children's clay.

Ryan's voice had a thick timber, but he could be underestimated because of his seemingly aloof demeanor. The truth was, he not only heard every word spoken to him but read the nuances in the rhythm and tone of the speaker, his or her posture, the smallest eye movement, even a flick of the tongue. People, especially potential suspects, were truly like open books to him. He scoured every aspect of their being and targeted anything that triggered his own suspicions. He was an observer's observer. It was as if Ryan Lee had a sixth sense when it came to crime detection, and this wasn't something that could be programmed, even in a genetic lab. It fell into the realm of talent.

Despite his achievements and his apparent emotional armor, Ryan was sensitive to critical eyes, to those who he knew expected him to fail. His CID psychologist accurately diagnosed his obsession.

"You want not only to be successful, Ryan, you want to prove you're just as good as, if not better than, the Natals. In your case, that extra motivation gives you an added edge. You'll hammer harder, turn over more rocks, sniff deeper cracks, go one more step than most of the trainees here. Just don't let it destroy you," he admonished. Then, with a smile, he added, "Ironically, you could lose your humanity faster than the rest of us."

The warning took a seat in the front row of his thoughts, but it didn't slow him down, not yet. He was still on that mission, and this was a prime opportunity toward completing it.

He drew a long, full breath and walked toward the police officer there to greet him. The policeman was accompanied by three women.

"Henry McCalester," he said, offering his hand.

"Ryan Lee, fifth level, CID."

"Glad you're here. This is Hattie Scranton and two members of her committee."

"Committee?"

"We're the Sandburg baby squad," Hattie said proudly, even arrogantly.

Although Ryan knew there were such groups in various cities and towns throughout the state, none of them had any real official sanction. They were the closest thing to old-fashioned vigilantes, and professional members of law enforcement were not happy about them or supportive. However, everyone recognized their political influence in their communities.

"I see," Ryan said.

"We asked Chief McCalester to let us accompany him to meet you today so you could fully understand what's going on here."

"Oh? What is going on here?" Ryan asked, noting how quiet and subservient the policeman was in their presence.

"It's a particularly nasty situation. The day before, this same girl was found with prenatal vitamins and pulled in by our baby squad to be examined."

"Was she pregnant?" Ryan asked quickly. It would hardly surprise him to hear that someone had battered an Abnormal to death.

"No, we believe she stole those pills or got them from someone who is, and you know what that can do to a community," Hattie replied.

"I see."

"We hope you do see. We'd like to bring this to as quick a conclusion as possible."

The woman looked as if she had a backbone constructed out of steel and oil running through her veins. The only colder eyes he had ever seen were the eyes of the dead.

"Those are exactly my sentiments as well," Ryan said, gazing around as if he couldn't wait to get out of this place.

"Everyone is looking at everyone else, everyone who is of the age to become pregnant, I mean," Hattie continued, not satisfied with his response. "A natural birth on top of this would be devastating for our community. We're here to see that doesn't happen."

Ryan winced but didn't clear his smile. No one had told the local police or anyone else about his own background. He could thank Lieutenant Childs for that, he thought. He was giving him a chance to prove himself in the field without any added baggage. Besides, if no one knew he had been born naturally, no one would hold back his or her thoughts, especially these women, Ryan concluded.

"I understand," Ryan said as firmly and convincingly as he could.

"We hope you do. We are going to make ourselves available at all times during this investigation. Chief McCalester knows how to contact us, and we'll do all we can to solve this as well."

Ryan reluctantly nodded.

"We welcome, no, we expect you to utilize us," Hattie concluded. She paused as though she believed her words had to sink well into his brain before she could leave. Then she glanced at McCalester and turned away.

Ryan and McCalester watched the three women walk to the terminal.

"They won't be looking over your shoulder,"

McCalester said. Ryan was about to smile when McCalester added, "They'll be *on* your shoulder."

"They haven't been on the crime scene, have they?" he asked.

"No," McCalester replied. "Not yet."

"I don't care if they want to parade around and show off their power, bullying people in your community," Ryan said, "but the moment it even looks like they'll compromise a murder investigation, I'll make them wish they were investigating the black market for dogs and cats instead."

McCalester laughed. "I'll be right behind you, about half a mile," he honestly admitted.

"Has the ME been to the murder scene yet?"

"Everything's waiting on you, detective. That's the procedure."

Ryan grunted. How many times had he seen the procedure adjusted to fit the egos of local authorities?

"Let's just get right to it, then."

"Sure."

"Tell me about the girl," Ryan ordered, avoiding any small talk. CID officers as a type didn't bother being overly polite. Once launched, they were robotic military machines. It was expected. People were going to jump when he made a demand, and he didn't want to do anything to give anyone any doubts about him or his abilities.

McCalester had so much to say, he talked almost the entire trip. Despite the size of the growing community, Ryan wasn't surprised at how much Henry McCalester knew about Lois Marlowe and her family. He had been brought up in a town not much larger or more populated than Sandburg and remembered how much everyone knew about everyone else. So much of what was once considered private was public when it came to people's histories. Employers had a right to view their candidates' health and physical records, including their genome descriptions as well as their entire education and behavior records. It was easily accessible. What weren't were the small nuances, the little things only small-town people knew about one another. When a wife complained about her husband's snoring or a husband complained about his wife's cosmetic bills, it was pretty common knowledge in a very short time.

Historically, people became accustomed to personal revelations years and years ago. One by one, the privacy laws were abandoned in the name of the public good. Big Brother was in your face at plane and train stations, even by remote from taxi cabs. Sociological historians argued it was the natural progression of things. Ryan had seen some of the vintage television programs archived in which people on talk shows described the most intimate details of their marriages, their family lives, their own eccentricities. Nothing seemed very sacred by the end of the twentieth century, so why worry about your prospective employer getting access to your personal history? The word *private* had almost dropped out of the lexicon.

"I roped off fifty meters in every direction," McCalester told Ryan as soon as they started up the gravel road to the lake. It was the prescribed procedure, and he wanted Ryan to know he was far from some small-town, bumbling policeman.

"Good. Anything resembling a weapon?"

"Not that we could see immediately, but remember, we just protected the crime scene," Henry made clear. He knew the CID hated local police authorities poking around before they had arrived.

"Right."

Butch Decker was leaning against his truck, talking with Carl Osterman, Henry's other deputy chief, when Henry and Ryan drove in. They stopped talking and looked toward the patrol car.

"That's the guy who found the body," Henry quickly explained.

Ryan nodded, grabbed his bag, and got out. He stepped forward, first to take in the environment before he even began questioning Butch, who looked at Henry and Carl and then, along with them, watched Ryan look first at the bike and then gingerly step around Lois Marlowe's corpse. As McCalester claimed, nothing had been disturbed. The ants were still feasting. Ryan looked down at the lake and turned slowly toward the clearing behind and to the right.

"Kids are always coming up here to park. It's a

regular lovers' lane. Been that way a long time," Butch offered without any prodding.

Ryan glanced at him, the short but intense look scrutinizing enough to make Butch nervous.

"Call the ME," Ryan told McCalester, who nodded at his deputy to go to the car.

Ryan then knelt at the bike. He lifted it with a small steal rod he drew from his inside jacket pocket and studied the frame for a very long moment before lowering the bike again.

"All right," he said, approaching Butch. "Tell me about the discovery."

"The discovery?"

"Finding the girl," Ryan snapped back, his eyes so fixed on Butch he had to swallow and glance at McCalester.

Did they think he had something to do with this?

"I just, I mean, I just came up here on a work order. Pole 7001," he stammered, "and started to eat my lunch first when I saw the bike."

"Not the girl?"

"Not from back here. Look for yourself if you want. Go sit in my truck," he said defensively. "You can't see her even sitting up there."

"But you did see the bike?"

"Right, and I wondered why it was there, so I got out and went to see, and that's when I saw her."

"What did you do then?" Ryan asked.

"I . . ." He looked at Henry. "I got sick for a minute and went down to the lake. Then I hurried back to the cab and called dispatch to get hold of Chief McCalester."

"Do you know the girl?"

"No."

"Did you touch her or the bike?"

"No. Hell no. I lost my lunch over that," he said, nodding toward the corpse.

"Did you see or hear anyone in this vicinity at the time?"

"No."

"Show me where you walked exactly," Ryan ordered. Butch did so, avoiding looking at Lois Marlowe. "Okay," Ryan said. He turned back to the crime scene.

"Okay?" Butch looked at Henry. "Does that mean I can go back to work?"

"Sure, Butch. Go back to work," McCalester told him. "We know where to find you if we need to find you."

Butch looked at Ryan, who was back at the bike. Then he opened his truck and started to take out his tools. He wanted to get this over with quickly and get the hell away from here. Probably for good, considering what would come to mind every time he turned toward this place.

Henry joined Ryan a moment later. He was kneeling at the bike again. After a moment, he looked up.

"No one hit her while she was on it," Ryan said. "This bike was laid down softly. Not a scratch on it, not the tiniest of dents." He stood up and looked at Lois Marlowe's body. "She definitely came here to meet someone, most probably a female."

"How can you tell that?"

"Look at the footprint next to the body." He pointed it out with his steel extender. "Whoever it was knelt beside her after she had been knocked down. When people squat, they put more pressure on the balls of their feet. You can see that here. The foot size would suggest either a small boy or a woman, and I just don't think this is the work of a small boy," he added, nodding at Lois's battered skull. "The victim is at least five seven, five seven and a half. The angle of these wounds suggests someone at least that height, if not a bit taller. There's a definite downward motion," he continued, using his steel rod again to point to ripped tissue and exposed bone.

Henry's eyes widened. "If you told me the killer was pregnant, too, I'd think you were some sort of magician."

Ryan didn't smile. "She's not light of foot," he said. "Look at the depth of the prints."

He opened his bag and aimed what looked like a small flashlight at the shoeprint indentations. It flashed a pulsating laser beam, and then Ryan turned the instrument and read some information off the small glass screen.

"Imitation-leather soles, chemical description pinpoints it to those primarily used for sneakers, because of the synthetics used, isolated to Rockers, a very popular brand."

He reached into his bag and produced a hand-held computer with a small microphone in its base.

"Sandburg, New York. Soft shoes, Rockers," he dictated.

Seconds later, words scrolled on the screen.

"Krupps Shoe Palace, Monticello Pavilion Mall, East Broadway, is the closest dealer. According to the description here, it's marketed primarily to teenagers but not solely. Apparently, it's their most recent style of sneaker."

"You think it might have been a pregnant teenage girl?"

"It's certainly in the realm of possibility," Ryan replied dryly. He gazed around.

"But . . . how would a pregnant teenage girl go on the black market for prenatal vitamins?" Henry asked. "She would have to have her parents' cooperation," he thought aloud. "That would center us on any Abnormal with a child. Why would they do it, though? Why would they take such a risk? Eventually, they would be discovered. It doesn't make sense to me," McCalester decided, shaking his head. "How about you?"

Ryan stared at him a moment. "I'm not saying it's a teenager. Lots of women buy these so-called young miss styles. The worst thing we could do is jump to any premature conclusions. Remember, a journey of five thousand miles begins with a single step," he replied.

"Huh?"

"You've got to make the small steps first before you get all your questions answered, Chief Mc-Calester. All we want to do at the moment is decide the direction," Ryan added, and turned back to the corpse.

"How do you decide that?" McCalester asked.

"She'll tell us," Ryan said, nodding at Lois Marlowe.

"She'll tell us?"

"The dead talk," Ryan said. "We've just got to listen. For now, take me to the hotel. I want to get settled in, make some calls, connect with my forensic center, and coordinate with the local ME after he makes his on-site examination. I have him down as Dr. Gordon Howard, correct?"

"Yes. He should be here in ten minutes, if you want to wait."

"No, no need to look over his shoulder. I have what I need at the moment."

"There are a number of television and newspaper people already hovering about. Just warning you," McCalester added when Ryan raised his eyebrows.

"Field officers from the CID never speak to the press. It's SOP they call the public relations officer at our central offices. I don't go through any local public relations office, either. You are aware of that, I'm sure. Tell whoever is worried that I'm a descendant of the Sphinx."

"Huh?"

"No one's ever gotten it to reveal a thing. Don't you know what I'm talking about?" Ryan asked with a small smile of incredulity when McCalester registered total confusion.

"Yes, of course," McCalester said, a little crimson with indignation. "All I'm doing is giving you some head's up," McCalester added, almost in a tone of whining.

"Thanks," Ryan said, but not with any real sincerity.

Henry looked at Carl Osterman, who shook his head with concern.

It was written on McCalester's face: this wasn't looking good. Possibly a pregnant teenage girl whose parents were part of the conspiracy to have a Natural, and here, under his watch. No, this wasn't looking good. It wasn't looking good for this community at all.

Wherever Natalie and Judy went, the chatter was about the murder of Lois Marlowe. The moment a sales girl or anyone heard or saw they were from Sandburg, it was brought up. For the first time since she had heard of the killing, Natalie considered the possibility that someone else was pregnant in Sandburg. The word out was that it could even be a teenage girl who might have committed the crime. Maybe it had nothing whatsoever to do with her missing pills. Maybe it was as she had considered: she simply had miscounted.

Very quickly, this became a hope, even though it made her feel guilty to have it, to wish for it to be so. Another pregnancy in the town would take all attention from her problem, she thought. It would serve as a good diversion for her as well. She needed that. She had to stop thinking about this, even for a few hours.

She and Judy went to Saks, bought the gift for Preston, and then went their separate ways to prepare for the celebration dinner. Bob had made reservations at Soy-Hoy, a fun Chinese restaurant in South Fallsburg that had private rooms with beaded portals. It was so authentic one could easily imagine entering a virtual reality travel machine and choosing Peking or Shanghai. Like most good restaurants these days, ambiance was almost as important as the food. It was a complete experience, with the restaurant running like a show. Customers felt as if they had stepped into a movie, complete with Suzie Wongs and Charlie Chans. They even had the Dragon Lady at the front desk, along with Jackie Chan and Bruce Lee look-alike waiters and an evening's performance of Chinese folk dancers.

Natalie thought all of this would provide wonderful distraction and keep her thinking about her problem for a while, but only for a while. Her D-day was coming, or should she call it her B-day, for *birthing*? She had to face the fact that she would either have to find an excuse to leave Preston for a few days and get the abortion which she abhorred or tell him the truth and see if he wanted this baby as much as she did. She was still confident he might, despite the danger and the risk to his career. They could surely pull it off if he wanted to do it. He had access to the paper trail they needed to leave in their wake, and they could easily forge a Natal.

On the way home, she checked her voice mail and heard Preston's message, reading the annoyance and irritation in his tone. She had forgotten to turn on her cellular. With what weighed heavy on her mind, she wasn't surprised. Who knew what else she had forgotten to do today?

Rose answered with as cheerful a voice as Natalie had ever heard Preston's secretary have.

"Oh, Mrs. Ross, congratulations to you, too. We're all so happy for Mr. Ross," she said.

"Thank you, Rose. Is he in?"

"Yes. One moment, please."

Natalie turned off Sandburg's Main Street onto Birch Place toward their two-story home at the center of the cul-de-sac. The sprinklers were going, sending up a pulsating fountain of man-made rain. Their irrigation system worked like a charm. She was proud of the way the bushes lined the walk and the driveway, proud of their flower bed at the crest of the lawn and the two tall hickories that flourished on each side of their frontage.

The house itself had a fieldstone cladding, a very large living-room picture window, and a large dining-room window, both of which provided a bright, airy feeling in the daytime. The dining-room window looked out on the undeveloped forest with trees still low enough to permit a clear view of the mountain range and the night sky. Very cozy, very romantic dinners for her and Preston had been held here.

Behind the three-car-garage, she had her writing office. Preston had his own home office on the opposite end of the nearly seventy-five-hundred-square-foot residence. There was a game room and two guest bedrooms as well, one of which she was hoping would become the nursery in a matter of months. They had a pool and a tennis court in the rear, with more gardens, walkways, and beautiful red maple trees. It was her dream home.

"Nat, where the hell have you been?"

"I forgot to turn on my cellular," she quickly explained. "I was with Judy. We went to the Cliff House for lunch to celebrate your promotion and then to do some shopping. Sorry. What's happening now?"

"Did you hear about the Marlowe girl?"

"That's all anyone's talking about around here," she replied.

"Bertram just received a call from McCalester. The CID is on the scene, and a preliminary investigation is confirming that the killer was female and very possibly pregnant," Preston practically whispered.

"Oh."

"It's not good. The *Times-Herald* has a reporter in Sandburg camped out at Benny's Deli. We just heard the television stations are sending out remotes, and there are calls coming in from New York City. We could be on the national broadcasts in a matter of hours!"

"I'm sorry," she said, as if it really was all her fault.

"I'm coming home early," he said. "We need to talk."

"Why?"

"I'd rather wait until I'm home," he added. "Where are you now?"

"Just pulling into the driveway."

"Stay there," he ordered, and hung up.

She stared at the garage door opening as soon as the laser eye read her car ID. For a moment, she didn't move forward. It was almost as if she wanted to back out, turn, and drive away, maybe forever and ever.

What was Preston rushing home to tell her? Did he know? Had she slipped up somewhere?

After she pulled in and entered her home, she prepared herself a glass of ice water. For hours now, she had felt as if she had a fever. Her stomach had churned all through lunch, and her nerves were like firecrackers. She had no reason to be this way, she told herself. She and Preston were as tight and as devoted to each other as any modern couple possibly could be. Everything in this house reinforced that belief.

The fireplace mantel in the living room, the piano, and the shelves all had beautifully framed photographs of her and Preston at various important affairs, on vacations, or just having a casual good time at a restaurant dinner. In all of them, they held each other closely, lovingly, his eyes on her telling anyone who looked at the pictures that he absolutely adored her. What was it Judy said about *A Summer Place?* The passion was palpable? Well, that was the way it looked in all their pictures, too: their passion was palpable.

When she entered her bedroom, she thought about all their lovemaking, their expressions of love, his wonderful reference to the Bible, telling her, "If you should die, I will hate all womankind." This was just their bedroom; it was their magic room because they touched each other so deeply and fully it felt like something beyond reality, something special. Sometimes they acted like two people with a big state secret, the secret being how much they were in love and how wonderful that made them feel. Neither of them was really superstitious, but they both knew what envy meant and how their affection toward each other could make less affectionate, less loving couples feel inferior and uncomfortable enough to cast an evil eye their way, to wish them bad luck.

"Sometimes when we're out, I feel like a man in chains," Preston had told her, and just recently, too. "I want to devour you, hold you, kiss you, but I know I've got to have self-control, and I hate it."

She laughed. How good he made her feel.

Just thinking about all this stimulated her creative juices. She wanted to get back to her novel. She would write a love scene that would sing on the page, bring a flush to the face of her reader, and fill her life with everything that was missing, even if it was only a vicarious experience.

That was where Preston found her when he returned home. She didn't even hear him come into the house.

"Hey," he said.

She turned from the Wordsmith.

"Hi. I just had to get back to this scene, but it's all right. I've got down what I needed to," she said, rising to go to him.

He stood in the office doorway. She hugged him, but she felt the stiffness in his body.

"What's wrong, Preston?" she asked, stepping back, her heart pounding.

"The Abnormal, the possible murderer . . ."

"Yes?"

"Bertram is worried she's someone who belongs

to a family of some stature in the community and not just some known Abnormal," he said. "He's very concerned about it and the impact it's going to have on all of us."

For a moment, she felt as if her heart had simply turned into a block of ice. Was he telling her he knew?

"What makes him come to such a conclusion?"

"You know Bertram . . . he's always paranoid, always looking on the darkest possible side of things. I know he can be quite a nervous Nelly warning us about real estate values and all that. The man is skeptical of everything. It comes with the territory, maybe even with being an attorney, but . . ."

"He's not wrong," she blurted.

"What?"

"Bertram's not wrong about someone of standing in our community being pregnant."

"You sound pretty sure of yourself, Nat," he said with a smile. He nodded after studying her face a moment. "I was coming here to tell you Bertram wanted us to be extra careful about whom we associate with these days and . . ."

"It's too late," she said.

"Too late? Why?"

"We're already associating with her, but she's not the murderer."

His smile faded quickly. He looked at the small settee across from her desk as if he were wondering if he could make it before he collapsed.

"I had that feeling, Nat," he said. "I know you'll laugh, but I had this feeling deep down in my gut that it was someone close to us."

He started for the settee and turned when he reached it to look up at her.

"It's Judy, isn't it? There's always been something about Judy that made me think of her as different. When did she tell you? How long have you known?" he asked. "I'm actually a little disappointed you never told me after she told you, Nat."

"She never told me."

He started to nod. "How did you find out, then?"

"It's not Judy," she said.

He started to sit back and then straightened up slowly, his face filling with renewed concern.

"What do you mean? Who is it?"

"It's me, Preston. I'm pregnant," she said.

Six

Preston just stared. It was as if time had stopped, the hands of every clock frozen. Even the wind was halted in midair. His expression moved from incredulity to a silly smile, the smile of someone who thought he had heard something so ridiculous he had to laugh. The next words out of his mouth would be *You can't imagine what I thought you just said, Natalie. It's so off the wall, I don't even know how to tell you.*

He would laugh, shake his head, and just go on as though none of that had occurred.

Natalie went to the antique French chair she had recently had refurbished and sat, her eyes down, her hands in her lap, waiting like someone in the eye of a storm, anticipating the worst was yet to come. It was a fool's respite, a beguiling stillness that would give her the courage to venture forth and then be carried off in the jaws of a hurricane.

"What are you saying?" Preston finally asked. He needed it repeated.

"I wasn't an NL1. My mother refused to go through the sterilization process, and eventually she became pregnant. Personal information about people wasn't as easily available when she was my age, as you know. They managed to keep her pregnancy a secret."

She paused, took a deep breath, and continued.

"Of course, my mother knew what this would mean for me. In those days, it was much easier to forge an NL1 certificate. There was that network of underground medical services that provided the old-fashioned methods of inoculations and treatments before the crackdown in the 2030s. When I was twelve, I went to the Underground Naturals classes, the training to help me and others survive in a world that considered us abnormal, learning how to cover up, deceive, survive."

"Why didn't you ever tell me the truth?" Preston asked, nearly breathless.

"In the beginning, I was afraid you wouldn't want me."

"But afterward, after we had gotten married, for Christ's sake . . ."

"I didn't want to burden you with it, and I loved you, still love you too much to risk losing you, Preston. There are many women out there who are like me and who have managed to keep the truth about themselves hidden, even from their husbands and families."

"So you've been buying contraband drugs from black market sources all this time?"

She nodded.

"That alone is a crime, you know."

"I know, but I didn't have a choice. It's like those poor women in 2010, when all abortions, for any reason, were outlawed. Thousands went underground, hundreds died in unsanitary conditions and at the hands of butchers, but many were going to die anyway, and who could blame a woman victimized by a rape or involved in something incestuous?"

"This is different, Natalie. Your life isn't at risk."

"No? What would my life be if the truth about me was revealed, Preston? Would you have married me? I like to believe you would have, but maybe you should tell me."

"Maybe you should have given me that opportunity years ago, Natalie," he countered.

She nodded. "Maybe I should have. You're right. I'm sorry."

"Sorry," he muttered.

"I want to have the baby, Preston. The child is really going to be our child, fully and completely our own, and not some laboratory creation with a few transferred chromosomes to give him or her some resemblances. We still have some heritage, bloodlines to pass on. You can't tell me parents who give birth to their own children don't have closer ties with them, Preston. You know it in your heart, just as I do. We've spoken about this from time to time."

He looked up sharply. "Yes, but that was always in the abstract or as a result of one of your romance novels. I never dreamed . . ."

He shook his head.

"God, Natalie, I work for a firm that argues before the Parental Review Board. I pass judgments and accept or reject couples who seek to have children. They just made me a partner and gave me full control of that division of the company's business. Can you imagine what would happen if this was known?"

"We can keep it from being known, Preston. You know how to do it, and you can get it done. I know you can, and you know you can," she countered with a frantic urgency. "I'm willing to do anything, go anywhere, for this child," she emphasized, and placed her palm over her abdomen.

Preston stared at her hand.

"This is your baby, Preston. He or she is you, entirely you and me, no genetics added, no element of our identities removed. You told me there were wealthy, powerful couples who have done just that."

"There are stories, but . . ."

"None of the husbands could be smarter or more capable than you are, Preston. Don't you want this, too? Deep down inside you, don't you? I think I love you more just knowing that you do," she said.

He looked up at her sharply.

"We're different, Preston. We've been different from the beginning, falling in love the old-fashioned way, really enjoying passion in our marriage. You know I'm right. Let's do something from the heart, totally from the heart and soul, Preston."

"But we'd have to . . ."

"What?"

"You would have to go away soon, Natalie, and then afterward."

"If it's a boy, Preston, there's nothing to do afterward except get hold of the vaccines." She smiled. "If men weren't in control of the government, would they have been exempt from the sterilization process as they still are? I often wonder if abortion would have been outlawed if men were capable of becoming pregnant. All the burden is still on the women in this society, regardless of the magnificent technological advances," she added.

He glanced at her and then stood up and went to the window. For a long moment, he just stood there gazing out.

"I'll do whatever you want me to do, Preston, but I want you to know I love you very much, and I look at this child inside me as the greatest possible expression of that love. That's not something from one of my romance novels, either," she said. "It's something from my heart, the heart of my very being."

He turned slowly and looked at her. "I love you very much, too, Nat. You know I do."

She smiled. "I live with that hope every day of my life, Preston, especially now."

He nodded. "Let me think about it all, how to do it."

"But you want to do it, don't you?" she asked quickly, and rose. "You see why it is so important and why you will love this child more than any other the state can create for us. You see that. I know you do, Preston."

He nodded again. "Okay," he said. "I'll figure something out."

She moved quickly into his arms and held on to him tightly. "Oh, I just knew you would say that, Preston. I just knew it." She pulled back and looked into his eyes. "I'm not afraid for us, Preston. I believe in you and in how smart you are and what you can do."

"I hope you're right," he said.

"I know I'm right."

They kissed. For her, it was like the sealing of a promise.

He grew thoughtful again, his eyes swirling with worry and concern.

"What?" she asked.

"You didn't know or have any contact with this teenage girl, did you, Nat? The one who was murdered?"

She shook her head. Should she tell him about

the pills? She wasn't positive they were missing. Why add such a complication now when she had him wanting to go through with this? Why chance losing his support?

"No. I don't even know the parents, do you?"

"Yes, of course. He's our insurance agent. He's been in this house, Nat. You met him."

"Oh, right. But not the girl. He never brought her along, did he?"

"No, but I just want to be very sure of all that. There's a CID man on the case, and he'll be scrutinizing every possible linkage to anyone or anything."

She shrugged. "It can't have anything to do with us," she assured him.

"Okay. How long have you been pregnant?"

"Five, nearly six months," she said.

"Six months!"

"My mother didn't show until she was nearly in the middle of her sixth month, and after that, she wore these girdles that kept her looking svelte for at least another month before she went away to have me," she quickly added.

"So all this business about being bloated, too much salt, all that was part of the deception," he concluded.

"I don't like to think of it as deception, Preston. For a while, I wasn't sure what we should do."

"Seems to me you made up your mind when you let it go this far, Natalie."

She was quiet.

He walked slowly toward the door. There, he paused and turned to her. "I assume no one else knows about this in Sandburg, Nat, not even Judy, correct?"

"No one else in Sandburg knows."

"What about your mother?" he followed.

Her mother lived in Palm Springs, California, now. She and Natalie's father had moved there more than ten years ago, and he had died there. California had more pockets of Naturals than any other state, and it had always been more comfortable for them, giving them a greater sense of security. Of course, Preston never knew those motivations.

"I haven't told her yet."

"Don't. We can't take a chance on anything slipping out, and you don't have to burden her with the obligation of keeping it all a tight secret."

"Okay," she said. "Whatever you say, Preston."

He shook his head. "I don't feel much like going out with the Normans, but we don't want to do the slightest thing that might give anyone any suspicions."

"It will be fun," she promised. "Bob booked Soy-Hoy."

He started to nod but stopped and then shook his head with a smile. "Here I was patting myself on the back all day, telling myself how brilliant I was, and I missed one of the biggest events in my marriage, something literally right under my nose."

"You are brilliant," she insisted. "I don't want you to blame yourself for anything, Preston."

"No, it's okay. This is good. It's a good lesson for me. Arrogant people make big mistakes. I needed to be reminded of my vulnerabilities. I don't know it all. You proved that, and to tell you the truth, Nat, I'm grateful."

She smiled. This was the Preston she had hoped to see and hear after she had confessed.

"Many of these things people are doing and are forced to do today diminish their humanity, Preston. It's good to embrace it once in a while. And that's not just the romantic in me talking," she quickly qualified. "It's the woman in me, and what is making you want to do this as much as I do is the man in you. That's really all we are, no matter what so-called miracles they accomplish in some laboratory, just a man and a woman in love."

He laughed. "Don't tell me you're not going to get this into one of your novels, Natalie Ross."

"I'll dedicate it to you," she promised.

He stared at her, his lips tight, his eyes full of that mystery and depth she so loved. "Matter of fact," he said, "you will soon have research to do on your next novel. It's going to take you out of town."

"Take me out of town?"

He nodded.

She stared, thinking, and then smiled. "Oh.

What a good idea. I knew you would come up with solutions, Preston. I just knew it."

"It's not a solution. It's a start," he said.

Then he turned and went down to his office.

She stood there for a long moment, her heart so full of love and hope.

She put her hand on her belly.

"Welcome to your home, my darling. Welcome to your family," she whispered.

Dr. Gordon Howard's preliminary examination held no surprises for Ryan. He spoke briefly with him over the telephone in his hotel room, where he had set up his own technical headquarters. He had to rely on wireless transmissions because the refurbished hotel was not even close to being up to date. This area of the Catskills had been a popular mid-twentieth-century resort region. In the 1970s, it began to experience heart failure and dropped into an economic coma until it was resurrected in the second decade of the twenty-first century. Small communities like Sandburg were able to attract some historic restoration, and this was the only real hotel to be a part of that recovery. Purists kept it from being like the techno-resorts prominent throughout the country.

The medical examiner had pinpointed the time of death to nine-thirty P.M. the night before. That science had been greatly improved. The one piece of information he was able to add to Ryan's information involved a trace of some hard plastic substance on the victim's skull. Ryan ran the description through his own computer analysis and determined it had come from a flashlight. He even had the make and the model.

More than likely, this was not the weapon of choice for a premeditated murder. It had been utilized in the midst of some rage. The obvious question was, why bring a flashlight to the scene? Was another exchange of some sort to take place in the darkness? Maybe it was part of what was needed to travel, either by bicycle or walking? Walking meant a closer proximity to the scene. Even biking limited the distance. Yet he still couldn't rule out a vehicle, even though he found no recent tire tracks. The car could have been parked some distance from the actual site of the crime.

Of course, there was also the possibility that Lois Marlowe had brought the flashlight, and it had been taken from her and used to kill her. He doubted it, because he saw no other signs of any sort of struggle. He felt confident the blows to her head came as a surprise.

He also felt the surprise came with no less of an impact to her parents, whose home McCalester was now driving him out to visit so he could conduct the necessary interview.

A veil of mourning had already fallen over the Marlowe family's home. The curtains were closed tightly. There was little light, and without any vehicles in the driveway, the garage door closed, the two-story Tudor had the look of desertion about it. The inhabitants, unable to cope with their tragedy, had fled. At least, that was the way it looked to Ryan Lee.

When he and Henry McCalester stepped out of the police vehicle, Ryan was taken with the silence. It was as though the birds were in mourning as well. The house was sufficiently off the main road to be undisturbed by the sounds of traffic. There was a true rural stillness here. The patch of woods and the long, rolling lawn were scenic, even somewhat pristine. In such an idyllic setting, misfortune and calamity seemed totally misplaced.

This should be the home of contentment, calm, balance, and bliss, he thought. A mother and a father should not be embracing each other in sorrow, asking themselves if all this wasn't just a horrible nightmare that would soon pass. They should be sitting at their dinner table, exchanging happy stories about their day, and talking about good things they were planning for their future, especially their child's future.

The state had manufactured what was considered a nearly perfectly healthy baby girl for them. They had met all the criteria for a stable, constructive family. All the *t*'s were crossed, the *i*'s dotted. This was supposed to be a guaranteed success.

Ironically, Ryan felt sorrier for these people

than he did for his own parents, who had to suffer through the degradation that accompanied having a natural-born child. These people, the Marlowes, in a real sense had been betrayed, lied to, defrauded. They had been asked to place their trust in the new world, in the hands of scientists and politicians, a government that would make the people for the people. The new world for parents was supposed to be relatively crime-free. It was almost as if someone had been vaccinated against one of those old diseases, such as polio, and then soon afterward contracted it.

"He's a pretty successful insurance agent," Henry continued, nodding at the expensive-looking home as they walked toward the front door. "She works at the Community National Bank, a loan officer. Both are in their late thirties. He was born and brought up in Ellenville, which is about fifteen miles away. She's a local girl. They met at the state university in Albany and married when he graduated. She was still in school, so he worked there for two years. That impulsiveness almost sank them with the review committee when they went for their parental license and baby acquisition, I remember. Spontaneity is not one of their highly regarded criteria," Henry added, lifting his right eyebrow.

Ryan nodded but said nothing. He had permitted Henry to do all the talking, absorbing whatever he thought might have some significance. He was here to learn, after all, not to teach. Why should he be talking?

Before they reached the front door, it opened, and Hattie Scranton and two of her women stepped out. For a moment, everyone froze, McCalester and Ryan and the women, and just stared at one another.

"What are you doing here, Hattie?" McCalester asked with more of a curious than an angry tone.

"We came to pay our respects, Henry," she said. She smiled coldly. "We're not heartless, just vigilant," she added, and then started toward their vehicle parked in the street.

"They can do damage to an investigation," Ryan warned.

"You'll have to be the one to tell them," McCalester replied with frankness.

"If I have to, I will," Ryan promised.

Henry rang the doorbell. The short pause was uncomfortable. He shifted his weight from one foot to the other and shook his head.

"Terrible thing," he muttered.

Jennie Marlowe opened the door. Her eyes were bloodshot, her face pale, her shoulders slumped. She had a green knitted shawl over those shoulders. Grief had filled her body as well as the house with a dark chill.

"Sorry to be bothering you again, Jennie, but this is Ryan Lee from the NYSCID. He's the one

authorized to investigate Lois's death," Henry Mc-
Calester emphasized.

Jennie Marlowe, shaking her head back and
forth slightly, turned her tired eyes toward Ryan.
He didn't smile. He simply nodded, and she
backed up to let them enter the house.

"Chester is in the living room," she said, and led
them.

Chester Marlowe looked asleep in the oversized
chair. His head lay on his right shoulder, and his
eyes were closed. He didn't move when they entered.

"Chester," Jennie said softly.

He lifted his head without surprise and looked
at the two policemen, his eyes redder than Jennie's.

"My sympathies again, Chester," McCalester
said.

Chester just nodded. He looked like someone
under heavy sedation, and for a moment, Ryan
considered that to be a real possibility. Usually,
the woman was the one under sedation in these
circumstances, he thought, but he also knew the
consequences of all this. When or if they returned
to the review board to apply for another baby acquisition, their failure with Lois would weigh in
like a two-ton gorilla, unless they had some very
significant political help.

"This is Ryan Lee from the NYSCID, Chester.

He has some questions that might help us get to the bottom of all this," McCalester said.

"Bottom?"

"Right, Chester."

"The bottom of all this is in a six-foot grave," Chester said dryly, his voice in a tired monotone. "Bottom."

"Mr. Marlowe, Mrs. Marlowe," Ryan began, taking over quickly, "have you any idea whom your daughter might have gone to meet at the lake?"

"Someone from school," Chester said. "Someone she was going to get to confess tomorrow. That's what she told me that night, but she didn't tell me she was going to try to get her to do it right away."

"How do you know for certain it was someone from the school?" Ryan asked.

Chester raised his eyebrows. "She said she was bringing this person in to see Ted Sullivan, the principal. She also said she had traded for those damn pills. She told Jennie she traded a rock DVD. Who else would trade for a stupid rock DVD besides another student?"

"What was the name of the DVD?" Ryan asked.

Chester looked at Jennie. She shook her head.

"I can't remember if she told me the name or not."

"Sorry," Chester said.

"If it comes to you, please let us know," Ryan

said. "Do we know if that student is a male or a female?"

The possibility of it being a male obviously hadn't occurred to either Chester or Jennie.

"No, but I just assumed . . . no," he answered. He thought a moment. "You mean, the blows might be too powerful for a girl to have thrown?"

"No, not necessarily. The foot imprints suggest a female at the scene, but I need to explore every possibility. I'm not yet sure they are the killer's footprints," Ryan said, sounding very official. "Can you tell me if you own a Radox flashlight, model number 2x5?"

"Huh?"

"Black, ebony black," Ryan added.

"I don't know. We've got flashlights all over the place."

"This model is about a foot long," Ryan added.

Chester thought a moment.

"We've got that big one in the kitchen," Jennie said.

"Can I see it?" Ryan asked.

She hurried into the kitchen and returned with a black flashlight. Ryan looked at it and shook his head.

"It's a Magnolight. Any others?"

"Not that big," Chester said firmly.

"Okay. I'd like to look at her room, if I may," Ryan requested.

"Sure, go look at her room. I guess we'll turn it

into a regular museum now," Chester muttered, and closed his eyes to lay his head against his right shoulder again.

Ryan studied him for a moment, glanced at Henry McCalester, and then turned to Jennie.

"Those women who were just here," he said.

"Yes?"

"Were they in your daughter's room?"

Jennie looked furtively at her husband, but he kept his eyes closed, his head turned away. She, too, glanced at Henry.

"Were they?" McCalester followed.

"Hattie said it was necessary," Jennie replied.

"Did they take anything from the room?" Ryan quickly followed.

"Not that I saw, no."

"Take me to it now," Ryan demanded. "They're way out of bounds here," he told McCalester.

Henry simply nodded.

Jennie led them up the stairway, each step looking as if it might just be her last and she would come tumbling back at them.

When she opened the door to Lois's room, she turned away as if she had confronted her corpse and began to cry softly.

"I'll just be a few minutes," Ryan told her, and entered the room.

Teenage girls were almost another species to him. He had no sisters or brothers and no significant high-school relationships. His peers always

knew he was a Natural, and despite there being
no obvious differences between him and them,
they always looked at him differently. He carried
the unmentionable stamp of a leper. What little he
knew about women from a romantic standpoint,
he knew through some very insignificant relationships, observation, and vicarious experiences. He
found it hard enough to understand women his
age, much less the impulsive, highly emotional
creature he saw teenage girls to be.

For example, despite their promiscuity, they
clung to childish things such as dolls and Teddy
bears, while teenage boys eschewed anything that
in the smallest way connected them to preadoles-
cence. Girls were far more sensitive to looks and
words and always seemed to totter on a tightrope,
threatening to fall to the side of tears or the side
of laughter. What made them lean either way
made no logical sense to a man like Ryan Lee.

On a number of previous occasions, he had
been alone in the room of a young girl or a young
woman and couldn't help feeling titillation. Touching, inspecting, searching a woman's underthings
immediately conjured up the woman naked. The
same sort of reaction occurred when he smelled
her perfumes or touched her lipsticks. Any intimate part of her being aroused him. He resisted it,
hated himself for having the reaction, and did the
best he could to hide it from his associates and superiors, none of whom seemed to have a similar

reaction. It would surely confirm his being different in their eyes and disqualify him as an objective investigator immediately.

Up until now, his relationships had all been unsatisfactory. He had even resorted to paying for sexual favors, treating it in his own mind as he would going to the dentist or doctor, a medical necessity. Fortunately for him, few people cared about his personal life.

He took a deep, quiet breath and fought back the wave of sexual interest that threatened to invade his deductive thinking. Lois Marlowe's room had shelves of stuffed animals on the wall to his right, and there were dolls on a shelf below that. She appeared to have kept everything ever given to her.

The wall on his left had movie and rock posters. It looked as if she had belonged to the Vig Tom fan club. There was an autographed picture of the prematurely gray-haired twenty-year-old albino rock star wearing his famous pink-framed sunglasses and an opened shirt revealing the tattoo of a jagged cross with hands at the ends. Girls who followed him were definitely left of center, Ryan thought.

He studied the desk, the computer, the top of the dresser, and the vanity table. He perused the closet and checked the shoes. There was no pair of Rockers. In many ways, Lois Marlowe didn't follow the crowd, he concluded.

He opened his bag and extracted his video-phone file researcher. Then he went to the console on the nightstand beside her bed and turned over the receiver. With his pocket screwdriver, he flicked off the brain cover and inserted his VFR. It clicked, and he turned the instrument over to look at the screen. He considered the date and time of each call, chose one in particular, and called for an identification. A split second later, the Robinsons' address came up.

He put the brain cover back on the receiver and his instrument back in his bag. Then he did a routine search of dresser and desk drawers. Finding nothing of interest there, he turned on the computer and with a few quick function key directions began to read her e-mail and Internet history, almost instantly centering on the Natural Birth Web site. He knew that it was coming from France. There was a continuous diplomatic effort to get the French government to shut it down, until now to no avail.

It both amused and interested him that more and more young people were fascinated with natural childbirth these days. He wondered what it meant. They all knew they were reading what society now considered pornography and they could be arrested for spreading it, yet they were determined to know, to learn, to question, despite the risk. Were they looking for something freaky, or were they part of a new generation that might someday challenge what was called progress? He wondered.

He ran down her e-mail history, made some notes of names and addresses, and shut off the computer.

McCalester had been standing in the doorway quietly observing. When Ryan picked up his bag and turned to him, he raised his eyebrows.

"Well?"

"We've taken a few more steps forward," Ryan said cryptically.

They marched back down the stairs. Jennie Marlowe waited in the living-room doorway.

"Did you find anything that will help?" she asked, her hands clasped at the base of her throat as if she were in the middle of a prayer.

"I believe so, Mrs. Marlowe," Ryan said.

"Good. Now what?" Chester Marlowe called from the living room. Ryan stepped past Jennie and looked in at him.

"We'll find the person who killed your daughter, Mr. Marlowe."

"And then what?" Chester pursued.

"We'll bring him or her to justice."

"And what do we do then?" Chester followed like some priest testing the catechism.

Ryan stared at him a moment. "Mr. Marlowe, you'll have to go to a higher authority to get the answer to that question, I'm afraid."

"What higher authority? God? I sometimes

wonder if he's a higher authority anymore," Chester said bitterly.

"So do I, Mr. Marlowe," Ryan said.

Chester turned with surprise.

"So do I," Ryan repeated, and headed for the front door.

Seven

::::::::::::

"**W**here is she?" Hattie Scranton demanded as soon as Esther Robinson opened the front door.

"Who is it?" her husband, Mickey, called with clear annoyance from the living room, where he had just sat back like someone easing himself into a hot bath. The county highway employee wanted to watch the Scooters' flip-ball game without any interruptions. It was the preliminary, and he had put twenty-five dollars on them to win by more than five points. They had one of the best flippers in the league, Marsh King, who could flip the disc close to full field.

"Where's who?" Esther fired back at the four women crowding the small entry.

Despite their demeanor and their influence on everyone in this community, they didn't intimidate Esther Robinson, who was a known Abnormal but who never let anyone think he or she was superior because of her birth. Nevertheless, it was a surprise to everyone that she and Mickey had qualified for a parental license and acquired Stocker a little more than sixteen years ago. Bertram Cauthers had weighed in on their behalf. Hattie had her suspicions and her theories about the reason, focusing mainly on Bertram's well-known sexual predatoriness, but she had never voiced an accusation or complaint. She had the diplomatic sense to know whom to bully and whom to leave alone. Bertram Cauthers was no one she could bully.

"Your daughter," Hattie replied, almost spitting the words back at her.

"She's finishing her homework. Why?"

"We have to talk to her. Now," she emphasized.

"Why?"

"She's been linked to the Marlowe girl situation." Hattie obviously enjoyed telling.

The impact was immediate. Whatever wall of defiance Esther had been able to put up between her and the baby squad immediately began to crumble. They were saying her daughter was linked to a murder.

"I don't understand," she managed to say.

"Who the hell is it?" Mickey Robinson screamed. He came to the doorway of the living room and looked past his wife. When he saw Hattie and the women, he simmered down like a pot of boiling water placed on a pile of ice. "Huh?" he muttered. "What's going on here?"

Esther stepped aside, and Hattie moved into the

house, the three women with her moving so in sync they looked almost attached to her.

"We have to speak to your daughter immediately," she said. "We've just come from the Marlowe house."

"Stocker?" He looked at Esther, but she seemed to have suffered lockjaw. "Why?"

"Either take us to her or bring her to us," Hattie replied. "We're wasting time."

He glanced again at his wife and then backed up toward the stairway.

"Stocker!" he cried, his eyes on the women who glared at him as if he were the murderer. "Stocker!"

The shouting woke Kasey-Lady, and she started to bark. Someone scored a goal in the flip-ball game, and the crowd roared over the television set. Missing that on top of all the commotion churned up Mickey Robinson's stomach, making him feel as if he had swallowed a dozen steel ball bearings.

Stocker had still not appeared on the stairway landing. He cursed under his breath and charged up the steps. When he reached her door, he pounded with a closed fist.

"Stocker, get the hell out here!"

No response brought a pitch of rage into his face that looked as if it would blow the top off his head. He practically ripped the door off its hinges when he turned the knob and pushed it open.

The sight nailed his feet to the floor.

Stocker was naked except for her virtual reality

glasses. She had an X-rated VRG movie running, and she was masturbating along with the two studs who had surrounded the voluptuous naked woman giving head to a naked man kneeling on the bed. Everyone's groans and moans were amplified, including Stocker's.

Mickey ripped the glasses off her head and looked down at her with bulging, furious eyes. She reached to pull her blanket over her and started to cry out, but he put his hand over her mouth and glanced into the VRG.

"Christ," he moaned, and then realized the situation. "The baby squad is downstairs," he said in a loud whisper. "Get dressed and come down immediately. We'll talk about this later," he added, holding up the VRG. He took his hand from her mouth.

"What do they want?"

"How the hell do I know? Get down there in thirty seconds," he ordered.

He turned and walked out, closing the door behind him. She leaped out of bed and put on her bathrobe. Then she slipped into her Rockers and shuffled to the door. Before she opened it, she took a deep breath and gained full control of herself. No one was going to blame her for anything, she vowed, and walked out of her room and down the stairs.

The women were standing in the small hallway, all eyes lifting to watch her descend. When she reached the bottom of the stairway, she folded her arms under her small bosom and looked from her mother, who was now nearly trembling, to Hattie.

"You gave Lois Marlowe those prenatal vitamins, didn't you?" Hattie began.

"Who said so?" Stocker shot back.

Mickey widened his eyes at her nasty, defiant tone. Didn't anything frighten her?

"You traded something for them, didn't you?"

"That's a filthy, stinking lie," Stocker said, her mouth twisted with wonderful feigned rage. "Those girls hate me. They're always making stuff up about me. They call me names and all because of my mother," she said, throwing a pail of blame at Esther Robinson. "People say nasty things about us all the time."

Hattie stared at her. She had always prided herself on her ability to mine the truth like some panhandler searching for nuggets of gold. She could shift her eyes, scan a face, read every revealing gesture.

However, Stocker was a match for anyone. She was a good liar because she knew how to convince herself of the lie and then defend it. She really believed she was the victim here, and she wasn't going to let that happen again, not this time.

"We found this in Lois Marlowe's room," Hattie said, and held out a notebook page. She didn't want to use the trump card so quickly. She was hoping for some sort of confession and then supporting it with the scribbling, but Stocker's façade of defiance and convincing show of anger demanded it.

Stocker took the paper and opened it. She smirked when she read it. "So?" she said, handing the paper back.

"What is that?" Mickey Robinson demanded.

"It's a list Lois Marlowe made of things she was willing to trade. Stocker's name is on the paper. Lois Marlowe told us she had traded for the prenatal vitamins." Hattie turned back to Stocker. "Did you trade with her?"

"Not for prenatal vitamins," she replied. Long ago, she had learned that offering a piece of the truth when she lied helped her get the lie accepted. This answer confused Hattie Scranton for a moment, as well as her women. One of them, Carol Saxon, was too frustrated and impatient to let Hattie continue the interrogation herself.

"What did you trade, then?" Carol asked.

Hattie shot a reprimanding glance her way. She didn't want her own momentum interrupted.

Stocker looked at her father.

"You better tell them and tell them now," he ordered.

Stocker looked down. "An X-rated VRG movie," she replied, her eyes still directed to the floor.

"What?" Hattie swallowed before she spoke.

"One of these, for sure," Mickey said, holding out the virtual reality glasses. "There's a filthy one loaded. I just caught her with it."

Hattie took the glasses slowly. The movie was still running in them. She brought it to her eyes and then lowered it and passed it to Carol, who looked, grimaced, and passed it to the others.

"A lot of the kids have them," Stocker defended. "I'm not the only one!"

Disappointment flooded Hattie Scranton's face. She smirked and then took a deep, thoughtful breath.

"How did you get this horribly disgusting thing?" Esther asked her when the glasses were finally passed to her and she had looked.

"Kids are trading for them all the time," Stocker said. "I'm not the only one."

"Someone has to talk to Mr. Sullivan about this," Esther told Hattie Scranton.

Hattie pressed her lips together harder. "That's a different issue. We don't have time for that. You parents should be taking more interest in your teenage sons and daughters. Parental licenses can be revoked, you know," she threatened.

Mickey gazed furiously at Stocker. "We might not fight so hard to keep it if this sort of thing continues," he threatened.

"I'm not the only one!" Stocker insisted.

A knock on the open doorway turned everyone around.

"Who's this now?" Mickey moaned, and opened the door.

Ryan Lee and Henry McCalester were standing there.

"What is this?" Ryan demanded when he saw Hattie and the others. "Why have you women come here?"

"We had reason," Hattie said curtly, then turned and marched herself and her followers out of the house. Henry had to step aside quickly. Hattie paused and turned back to Stocker. "We're not finished with you, young lady."

She and the others continued to leave.

"You're interfering in a state criminal investigation," Ryan called after them. "I'm warning you."

Hattie didn't respond. She walked faster to her car. The women got into it quickly.

Ryan and McCalester turned back to the Robinsons.

"This is Ryan Lee from the state criminal investigative division, Mickey. He's here to find the person who murdered Lois Marlowe. He wants to talk to Stocker."

"If this is about her doing some sort of trade with Lois Marlowe," Mickey began, "we've just been through it all. That's what brought Hattie here. These kids have been passing X-rated VRG movies among themselves for who knows how long."

"No," Ryan said. "It's about a phone call that was made to this house right before Lois Marlowe was murdered," he said, and stepped farther into the house.

Esther turned to Stocker. "You're going to give me a heart attack tonight," she said. "Tell them everything you know, Stocker, and tell it to them immediately."

Stocker looked at Ryan. Lying to Hattie Scranton had been easier than she had anticipated. It filled her with confidence. "She called me, yes," she admitted.

"And?" Ryan said.

"She wanted that," she said, nodding at the glasses in her mother's hands.

"What's that?" Henry asked.

"One of those disgusting movies," Mickey said.

"It's the best one. Everyone says so," Stocker continued. "I was just lucky to have gotten it. Everyone was offering me stuff, and I kept saying no, not enough."

She spun on Mickey.

"You taught me to be like that, Daddy," she told him in a tone of accusation.

"Huh?"

"You said, don't sell yourself too cheaply. The successful person always has patience and waits, and sure enough the price goes up, so I did that."

"I wasn't talking about something as disgusting as this, for God's sake!"

"Why did she call you?" Ryan pursued, his eyes not leaving Stocker.

"She said she was getting me what I wanted."

"Which was?"

"Five hundred dollars."

"Five hundred dollars!" Mickey cried.

"How was she getting it?" Ryan asked.

"She was meeting someone who was going to give it to her. I asked her what she was trading, and she said a secret this person didn't want anyone else to know. She promised she would have it in a day or so. I didn't say anything to anyone because . . . because I didn't want anyone to know about that," she said, nodding at the glasses. "I knew you were going to be mad, Daddy," she wailed. "But everyone is doing it."

"Everyone's doing it? Everyone's doing it!" Mickey screamed at her. He ripped the glasses from Esther's hands and dropped them to the floor. Then he stamped on them, smashing the instrument to pieces. "Now you're *not* doing it."

"Nooooo!" Stocker cried. "I had other movies, Daddy!"

The dramatics and the violence gave her an opportunity, and she seized it. She turned and ran up the stairs, sobbing, and slammed her door shut.

No one spoke for a moment.

"I'm sorry about all this," Esther told Henry McCalester.

Mickey, still fuming, stood staring down at the wreckage he had visited on the rather expensive equipment. It had been Stocker's sweet sixteen present, and they had saved for almost a year to get it for her.

"It's all right, Esther. Ryan?"

He was still looking up the stairway. After a moment, he turned to Esther and Mickey.

"Do you have a foot-long, ebony black Raydox flashlight?" he asked.

"Flashlight? Yeah, I think I do. Why?"

"I'd like to see it."

"What the hell . . ."

"Please, Mickey," McCalester said.

Mickey Robinson turned and went through the hallway to a closet near the rear door of the house. He turned and held up the flashlight.

Ryan joined him and looked at it.

"It's what we use . . . highway department issue," Mickey said. "I get called out sometimes and need stuff here," he added to cover up any petty thievery.

Ryan set down his bag and opened it, plucking out a long-nosed instrument that looked like a small torpedo. He flipped a switch on the rear end, and the entire tip of the cone glowed.

"What's that?" Mickey asked.

"We call it a bloodhound," Ryan said, running it over the light. "It detects human tracings."

"Human tracings? What's that?"

"Blood, skin, saliva, semen, to name a few examples."

The instrument glowed but remained silent. Ryan switched it off and handed it back to Mickey.

"Any more?"

"I don't think so. In my truck, of course."

"Where's your truck?"

"In the garage," he said, and they went through a side door. Mickey turned on the lights and reached into the rear of the truck to produce a tool chest. He snapped it open and looked inside. Ryan waited beside him. McCalester lingered in the doorway.

"Well?"

"I don't seem to have one. Might have left it at the plant or at a job. I don't know."

"Let us know if you figure it out," Ryan said dryly. He and Mickey returned to the hallway, where Esther waited, looking as if she had been holding her breath.

"Is everything all right?"

"No," Mickey snapped. "Far from it."

"I'll be back to speak with your daughter again," Ryan said. "In the meantime, I want her to search her memory about that last conversation she allegedly had with Lois Marlowe. Any detail, no matter how small or insignificant it might seem, is important to me."

"I'll make her remember," Mickey promised.

"Make her remember only the truth," Ryan instructed.

He and Henry started out. Just outside the door, he turned to McCalester.

"Notice anything on Stocker Robinson?" he asked the policeman.

"Like what?"

"Her footwear. 'Rockers' was printed along the sides, the company trademark."

McCalester looked back at the closed door. "Let's go back in."

"No, not yet. I have some other things to do first," Ryan said, and headed for their vehicle.

Inside the house, Esther immediately began to clean up the shattered electronics. When the door had closed, Mickey turned back to the living room.

"Damn!" he screamed. "They've already gotten three goals, and I haven't seen one."

Upstairs in her room, Stocker finally started to tremble. She had done well, but she sensed it was far from over. There was one more thing to do, and she knew just how she was going to get it done.

That knowledge and her success finally stopped the shakes. It was all quickly replaced with rage at her father for smashing the VRG.

Where the hell was she going to get another pair of virtual reality glasses now? And what was she going to do for the money to buy them?

She decided to soak in a warm bath and think and plot. She realized that what she had told them Lois was going to do wasn't such a bad idea after all.

I bet I could get at least five hundred dollars from her, she thought. *Maybe even a thousand dollars. She's rich. She would pay it.*

But could she do it? It was one thing to intimidate another teenager, but an adult?

She could do everything else, and she hadn't done badly against adults up until now.

She closed her eyes, lay back, and tried to revive the images of that X-rated VRG movie as she ran her hands over her own breasts and erect nipples.

She could do it all.

Why not?

Both Bob and Judy Norman were in such a festive mood right from the beginning of the evening that neither noticed how tense and nervous Preston and Natalie were at dinner. The Rosses thought all of the gaiety resulted from Preston's impressive promotion, but right after they had their cocktails served and Bob proposed a toast to Preston, he paused, smiled at Judy, and turned back to them to say, "We have something else to toast tonight."

"Oh," Preston said cautiously. "And what might that be?" He held his smile.

For some reason, Natalie felt her heart begin to pound with anxiety.

Bob reached for Judy's hand first and then turned back. "We've decided to apply for a child, counselor, so you can expect a new application on your desk this week."

"You stinker," Natalie told Judy. "We were together all day, and you never said a word, not a hint."

"Bob wanted to make the announcement tonight when we were all together," she explained.

"We appreciate that," Preston said quickly. Then he smiled again. "I look forward to reviewing your qualifications for parenthood."

"Have you decided whether you'll have a boy or a girl?" Natalie asked.

"We've decided on a boy for our first child," Bob said. "Right?"

"Yes," Judy said. "I can tell you, as long as you don't hold it against us, Preston, that I'm absolutely terrified of the whole thing. One day, there's us, and the next, there's us plus one. Motherhood," she added with a sigh. "To suddenly care for another as much as you care for yourself."

"Even more," Natalie said.

"Yes, even more. Sometimes," she added in almost a whisper, "I wonder if the old way wasn't better . . . carrying a child inside you for nine months. You can bond faster when the child is born. At least, that's what I've heard."

"Ridiculous," Bob said quickly. "What anyone who has had any experience with that tells me is it's such an ordeal many of the Abnormals actually resent their children. That's why underground abortions still rage at the numbers they rage."

"None of that is confirmed," Preston said. "I'm sure the numbers you hear are exaggerated."

"Well, I suppose you would know better than I would," Bob said with a shrug. "Still, I wouldn't trade our system for anything in the past, would you, Natalie?"

Natalie smiled. "I wouldn't change anything in regard to myself," she said.

Preston shifted his eyes to catch the glint in hers and then looked at the menu. "Actually," he said while reading it, "there is one more thing to announce tonight."

"Oh? Don't tell me you guys have decided to become parents, too."

"No, not yet," Preston said. "Natalie has had a new book offer, to do a series, in fact."

"Wow!"

"Talk about keeping secrets," Judy countered. "You didn't mention anything or give any hints, either, today."

"I didn't know until I went home," Natalie said. "The message from my publisher was waiting for me. They liked an outline I had created. I'm setting the whole series in Cape Cod."

"Congratulations," Bob said.

"Thank you."

"What Natalie is trying to tell you, however," Preston continued, "is she is leaving for some prolonged research."

"Leaving?" Judy asked.

"Yes. You know how I like to feel the places I write about, taste them? I want a real sense of authenticity about this series."

"What does that mean? Leaving?"

"I'm just going to do a little traveling on the Cape, Judy, stay at a few bed-and-breakfast places. My publishers are putting it all together for me. They're even paying for it!"

"Wow again," Bob said. "But what about you, counselor?"

"We'll join up in a few weeks or so," Preston said. "I don't want to distract her from her work. I'll spend a weekend or so on the Cape and then return, and she'll be back when she's got what she needs done."

"Well, what am I supposed to do?" Judy cried. "I'm getting a child, and I won't have my best friend at my side. Who's going to listen to my complaints?"

"I'll call you on a daily basis," Natalie promised. "Or as much as I can," she added. Judy didn't smile. "Please, be happy for me, Judy. I'm happy for you."

"Oh, I'm sorry. Of course, I'm happy for you, Nat. You're going to be a real bestselling author. And I'll be able to say you're my best friend, right?"

"Always," Natalie promised. "As long as you want."

"Well, I want it forever," Judy declared, as if it was the most obvious thing of all.

Everyone laughed.

The waiter approached.

"Let's order. All this excitement has made me hungry," Bob said.

Preston nodded. He looked at Natalie.

She smiled at him. He could do it all, after all. Just as she had thought. He was smart enough, and he loved her enough, and they would be fine. They would all be fine, she, he, and their child.

What would she have?

Was it more or less exciting not to know?

Whatever it is, boy or girl, she thought, *the baby will be more of us than Judy and Bob's will be of them.*

And that has to be more exciting.

She hoped.

Despite the commotion in her home earlier, it was easier for Stocker Robinson to sneak out of her house than it had been for Lois Marlowe to sneak out of hers. Stocker's mother, emotionally exhausted, went to bed early, and her father, angry, frustrated, drank too many beers and fell asleep in the living room with the television still droning, its dull white light flashing shadows on the wall behind him. She could hear him snoring when she reached the foot of the stairway and turned to go out the rear door, pausing at the pantry to get a pair of plastic gloves. Nothing she did attracted the slightest attention. Stocker couldn't recall how many times had she successfully snuck out of this house. She had done it too often, most of the time to go up to the Lakehouse and spy on the lovers, of course.

A heavy, overcast sky thickened the darkness. It was so difficult to see, in fact, that she moved like a blind girl, depending more on her memory than on her vision as she crossed the yard to the unattached garage. She heard Kasey-Lady stir, but it took only one sharp, guttural command to send her cowering back into her doghouse before she started to bark.

When she was inside the garage, she paused to acclimate herself in the dark. She didn't want to put on the light. Her father might wake and see it. Instead, she moved as carefully as she could to her Compubike and unlocked it. Then she struggled a bit to get it out through the side door. Lifting the garage door would have been far easier, but that was out of the question. That much noise would surely alert dear old Dad.

Once the bike was out, she put on the plastic gloves and returned to the garage. Like a rat, she burrowed under old rags and a discarded blanket her father threw on the floor if he ever had to get down on his knees to do anything under their vehicles. She felt around until she found the heavy flashlight and brought it out carefully. Then she took one of the rags and meticulously wiped the handle of the flashlight.

It wasn't until she had pedaled and motored with the assistance of the computer generator a good half mile from her house that she stopped and bathed the flashlight in the bike light to inspect it. The bloodstains were dark and dry around the lens, but there certainly was enough there for the CID man to describe the flashlight as a murder weapon.

Buoyed by her own cleverness, she sped up. As she rode, she reconstructed the scene with Lois Marlowe. In her new version, she saw herself come upon Lois after Lois had been struck. She knelt beside her body and realized she was dead, and the sight of that death, the impact on her, was so traumatic that it sent her fleeing into the night. She then had put it out of her mind for fear of nightmares.

This was not a story she was developing for any police authority. Rather, it was what she would come to believe herself, referring back to her good techniques for falsification: first you convince yourself, and then you can convince others. Reality was pliable. Details could be refitted, events reconstructed and then put back in their new form, as firmly and as authentically as they had been.

In the event she would be questioned again, she would be convincing because she had convinced herself.

The Rosses' house was dark except for two lighted windows upstairs she knew to be their bedroom. Because her mother was so trusted a housekeeper and domestic assistant, Natalie and Preston Ross told her where they kept their emergency key. It was in a fake rock at the rear of the house. Stocker knew that the Rosses' electronic field security system would not go on until all the main lights had gone off. Everything was tied in through the house computer.

Nevertheless, she stopped a good hundred yards from the perimeter of the house and gently laid her bike down. She moved through the shadows as quickly as she could, found the fake rock, extracted the key, and went around to the side door of the attached garage. Once inside, she turned on the flashlight and studied for a potentially good hiding place. Then, she thought, that made no sense. Someone who was afraid of the flashlight being discovered would have gotten rid of it, not taken it home. No, this was an impulsive act of rage, not a premeditated, well-planned murder. Natalie Ross was no professional killer. She returned home, terrified by what she had done, and just put the flashlight back in one of those drawers. Then she went upstairs and took a mood balancer.

Or maybe not. She was, after all, pregnant. Her underground doctor might have forbidden any drugs or significant alcohol.

What does any of that matter? she asked herself. *Get this over with.*

She chose a deep drawer and put the flashlight in the back of it quickly. Satisfied with how innocent it looked there, she closed the drawer and retreated. She returned the spare key to the fake rock and hurried through the shadows to her bike. On the way home, she felt the breeze lift her hair and caress her cheeks. She felt as if she were actually flying. She was ecstatic and felt larger than life. She could sail above events and time and change fate. She was godlike and could give people life or death, years of sadness or years of happiness.

How dare Daddy smash her VRG? Didn't he understand? She would get another one easier than she had gotten the first. Punishing her was a futile activity. He should just accept her, be grateful that she didn't turn her fury and her power on him. If he continued to behave this way, she just might do that.

When she entered the house, she discovered he had finally gone up to bed. She tiptoed through the downstairs hallway to the stairs and went up to her room. It wasn't until she went to the bathroom that she realized she was still wearing the plastic gloves.

That was a mistake, she thought unhappily. She could have been caught with them on and would have had to come up with some amazing fabrication to explain them. It put a little doubt and fear into her wall of arrogance. She shouldn't have taken such pleasure in the ride home. She should have stayed with the program, reviewed every moment to be sure she made no mistakes.

Let this be the one and only, she chanted.

It wasn't a prayer. She didn't pray.

She never prayed.

The night was always too dark and too empty for her to believe in anything greater than herself out there or above her.

Besides, wasn't it mankind that made life and took life, cured diseases, repaired the environment, managed nature, and created destiny?

God was out of work, unemployed, like some parent caught by surprise and faced with the incontestable fact that he was no longer necessary.

That damn old Tree of Knowledge, she thought recalling the religious mythology she was once taught. That was surely dumb on his part. Why in hell did he ever plant it in the first place?

Look what it had wrought.

She fell asleep with laughter on her lips.

Eight
::::::::::::

Hattie Scranton, Carol Saxon, Betty Prater, Sally Morris, and Fern Ridley sat in a semicircle around Suki Astor. All eyes like pairs of laser drills were fixed intently on her. Despite this, the petite seventeen-year-old girl with rich, strawberry-blond hair trimmed, cut, and styled with a graceful sweep back, looked as fresh, relaxed, and perfect as she had the day she had her hair done.

Suki wasn't dressed like this in anticipation of company. Neither she nor her parents had any idea that Hattie and her baby squad would be swooping down on them this evening. Suki was always well put together, fashionable, sophisticated, and certainly not the typical teenage girl. When it came to her appearance, she was rarely taken by surprise. Her girlfriends had long since nicknamed her Chichi.

The Astor family was one of the wealthiest in the community. Philip Astor was the owner of the county's biggest construction firm. They lived in a virtual mansion, a three-story Greek Revival with four Ionic columns. Built on a knoll overlooking the valley, it looked as if it could be the governor's mansion. Suki's room was as big as the master bedroom in any one of the baby squad's houses. One could almost taste the joy they all felt for having bullied their way into this exquisite home and wealthy family.

Suki's beautiful black eyes shifted from one scrutinizing face to the other. She tried desperately to look innocent and calm. Her parents hung back near the doorway, her mother pressing her upper lip down over her lower, her arms wrapped so tightly around herself she resembled someone wearing a straitjacket. Her father scowled, indignant, close to a rage, chafing at the bit. He was not used to being told what he had to do or whom he had to permit to enter his home.

However, Hattie had come armed with information she had already browbeaten out of another girl, Shirley Keefer, a far less self-confident teenager who had practically burst into tears at the sight of the squad.

"I will begin by telling you what we know for a fact, Suki, and I will ask you some questions and expect an immediate, honest reply to each one. Is that clear?" Hattie demanded.

Suki nodded and looked again at her parents. This was going to be bad. This was going to be very bad, she thought.

"We know you, Shirley Keefer, Lois Marlowe, Clair Kaufman, and Arlene Letz have been members of what you girls call the Pregnancy Club. We know this has been going on for some time. We know what you do at these so-called club meetings. We have seen those ridiculous pictures of you as well as the others simulating late-term pregnancy. We have confessions and testimony. We know you have violated laws, abused access to information, and actively tried to recruit other young girls. Do you deny any of this?"

Suki gazed at her father. His rage had begun to dissolve into a look of fear.

"I'm not pregnant," she said in reply.

"We know you're not pregnant," Hattie said with a small, tight smile. "We know you just pretend to be pregnant. I'm not going to march you out of this house and have you examined," she added, sounding very reasonable, almost sympathetic. It had the effect of lowering Suki's defensive demeanor. She had heard what had been done to Lois, but maybe she could get out of this undamaged after all.

"Lois Marlowe was your leader, wasn't she?"

"Yes," Suki admitted quickly. On any other occasion, in front of a different audience, she might resent that. She had just as much to do with the creation of the club, and she had brought in ideas everyone liked and activities everyone performed.

"You met here on various occasions? Most occasions involving your so-called club?"

"Yes," she said, shifting her glance at her mother, who muffled a cry.

"In fact, your home eventually became the clubhouse, so to speak, right?"

"I guess," she said.

"You guess? You more than guess, Suki. You know. This is where you simulated a natural birth, where Lois Marlowe pretended to have labor pains, isn't it?"

Suki nodded. How did they know all this?

Her mother looked so devastated. Her father had transformed from a powerful executive to a very frightened man. He actually lowered his head like someone waiting to be sentenced to imprisonment or death. The sight of his weakening increased the terror in her own heart. She had always believed her father to be one of the most powerful men she had ever known or could ever know.

"Lois had chosen herself to be the pregnant woman, right?"

Whoever told her this was lying to protect herself, Suki thought. The truth was, they had competed for the honor, but again, she did not disagree. "Yes."

"After that, it was Lois who acquired the prenatal vitamins to continue this awful pretending, is that not so?"

"Yes, that's so," Suki said.

"You continued to meet here in this house?"

Suki nodded.

"Where you actually had a doll with a fake umbilical cord. You, yourself, delivered this imaginary baby, cut the cord, correct?"

How did Hattie Scranton know all this? Who gave her so much detailed information? Was she being made the fall guy? Was she going to take all the blame? "We used cards to see who had the highest card and who would be the midwife."

"Midwife," Carol Saxon muttered through her clenched teeth. It sounded like profanity when she pronounced it.

Fern Ridley groaned and looked at Suki's mother, who just shook her head in disbelief.

"You and your club members created a nursery for the imaginary baby in this house as well, is that right?" Without waiting for Suki's confirmation, Hattie added, "In a moment, you will take us there and show us the doll in a bassinet, won't you?"

"What?" her father cried, raising his eyes from the floor. "A doll in a bassinet?"

"Well?"

"Yes," Suki said, her lips finally trembling, her eyes filling with tears. "But that wasn't my idea."

"It was Lois Marlowe's idea, wasn't it?" Hattie pursued.

"Yes, it was Lois's," Suki accepted quickly.

"You sat around and read aloud to each other those X-rated books about infant care, postpartum blues, all of it, didn't you?"

Suki took a deep breath. Was there anything she

didn't know? If that were true, why were they here? What did they want?

"How could you do this?" her mother asked, starting toward her. "And in our house?"

Hattie held up her hand without turning to her, and her mother stopped abruptly as if she had been slapped. She remained where she was.

"Where did Lois Marlowe get those prenatal vitamins?"

"She said she had gotten them from Stocker Robinson," Suki replied quickly.

Hattie glanced at the other women.

"Did she trade a music CD for them?"

"That's what she told us."

"Did she have an X-rated VRG movie that she had received from Stocker Robinson?"

Suki shook her head. She felt safe about this. No one would have told her that they all had watched those films at one time or another.

"If you lie about any of this, you will pay a very severe penalty, Suki," Hattie warned.

"She never told me she had traded anything for any X-rated VRG movies," Suki answered. The care with which she formed her sentences and chose her words was not lost on Hattie Scranton. She studied the girl a bit more. She didn't want to be made the fool here, to go off armed with misinformation and be shown to be wrong. That could do her and her squad a great deal more harm than doing nothing at all.

"Was Stocker Robinson ever at any of your club meetings?"

"No," Suki replied quickly, and even grimaced.

"You don't like her?"

"No one likes her."

"You wouldn't make things up to get her into trouble, now, would you, Suki? That would end up being worse for you and your friends, you know," Hattie warned.

"I don't care about her enough to make up anything about her," Suki said.

It was a good answer.

"Okay," Hattie said, rising. "Show us the nursery."

Suki got up slowly. Her mother was crying unabatedly now, and her father's face was so red he looked sunburned. Without so much as glancing at her parents, she led the women out of her room and up the stairway to the attic of the house. Her father and mother trailed behind, obedient puppy dogs, restrained and defeated by the revelations Hattie easily extracted from their daughter.

Suki flipped on the light and took them to the rear of the large attic, where she uncovered a small bassinet in which a doll had been placed.

All of the women looked at it as if it were really a living infant, their eyes wide, their lips stretched into ugly grimaces of disgust. They saw the baby bottles, the boxes of disposable diapers, the powders and oils, as well as the bottle of liquid infant vitamins.

"We want to know how you acquired each and every item here," Hattie said. "What store owner in what town sold any of this to you. We want names and dates and times. Is that clear?"

Suki lowered her head.

With her forefinger extended and accusing, she would bring terrible devastation to people who had no idea what she and her girlfriends were up to. They had done so good a job of pretending to be helping legal mothers. Of course, the store owners and sales clerks should have been more careful. They should have not sold these things to them without the proper license cards.

But what could she do about that?

It was save-your-own-skin time. Aside from blaming all she could on Lois Marlowe, who was beyond pain and disgrace, there was little other choice.

"Well?" Hattie pounded.

"Yes," she said. "I will."

"We'll contact you tomorrow and tell you where to be," Hattie declared. She looked at Suki's parents. "I'd advise you to get rid of all this immediately."

"How?" Philip asked. At this point, he wanted to sound as cooperative as possible and wanted to follow any prescribed procedure.

There really wasn't any precedent for this sort of thing.

"Take it out and burn it," Hattie suggested with disgust.

The women filed out of the attic, moving with an air of mourning. When their footsteps echoed on the stairway, Suki turned slowly and looked at her parents.

"We're going to be at the center of a terrific scandal. We don't deserve this," her father said.

"It was just for fun, Daddy. We never meant to hurt anyone," she cried.

"You haven't hurt just anyone," he said, his voice in a dead monotone. "You've hurt your family. You've hurt yourself. Go back to your room. Get more and more familiar with every aspect of it, no matter how tiny. It will be your world after school for the rest of this year," he said, pronouncing sentence. "Your phone will be gone in the morning. If anyone wants to talk to you, it will have to be through ESP," he added, and left.

She looked at her mother.

"Lois Marlowe is dead. It could have been you," her mother said.

"I wish it was," Suki replied.

Natalie pressed her body against Preston's and kissed his cheek and his lips. For a moment, she thought he wasn't going to react, but then he turned abruptly and kissed her on her lips, his kiss harder, longer. She felt him stirring with sexual interest.

Suddenly, he paused and pulled back.

"I don't know anything about this . . . this natural birth thing, Nat," he said, nodding at her stomach. "Can we still go at it at this late stage of pregnancy?"

"Of course," she said with a smile. "And don't worry. You can't make another until this one is born."

He laughed. "I know that much, at least."

He started toward her again.

Preston had always been what she thought of as a gradual lover, not that she had all that much experience at making love. She had a serious romance in high school that was very passionate but also rather short-lived. Natalie had always been more selective about her boyfriends and her relationships with men. Other girls her age almost reduced love itself to just another computer game, clicking on and off boys the way they would click on and off icons on a monitor. They made sexual activity seem like little more than a handshake. Making love with a man didn't mean you were serious about him or he was serious about you. People enjoyed one another the way they enjoyed different flavors of ice cream. At least, that was the way it seemed to her. She told herself that was why she had become a romance writer.

In her heart of hearts, she truly believed other women, even men, wanted something more, something deeper and more substantial in their relationships. It was almost an admission of weakness to reveal this, however. The philosophy that governed relationships in this country, this world, was the idea that everything that happened occurred for specific, tangible, and explainable reasons. There was no such thing as kismet or magic between two people. If they were attracted to each other enough to want to marry and live together in the hope of qualifying as parents, they did so because their genetics steered them toward each other. They fit like two well-made pieces of machinery. It made electrical and physiological sense. That's all.

And yet books like the ones she wrote still had a significant audience, albeit an audience that either had to consider or did consider what she did little more than distraction, the new form of comic book. She wrote with the passion she wanted to see in her own life, and she was eloquent enough to pass that need into her words, into her characters, into her plots.

She tried to employ it all in her own love relationship, but Preston could be close to mechanical when he made love sometimes. He would move over her body as if he were following a schematic drawing, kissing her neck here, strumming a nipple, licking it, nibbling around her breasts, kissing her on the mouth, moving his tongue over hers, scooping under her rear, moving his hands between her legs, moaning almost on cue, doing it all in the same pattern as if he were painting by numbers.

She would tell him how much she loved him and how good he felt to her, and either he would grunt in agreement or he would finally realize he was just going through motions and stop, look down at her, smile, and then say, "I love you more, Nat. You can't possibly love me as much as I love you."

"Why not?"

"Because I'm bigger. I have more love in me to give to you," he told her, and they both laughed, and their lovemaking was better, really passionate, full of feeling and care, but often it took that little extra effort on her part, that prodding.

"Are you happy with me, Preston? Are you happy I am carrying your baby, your complete and real baby?" she asked when he pulled his lips back from hers this time.

"Yes, Nat. I am," he said.

"You're not afraid? You're not nervous about it?"

"Of course I am, but so what? It makes it all that much more exciting, doesn't it?"

She tilted her head.

Was he serious? That wasn't what she thought he would say. She wasn't sure she liked it put that way. It wasn't just an adventure, a ride on a roller coaster in some fun park.

He sensed her displeasure. "What's wrong?"

"I didn't expect to hear you say that, Preston."

"I'm just trying to make you feel better, more at ease, Nat," he said quickly. "Let's not dwell on it to the extent that it takes us over, or we will make mistakes. Okay?" he said quickly.

She thought a moment and then nodded. Maybe he was right. He knew best about strategy when it came to dealing with people, especially important people. Look at how well he handled the Cauthers. "Okay."

They kissed again, and they made love until they were both exhausted, breathing hard, sweating with each other's heat.

It turned out to be wonderful. It was what she wanted it to be, always wanted it to be.

Afterward, he turned on his back and looked up at the ceiling. She took his hand and did the same. For a while, neither spoke.

"Sometimes, when we lie quietly beside each other like this, I feel like we're traveling through space together, moving faster than light," she said.

"Maybe we are. You heard that lecture last month at the club, the one on quantum energy and the human condition."

"No, not like that. I mean spiritually," she insisted. "Out of our bodies completely."

"Oooooh, Judy Norman's spiritual voodoo," he quipped.

"Not just Judy Norman. Me, too, Preston. I believe in much of that, in the unseen, untouchable part of ourselves."

He was quiet. "I made a call this afternoon," he said finally. "I'll hear back tomorrow."

"A call? What do you mean? A call to whom?"

"To where you have to go, where you'll be safe, away from prying eyes, away from people like Hattie Scranton and her henchwomen, in particular."

"Oh."

"It's possible you could go tomorrow, Nat," he said. "Pack in the morning."

"Tomorrow? So soon?"

"No sense waiting any longer than we have to and taking any chances, Nat. You understand that we will have to have a period without the baby, right? You understand you can't come home with a child in your arms?"

"Yes," she said sadly.

"In the meantime, I'll make out that we're applying, and soon after you're back, we'll have our child. Okay?"

"And our baby will be well looked after?" she asked. "I mean, until he or she is brought back to me?"

"Absolutely. I've been assured of that."

"By whom, Preston?"

"It's complicated, Nat. If I start giving you all the nitty-gritty, it might spook you. You'll have to take my word for all this, okay?"

"Okay," she said in a small voice.

He sat up to lean over and kiss her softly. "It

will be fine, Nat. It's going to be all right. Trust me," he said.

She put her hand on his cheek. "We trust you, Preston."

"We?"

"Me and you know who," she said, gently tapping her stomach with her left hand.

He looked down and nodded. "Right," he said.

"I can speak for both of us, Preston. I really can. That's the magic. I feel everything, know everything. It's really what should be," she said excitedly.

"Probably so," he said, and dropped back to his pillow. "But until the rest of this society sees it that way, we'd better tiptoe around them."

"Just think," Natalie said, "Judy and I will have children about the same time."

"If the Normans are approved," he said.

"There's no chance they won't be, is there, Preston?"

"Nothing is certain except that nothing is certain," he replied.

She didn't like that.

She didn't like it when he was coldly realistic.

At a time like this, who needed realism?

Romance, hope, dreams, fantasies, all of it had a reason to be, just as much as anything else.

People still had candles. They could light up the world if they wanted with their electric power, but they still had candles. Why?

Because there was still something about a small

flame, still some promise in its light, still some beauty in the shadows it threw. That's why they still put them on birthday cakes and lit them at special dinners, she thought.

Preston pressed the button, and all their lamps went dark, instantly lighting their alarm zone around the house. He turned over, snug, safe in their electronic cocoon.

"Good night," he said.

"Good night," she said.

I have one hope, she prayed after she closed her eyes, *one hope . . . that my child will not have to hide herself if she's a girl and will not want anything but his own child, fully, if he's a boy.*

Amen to that, she thought.

And then, in her mind, the candle flickered and went out.

Despite the wonders of modern police forensics and investigative science, Ryan Lee had confidence in his own instincts. Perhaps because he was a naturally born child, he had more faith in what others would call mumbo-jumbo, especially his superiors. He believed he had a sixth sense and that extrasensory power gave him the ability to be a highly successful investigator.

The bottom line was he didn't believe Stocker Robinson. Alarms had gone off when she gave her explanations and told that story about Lois Marlowe and the mysterious victim of her blackmail plot. Although it wasn't scientific, he noted movements in Stocker's eyes, the way she looked at her parents and avoided looking at him, and the nuances in her tone of voice. He often told himself he had an air for detecting liars and lies. They settled in those soft places in his brain where they could be dissected quickly, their falsity easily uncovered.

Without any more concrete evidence than the fact that she wore Rockers, he didn't want to confide too much in Henry McCalester, even when McCalester commented about Stocker.

"That's a weird one," he said. "Of course, you have to consider her mother is an Abnormal."

"Oh? Mr. Robinson works for the highway department. Does Mrs. Robinson do anything more than keep house?"

"Esther Robinson is what we call a domestic engineer," McCalester said, smiling.

"Cleans houses?"

"Well, I suppose with all the sophisticated cleaning equipment some people have these days, you just can't get any old body to do that sort of work anymore. Her clients are the most respected people in the community. You'd be surprised at how much money she makes. Thus, the term *domestic engineer*," he said with a sardonic smile. His smile faded quickly as a preamble to the question that followed. "You think she's the one, then? The shoes and all, right?"

"We'll see," Ryan said.

"Why don't we just bring her in and interrogate her? I know you guys have all sorts of sophisticated training for that sort of thing."

"Soon," Ryan said. He saw that McCalester looked nervous and unhappy about his hesitation. "I realize all the pressure on you, but we don't want to make a mistake here."

"Right," McCalester said, but not with any sincere note of agreement.

The state had McCalester provide Ryan with an undercover vehicle, and he parted company with him shortly after, but instead of returning to the hotel, he drove back to the Robinson residence and planted himself and his vehicle in the darkest possible shadows, settling in for a few hours of surveillance. As was often the case, he didn't have any specific expectations. Guilty people simply exposed their guilt on their own if you left them to their own devices, Ryan thought. Patience was still a virtue, regardless of the speed with which answers could be acquired through the variety of tools in his CID investigator's bag.

At first, he wasn't sure he saw someone leaving the house. She was so well melded with the shadows, like just another silhouette carved out of the darkness when a cloud shifted to permit some starlight to rain down. Then he clearly saw her emerge with her bike and start down the street.

With his car lights off, he followed, lagging far enough behind to remain almost invisible.

He had no idea whose house it was that she made her final destination. His mind was running along the theory that she was visiting a friend, someone who knew her lies, perhaps, someone she had to count on to support her fabricated story and explanations.

When she finally stopped at a house, he parked far enough away to get out of his vehicle and track behind her, still using the shadows to disguise himself and his movements. He watched through his night glasses with curiosity and interest as she scurried like some creature of the dark, keeping herself out of the dim glow of illumination that spilled from the upstairs windows of this home. He saw her take something from under a rock and then go to the garage. He moved close enough to see that she was carrying a flashlight, possibly the one he had identified. It looked that long. However, his first impression was that she had brought it along to see her way to something. His suspicions were aroused when she never turned it on and went into the garage.

When she emerged, she did not have the flashlight with her. He watched her put the key back under the rock and hurry to her bike. She took off down the road, pedaling and then using her electric motor to speed away. He lingered a moment, noted

the address, and returned to his vehicle. Seconds
later, he had the names of the residents. Their histories and identities scrolled on his pocket computer
screen.

What was her reason for leaving the flashlight
behind? Very likely, it was the murder weapon.
Was she trying to frame one of the residents of the
home, Mr. or Mrs. Ross? How could she hope to
do that?

With the flashlight as the weapon and with his
knowledge that he had placed her at the crime
scene, he felt confident that he had already found
his killer. He didn't know her motivation, and he
didn't have the pieces put together yet, but he would
have it all done within the next twenty-four hours.

Then he would make his arrest and return to
headquarters.

He envisioned it all. He would receive an impressive commendation and perhaps a promotion
that would trigger a salary raise.

However, the looks on the faces of those who
thought him inherently inferior would be the best
reward of all.

Something stirred in the bushes behind him,
and he spun around and studied the darkness. He
saw nothing. It could have been a deer or some
other field animal, he thought.

The lights went off in the Ross house, casting
the entire area in a deeper darkness but permitting
the stars to brighten and emerge.

He turned back to the Rosses' property and watched the tiny red electric field alarm lights illuminate like the eyes of a nocturnal beast waiting in the shadows, eager to attack some unwitting prey.

The sound of footsteps on the road spun him around again. He listened hard. Moments later, he was sure he heard a car engine start and then a vehicle not five hundred yards down the road drive off in the opposite direction.

There weren't any other houses here, not for a good quarter of a mile in either direction. Who the hell was that? He went to his car and got his own flashlight and his evidence bag, then tracked back until he saw tire tracks. In minutes, he had the information he needed to determine who might have been here.

He hurried back to his vehicle, started it, and slipped back into the darkness, turning on the headlights and blowing the night out of his way.

That car behind him might have been nothing, or maybe it was important. Maybe he didn't have it all figured out, after all.

Maybe there was something else out here, some other reason all this had happened.

That commendation and promotion might take a little longer than he had hoped.

Nine

••••••••••••
:::::::::::::

As Preston had suggested, the call came while they were at breakfast. Unlike some recent mornings, Natalie woke almost simultaneously with Preston and showered when he showered, dressed when he dressed. She was down a few minutes before he was and had started the juice machine and coffee maker. She had just put out his favorite dry cereal and put a cinnamon slice in the toaster for herself when he arrived, poured his juice, and turned on the television monitor to read the Wall Street report.

Then the phone rang.

They looked at each other, she freezing for a moment. Now that she had shared her secret with someone else, she couldn't help this sense of paranoia. It wasn't that she thought Preston would reveal it to anyone accidentally or otherwise, so much as it was this oppressive sense of impending doom, as if the walls had ears, as if Hattie Scranton and her baby squad had psychic talents.

Preston lifted the receiver, said hello, and then just listened.

Finally, he said, "I understand. Thank you."

He cradled the phone gently and nodded at her.

"They'll be by in an hour, Natalie."

"They'll be by in an hour? Who?"

"The limousine taking you to the safe house," he said. "It's where everything will be taken care of. It has the staff and the necessary equipment and facilities."

She felt her heart start to thump. "But . . . I didn't really get started packing and . . ."

"You've got an hour, honey," he said softly. "You don't need all that much. I'll bring the rest when I come to visit you. Just take what you need for the first week or so," he instructed.

"Where am I going, exactly, Preston?"

"Farther upstate, actually, a very rural, out-of-the-way area. You'll probably like it a great deal, Nat. It's woodsy, the nearest village about ten miles away, a lake nearby, streams, truly back to nature, just like in your novel *In the Arms of the Oak Tree*."

"You remember that one?" she asked, smiling.

"Kinda my favorite," he admitted. "Especially the man, the naturalist living in that cabin. Don't wander off and run into any strong woodsman types before I get there," he warned with feigned concern.

She laughed. The toaster popped, and she scooped out the slice of cinnamon bread, stuffing it into her mouth and grabbing herself a glass of juice as she started out of the kitchen. She paused in the doorway.

"How did you find this place so quickly, Preston?"

"Got to keep it a secret," he said. He smiled and added, "If I tell you, I have to kill you right afterward."

"You idiot. An hour! I can't believe it!"

She hurried to the stairway.

"Remember, don't take too much, Nat," he called after her. "I'll bring what else you need."

"Right."

What did she need now, anyway? Running through her wardrobe and making the choices put her into a frantic pace. Surely, she would forget something she would want the moment she got there and realized she didn't have it, she thought. She definitely would take her portable Wordsmith. She had to finish the novel and keep herself occupied. She considered her cosmetics and rejected taking most of them. This wasn't exactly a vacation. She also rejected most of her jewelry. Why would she need any of it?

Even her supply of black market prenatal vitamins wasn't important. Surely, the safe house would have everything she needed medically, but she did decide to take them and the birth control pills anyway. No sense leaving that sort of thing lying around now, she thought. The crush of an hour's packing wasn't as bad as she had anticipated once she considered what she really did and didn't need. Nevertheless, she still wasn't quite emotionally prepared when Preston came up to tell her the limousine had arrived.

"Already?"

"It's right on time, honey. I guess you didn't realize how long you've been up here."

He picked up her two suitcases and shoved her portable Wordsmith under his arm.

"I feel like I'm being scooped off," she complained.

"You are. That was the idea, wasn't it? You're too far along to waste any time, Nat."

"I know," she said, gazing around the bedroom, "but now that it's actually happening . . ."

"You told me to get on it, to do what had to be done," he said.

"Right. Of course." She smiled. "Why shouldn't I expect you to be efficient, effective? It's why I have so much faith in you to start with, Preston."

"I'm not saying I'm not nervous about all this, Nat. Inside, I'm shaking as much as you are, I bet."

Her smile widened and softened even more. "I'll miss you, even for a week."

"I'll be at your side first chance I have," he promised. "Come on," he urged.

"Coming," she said. She took one last look around the bedroom to be sure she wasn't leaving anything she would need immediately, and then, with a deep sigh, she followed him, holding her breath all the way down to the front door.

When it was opened, she saw the stretch pearl-black limousine. The chauffeur stepped out to help with the luggage. He wore very dark sunglasses and was a tall man with a military demeanor, his back and shoulders firm, straight, his body strong but trim. He barely glanced at her as she walked to the vehicle. He and Preston put her things in the trunk, and then he returned to his seat and stared ahead like some kind of mindless robot.

She stood there with Preston.

"It's happening so fast," she whispered.

"It's what you wanted, Nat. I'm doing what you wanted."

"And what you wanted, too," she emphasized.

He nodded. "Yes, but it's really all falling on you, Nat. You're the one going through natural childbirth, not me. Are you sure you still want to do it?"

"Yes. More than ever," she insisted.

"Okay, then." He opened the door for her.

She looked into the rear of the vehicle, darkened by the tinted windows that behaved as mirrors. Her home was reflected in the glass, her wonderful home, her dream house. She would miss it almost as much as she would miss Preston.

Tears came into her eyes. She sucked in her breath, turned to him, kissed him, and slipped into the limousine.

Preston gazed at her, smiled, and closed the door.

Almost instantly, the vehicle started away. She felt as if she had been swallowed up in it. There was so much room for just one person.

"Cold drinks are in the small refrigerator on the right side," she heard the chauffeur say. "The television remote is in the cradle by the glasses. You can ask me for anything you want. There's a built-in intercom. Just speak at will, Mrs. Ross," he concluded.

"Thank you," she said. "Oh. How long is the trip?" she asked.

He was silent.

"Excuse me," she followed. "How long is the ride?"

"That's confidential, Mrs. Ross," he replied. "I'm sure you understand. It's for your own protection as well as ours."

"Really?"

As they turned onto the main highway that would take them away from Sandburg, she heard the whir of an electric motor, and then, to her shock and surprise, metal curtains came sliding down and over the windows, shutting off her view of the world outside, locking her in as if she had been put in a moving casket.

"What are you doing?" she cried.

"It's standard operating procedure, Mrs. Ross. Relax. The air system is filtered and set at a comfortable temperature. If you get too cold or too warm, I can make instant adjustments."

"But . . . I like to look at the scenery."

"Television remote is by the glasses," he repeated. "Relax," he said. It sounded more like an order. "You'll be fine, ma'am, just fine."

The soft sound of the vehicle's cushioned movement over the highway was seductive, hypnotic. She closed her eyes and told herself there was just this little inconvenience for a while and then great happiness. No reason to worry about anything. She was safe. Preston was in charge. She and her baby were safe.

Hattie Scranton usually rose from bed seconds after her eyes opened. She despised wasting time. It actually made her sick to her stomach whenever she was in a situation where she had nothing to do but wait. From the moment she rose until the moment she laid her head back on her pillow at night, she was on the move, doing practical and useful things. After all, she had a major responsibility. In her way of thinking, the lives of hundreds, if not thousands, of people were dependent on how she carried forth.

Her husband, William, was no match for her when it came to this show of energy. He was a

rather quiet man, plodding along, a true journey-
man, never initiating anything new or creative, not
even changing the decor in his offices. He was the
community's most successful ophthalmologist, a
good technician utilizing the computerized laser
machinery that could eliminate most eye maladies.

As tall and slim as Hattie, he had a far softer
look, practically a look of defeat, in his dull brown
eyes, long nose, and weak mouth. Hattie was always chastising him about his posture, the way he
dipped his shoulders and let his arms dangle
loosely when he walked.

"You look moronic, primitive," she told him.

William accepted her criticism with the indiffer-
ence of a man resigned to pain, to whipping. It
was almost as if he viewed his marriage as punish-
ment for some ancestral sin passed down through
the genes that were continued into his human
genome. Marriage to Hattie was his burden.

They had been brought together by technology.
The Cupid computer, as it was informally known,
spit out their names after analyzing their genetic
histories and predilections. Those who were objective, who dared to challenge the infallibility of the
modern world, concluded Cupid had made a gross
error. Two people couldn't look more incompati-
ble. They always looked like strangers standing side
by side at social events, waiting to be formally introduced to each other. No one had ever seen a
sign of affection between them. William's typical

responses to Hattie's conversation were usually nods, monosyllabic words, shrugs, or slight shakes of his head.

Most significantly, Hattie and William Scranton had never applied for a parents' license. Early in the marriage, William had brought up the possibility, and she had told him they weren't ready. She said she would let him know when they were. She had yet to do that, and after a while, he gave up on the whole idea, harboring the belief that it would be cruel to permit Hattie to mother any child.

He contented himself with his work, his detective stories, and his one secret: his pornography VRG films hidden in the basement wall of their home. Sex between him and Hattie had always been mechanical. She made him feel as if he were participating in a bodily necessity, not much more than going to the bathroom. Lately, he had trouble reaching a climax with her, but she didn't seem to notice or care. She literally left him hanging.

Being married to a woman who carried so much informal authority in the community had its pros and cons. He recognized that it brought him far more respect than he would otherwise enjoy, even with his medical skills. However, he also sensed the fear people tried to cloak in his presence, their anxiety, and their nervousness. It forced him to remain further aloof from his patients than he would like. Women, especially, were overly ingratiating. He could read it in their eyes. They believed he could turn Hattie and her squad on them with a simple suggestion. He once complained about this to Hattie and asked her, "Do you know how hard it is to look into the eyes of people who are afraid of you and ask them to look forward, look at me?"

She smirked at him as if he had said the most ridiculous thing and replied, "Only the guilty look away."

She had no idea, he thought. She didn't have the talent, the perception to be doing what she was doing. He half expected this would become evident to the community after a while, and she would lose her grip on it, but this had yet to happen, and to him it indicated that the eyes he improved still remained blinded by the cataracts of fear they created in themselves.

William usually rose before Hattie on weekday mornings. To any casual observer, it would appear that he wanted to flee the bed they shared. Often, he would get up in the dark and tiptoe through the bedroom, barely running the water in the shower so as not to wake her. His coffee cup tinkled at breakfast. He moved like someone in a silent film, performing a dumb show in the kitchen below and then leaving the house like a soft breeze that had passed through, the door closing gently behind him. He was a ghost of himself and thought he wouldn't be surprised if he passed a mirror and saw no image, not surprised at all.

Hattie didn't mind his silent, swift morning

exit. Waking up beside him and gazing at his sleeping face actually nauseated her. His mouth was always open too far, the air whistling through his lips carrying a sour halitosis that churned her stomach. His dark brown hair fell loosely over his creased forehead. He always looked as if he was having painful thoughts. It actually enraged her. Somehow she had been cheated. She had been denied romance, love, affection. Now, she was comfortable believing they were all illusions, anyway. It helped her to endure. She never revealed this to anyone, of course. She had devoted and loyal followers but no one she could rely on, confide in.

But this wasn't her greatest secret. Her greatest secret related to her horrifying fantasy. She had learned that many women experienced it, but she had refused to acknowledge to anyone that she did, too. It was the fantasy of childbirth, the incredible sense of being pregnant, feeling a fetus turn and kick inside you, and then, on occasion, being inflicted with terrible cramps resembling labor pains. Some women even confessed to pushing an imaginary fetus from their wombs. Psychiatrists had been conjecturing about this phenomenon lately, comparing it to the sensation people with amputated limbs have, the feeling that the limb is still present. A radical theory that practically had the theoretician ostracized was the idea that the female body craved pregnancy and that to deny it that experience was to diminish its essence.

All of this helped to fan the flames of Hattie's fiery determination to hunt down Abnormals and keep the community pure and successful. She was a woman on a mission to justify her own existence, her own identity. It was her vigilance, and her vigilance alone, that made them successful. She didn't exactly think of it as a divine ordination. It was more like a genetic predisposition, her destiny determined before she was actually created.

This faith in herself, in her own perception, filled her with suspicions. Their cross-examination of the teenage girls was successful, but she couldn't help feeling there was something else here, some darker, deeper thing to uncover. And now she had some reason to give that theory credence.

Today, she thought, she would focus on it intensely, and by the end of the day, she would expose it. She would be far more successful than that CID officer. He was too narrow of purpose, anyway. The murder was the least of it.

She practically leaped out of bed, a woman with a mission, impatient, determined, and, of course, heroic.

Perhaps nowhere was a secret more in jeopardy within the Sandburg high school building than in the girls' bathroom. Much of the school was under surveillance. Cameras, microphones, metal detectors, alarms were in nearly every room. The only area left somewhat sacrosanct was the girls' toilet stalls; however, there were built-in smoke detectors and explosive material detectors. If the stall door was closed, a sensor would detect more than one body in the stall by recording the body heat. However, the girls knew that if they left the stall door open, they could stand around outside the stall and whisper among themselves relatively securely. They ran faucets and flushed toilets if they had to cover up some dialogue as well.

Suki Astor, Shirley Keefer, Clair Kaufman, and Arlene Letz met in the girls' bathroom shortly before the final bell for homeroom. It was their standard operating procedure. This morning, they were more anxious than ever to talk and share what they knew about Hattie and the baby squad's investigation. Suki was raging with anger the moment she had stepped into the school. She practically ran to the girls' room, impatiently awaiting the others.

"Someone here got me into a lot of trouble!" she accused as soon as they were all gathered around the stall. She sat on the toilet seat. "I'm grounded for the rest of the year!"

"They already knew a lot," Shirley volunteered. It was as good as a confession. "They did!" she emphasized when the others glared at her. "They knew all our names, and they knew where we had met, and they knew lots of stuff. I couldn't lie. I told them about Stocker," she added, nodding and smiling. "That's all they really wanted to know, anyway."

"You didn't have to tell them about the baby and the crib and all that," Suki moaned. "You told them exactly where it all was. We didn't have a chance to get rid of anything."

"I couldn't help it."

"You could have called and warned her they were coming," Arlene pointed out.

"My father ripped the video phone out of the wall as soon as they left our house," Shirley sobbed. "I'm grounded, too."

"I guess that's what I've got to look forward to later when I go home today," Clair said.

"Me, too," Arlene added, her rage whitening the corners of her mouth.

"Stocker Robinson. I hate her," Suki said through her clenched teeth.

"You think she really killed Lois?" Clair asked.

"She's a maggot. She's capable of anything," Suki insisted.

"A piece of vermin," Arlene said.

"An ugly, disgusting, horrid thing," Shirley contributed. Having someone on which they could unload their anger and deflect it from one another was very helpful.

"Maybe she's pregnant, too, and that's why she had those vitamins in the first place," Clair suggested. "Her mother's an Abnormal, isn't she? How do we know she really is an NL1?"

They were all silent for a moment, twisting and turning their anger and rage into some form of revenge.

"We'll say we know that to be true, her pregnancy," Suki suggested. "We'll spread the story."

"They'll drag her out of here in disgrace to the clinic," Clair said.

"Everyone will talk about her and forget about us," Shirley hoped aloud.

"Let's go to it," Suki said, rising. She flushed the toilet. No one had even noticed that she had peed.

Hattie and her baby squad hadn't told any of them not to say anything about their interrogations. Without fear or any hesitation, they fanned out to spread the stories as quickly as they could, often deliberately doing so in front of or near microphones and cameras. By lunch hour, the whole school was abuzz with rumors about Stocker Robinson. Stocker could feel the eyes of her classmates on her like a swarm of angry killer bees.

More furious than frightened, Stocker cut her last class of the morning and fled the building, even though it was a nearly impossible thing to do. Every student at the Sandburg high school as well as most every public and private school in the country wore an identification badge that carried a homing device enabling school authorities to tell where that student was located at all times. The entrances and exits of the building were armed with sensors that would ring on the central office monitor if a student left the building or attempted to leave at an unauthorized time. One had to receive permission for an early dismissal, and that was then programmed into the system.

The system not only made the structure impenetrable but also made it virtually impossible for a young person to go AWOL from school. Runaways as they were known in the twentieth century were rare, and if a young person did attempt such a thing, he or she was immediately brought to the juvenile authorities, and a homing chip was surgically implanted in the back of his or her neck. Not only was it difficult and painful to remove it, but it would set off an alarm and make the young person even more of a fugitive. That was punishable by imprisonment at a high-security juvenile facility.

Stocker was fully aware of all this, but she was also aware of a way to exit the building undetected. It wasn't exactly a graceful portal of escape. She had to go down to the school basement and slide out the garbage chute, which would drop her into the Dumpster, usually full of food remnants by this time of day. She had done it once before at the end of the day just for the excitement and had not been caught since she had no class to attend where she would be missed.

This was different. They would be looking for her, but she was enraged and could no longer stand being treated like some sort of leper. She would not be a victim. She was going to see to that now.

She walked and ran most of the way back to the village and cut through some yards and some woods and fields she knew. Being a loner most of her life, she had spent a good deal of her time on solitary hikes, sneaking around other people's homes, looking in windows for hours at a time, watching happier young people in their more loving homes. Having a mother who was a known Abnormal made life very difficult for her. She resented it and blamed her grandmother for giving birth to her mother the old-fashioned way. Stocker had her NL1 certificate prominently displayed on the wall of her bedroom, but who ever saw that? She had never had any girlfriends over to her home. The only people other than her parents who had been in her room were the members of that damn baby squad, and most of them looked as if they didn't believe it, anyway.

Nearly an hour later, she cut through a patch of woods and emerged on the southeastern side of the Rosses' home. She knew her mother was not working in the Rosses' house today. She didn't see her vehicle anywhere, and so she was confident there had been no change of schedule.

Even so, Stocker's plan of action wasn't completely clear to her yet. She thought she would confront Natalie Ross first, make her demands, and then, if that didn't work, call her husband perhaps. If none of that worked, she would place an anonymous phone call to Chief McCalester or maybe even Hattie Scranton herself and let them know where the murder weapon could be found. One way or the other, she would lift the burden of all this guilt and anger off her and transfer it to where it belonged. In her way of thinking, all this was Natalie Ross's fault, anyway. If she wasn't pregnant and didn't have those pills, none of this would have happened. It was a good way to rationalize her own responsibility away. She was very pleased with herself for thinking of it.

She approached the house cautiously and then pushed the door buzzer, deliberately looking into the camera. A door responder came on immediately, speaking in a mechanical computer voice.

"There is no one at home. Please leave a message in the door responder. If this is an unauthorized solicitation, be aware that the inhabitants do not receive such solicitations at any time. If this is a postal delivery, please leave the delivery in the package box. If the delivery requires a signature, please submit the signature card in the signature slot. Thank you."

Stocker stepped back, her disappointment sharpening her rage. What was she supposed to do, return to school? Where was that bitch? Patience was not one of Stocker's virtues. Her eagerness swirled inside her. She felt like Kasey-Lady lunging against that perennial leash and collar, and she had no tolerance for frustration.

I'm going to make a phone call, she thought. *I'll get what I want, and I'll get it now.*

Rather than return to school or even to her own home, she went to the rock and slipped out the spare key. Then she went into the garage and retrieved the flashlight, taking care to keep her fingerprints off it. She would tell Mrs. Ross she had found it in the house, if Mrs. Ross came home first. She would show her the bloodstains, and the woman would believe her husband might have killed Lois. If Mr. Ross returned before Mrs. Ross, she would tell him the same thing, and he might wonder if his wife hadn't killed Lois. She had seen something like this in a movie she had watched just last week on her virtual reality glasses. It would be more exciting, more titillating, to do it this way anyhow, she thought and returned to the front door.

Using the proper key disarmed the alarm system, and she was in without any difficulty. For a moment, she just stood in the entryway, feeling this great sense of power, this wonderful voyeurism, invading the Rosses' privacy. It was what made it so exciting when she had managed to slip away from her mother that day and sneak into Natalie Ross's bedroom, at first just to explore and then to discover the pamphlets about pregnancy and the pills, obviously black market, hidden. Under a magnifying glass, she read the engraved "PNV" and felt the surge of excitement. She hadn't discovered only contraband drugs; she had uncovered an Abnormal, a pregnant woman, and in this house, this important and powerful couple!

At the time, it wasn't the information and knowledge that she found to be salable, however; it was the pills. Now it was an entirely different story. Now it was information.

She went upstairs to the bedroom and paused in the doorway. Drawers were open, and the closet door was open. It looked as if someone had robbed them. Curiosity growing, she went into the closet and searched for the cache of pills. They were gone! She stood in the bedroom thinking.

I better move quickly, she thought. *There's something going on here because of all the turmoil in the town.*

Without hesitation, she went to the video phone and pressed for information. When Preston's firm came up, she initiated a call.

"Mr. Ross," she demanded when the receptionist answered.

"Who's calling, please?"

"His niece," she replied. Might as well be a member of the family, she thought with a smile.

Preston had just closed a folder and marked it with a red-ink rejection when Rose buzzed him.

"My niece? I have no niece."

"You want me to refuse the call, Mr. Ross?"

He thought a moment. Maybe it was some sort of disguise Natalie was using, although she shouldn't be able to call him from the limousine.

"No. I'll take it," he said.

He pressed the button and sat back as the screen formed a picture.

His eyebrows lifted. It was a teenage girl, but she looked as if she was in his bedroom. *Huh?*

"Hello. Who are you? What do you want? Where are you?" he fired.

Stocker smiled for the video phone camera.

"I know about your wife," she said.

Ten

::::::::::::

"The Rosses? Why would you want to know about them?" McCalester asked Ryan.

"I know about them. I want to know what you know about them," Ryan replied dryly.

They were sitting in his office. Ryan was thinking it was pathetically small, almost no larger than some walk-in closets he had seen in the homes of wealthy people. McCalester's desk was so small the big man looked as if he were sitting in a room full of children's furniture. The dull gray walls were inundated with framed pictures of a younger McCalester standing with state politicians and county officials. Here and there were pictures of him with celebrities, movie and television stars who had come through the area or attended an event nearby.

"Well, they're a great couple. She's a very attractive woman, and he's a good-looking man and, as you probably know, a very successful attorney. Matter of fact, he was recently promoted to partner in what you also probably know is the county's most successful and important law firm."

"I saw nothing about children. They've been married long enough to qualify," Ryan said.

"Can't tell you about that. I guess they'll have children when they want to, any time they want to. You know she's a novelist, writes these romance stories. I understand the people who read that sort of thing think they are very good, and I see them being sold everywhere."

"I read one this morning," Ryan replied.

"You read one this morning?"

"Not exactly rocket science," Ryan muttered. Actually, he enjoyed the book, but he didn't want to reveal that.

"Why did you read one of her books this morning? I don't get this. What did you expect to learn from that? How are the Rosses involved in all this?"

"You know Esther Robinson, Stocker Robinson's mother, works for them, cleans their home?"

"So?"

"I have reason to want to speak to all the parties concerned," Ryan said without offering any more information.

McCalester squeezed his heavy eyebrows toward each other and curled in the corners of his mouth before sitting forward and putting his big arms on the small desk.

"Your questioning someone as important and

influential as Mr. Ross and his wife about a murder in this community might be politically incorrect," he said. "It'll get around, and just questioning someone can taint him or her. Bertram Cauthers, the senior partner in Ross's firm, is very connected. I'd be extra sure before I tapped on those doors."

"I'm not running for any office," Ryan replied.

McCalester smiled and sat back again. "We're all running for office all the time, Detective Lee. I'm sure you've got your eyes set on some promotion, some higher goal."

"I don't compromise my investigations," Ryan said sharply, "to ensure personal goals."

McCalester's smile wilted. "I don't, either. I'm just trying to give you some sage advice. Take it or leave it. If you screw up here, one phone call from Bertram Cauthers will have you yanked so fast and hard you'll end up investigating ice-cube thieves at the North Pole."

Ryan stared coldly at him and had just started to stand when McCalester's phone rang. McCalester pounced on the receiver.

As he listened, his eyes widened, and he nodded at Ryan, who paused and sat again.

"When? What have you done about it? Okay, we'll get on it."

He hung up.

"That was Ted Sullivan, the high-school principal. The Robinson girl is AWOL from school.

Didn't show up for her class, and her homing badge isn't registering her in the building. They've gone through all their monitoring systems."

"As far as I know about that security system, she couldn't take her ID badge off and leave, or it would have sent an alarm to the central office, right?" Ryan asked.

"Right. Which means she must have found a way out. The question is why, and where did she go?"

He pressed a button on his console.

"Charlie, check the monitors and the tapes. We're looking for Stocker Robinson. See if she entered the village during the last hour."

"I'm going to her home," Ryan said, standing. "I wanted to interview her mother again, anyway."

"Let's be sure she's there first. She might be on a job," McCalester said. He made the call, and Esther Robinson answered, telling him she had just arrived.

"What's wrong now?" she asked.

"Is your daughter there, Esther?"

"My daughter? She's at school. Isn't she?"

"No. She made an unauthorized exit, I'm afraid."

"Oh, damn. On top of all the rest! Mickey's going to be beside himself," she said.

"Let's hope that's the least of it, Esther," McCalester said. "We'll be right there."

He cradled the phone and joined Ryan at the door.

"It's not necessary for you to come along," Ryan said without any belligerence.

"Hey, this is the most exciting thing to happen for some time. Besides, and this is a state secret, I haven't much to do here, anyway."

Ryan smiled and shrugged. "Suit yourself," he said.

On the way out, they checked with Charlie Krammer, who had nothing to report.

"Might as well take my car," McCalester suggested. "I've got to justify the gas allotment."

They got into McCalester's vehicle and shot away from the station. An increasingly graying sky had darkened, and small drizzle had begun. McCalester turned on his rain blowers which kept the drops off the windshield, and readjusted the braking system to prevent any planing on slick roads. There was no need to slow down.

"So, you're tying this Robinson girl to the Rosses somehow, is that it?" McCalester asked Ryan as they turned off Main Street and headed toward the Robinsons' residence.

The silent moments that followed made him think Ryan was just not going to answer.

Instead, he turned to him and said, "If you call Bertram Cauthers and tell him so, you'll endanger this whole investigation."

McCalester felt himself go crimson in the face and neck. "What makes you think I would do something like that?"

"We're all running for office all the time," Ryan replied. "Remember?"

McCalester glanced at him and then smiled. "I guess there's something to all those myths about the high intelligence of the Asian, genetic engineering or no genetic engineering."

Finally, Ryan Lee laughed.

"What's so funny?"

"What a dull world this would be if we lost all our stereotypes and prejudices, after all," Ryan said.

A little more than an hour out of Sandburg, Natalie reached for a bottle of water and poured herself a glass. Her throat had become so dry she couldn't swallow. Despite the television set and the availability of music any time she wanted it, she couldn't help feeling claustrophobic. Her driver hadn't said a word for nearly two hours, and the tinted window between them made it impossible for her to see him. She had the sense that he could see her whenever he wished, however.

Natalie appreciated the need for secrecy and the importance of protecting everyone involved, especially Preston, but she wished she could have a little more control of her destiny. At the moment, she felt like one of those poor astronauts who had lost their lifelines to the mother ship when repairing a satellite. They drifted off, out of control, counting down the minutes to the end of their oxygen supply and their impending death. With so much time to consider their plight, did they panic, or were they stoical? The messages they sent back were kept secret out of respect for them and their families. If any had panicked or died screaming for help, it was surely to be kept classified. As far as the rest of the world was concerned, they were the best of the best, and any human weakness had to be kept hidden.

What was her attitude supposed to be? Was she to keep her eyes closed and be patient, calm? Was she simply to obey every order, or could she exert her will, express her feelings, have some say, no matter how small and insignificant, in her own immediate future? Would she embarrass Preston? Compromise his efforts? Put him in any danger if she didn't do everything she was told?

This wasn't meant to be a picnic, Natalie, she told herself. *It's the path you and Preston have chosen to take. Grin and bear it. Swallow down your panic and your anxiety, Natalie Ross. You're an astronaut of sorts. You're dangling in space, and the lifeline is very fragile. Believe that.*

"Is it much longer?" she finally dared to ask.

"Another half hour," the driver replied. "Are you comfortable?"

"Yes."

"Okay, then," he said. It sounded like *Why the hell are you bothering me, then?*

She closed her eyes and lay back. Less than a

hundred years ago, a pregnant woman was a proud and happy woman. People smiled at her and asked her how she was. Soon-to-be grandparents were excited and eager. Her husband doted on her, cherished her. Together they planned and dreamed of their future as parents. They enjoyed sorting through names. They talked about ways they were going to make life better for their child than it had been for them.

They weren't fugitives.

They didn't have to be clandestine.

Why was it so difficult for everyone else to see the beauty in all that?

Today, the natal lab created a child to order, molded and carved his or her very being. The child's future was clear. There were even programs to help choose a name that was appropriate. Once the decision had been made to apply for parenthood, the rest was predetermined. The husband and wife didn't even talk about the child until it was time to retrieve him or her. She had seen enough instances of that. At least 95 percent of the mystery of life was gone. It was like reading the end of a detective story before it was begun. People walked about with smug confidence. They knew who the future doctors, lawyers, teachers, and scientists were. They knew who had talent and who had other attributes.

They went to sleep with confidence. No one tossed and turned in a sea of anxiety. But even though she didn't enjoy all this, Natalie was confident, too. She was confident that there was still that strange tickle, that ongoing question running continuously behind the mask of their complacency. Something was missing. They surely sensed it. Something wasn't right.

What?

What, indeed, Natalie thought. She smiled to herself. She knew, and she had chosen the way not only to find the answer to the question, but to stop the question to find a greater satisfaction.

Just a little more time, she thought. *Just a little more effort, and I'll be happy.*

We'll be happy, so happy the others will sense it and try desperately to understand why and how they could be as happy as we are.

They can't.

She drifted into a restful sleep, cradled in contentment until she heard the driver's voice.

"We're here, Mrs. Ross," he said.

She heard the whir of an electric motor, and the metal window covers began to rise, revealing a plush green roll of lawn. Behind it, dark patches of elm, birch, hickory, and oak trees filled the horizon. She spotted a white-tail deer feeding in the tall grass, lifting its head to gaze their way and then returning with nonchalance to its dinner. A tall wall of hedge came into view. It loomed at least eight or nine feet high and was very impressive. It seemed to run for a good half a mile along the roadway until they reached a gated driveway and the limousine turned in.

The chauffeur reached over and inserted a white card in the sentry box. It read the card and spit it back out. He took it, and the gate began to slide open. The windows of the limousine were still up. All of them were triple-layered and well insulated from sound so that to Natalie everything looked as if it were happening in the world of the deaf.

They started up the drive. She looked back and saw the gate closing much more rapidly than it had opened. It looked as if it slammed shut. Along the driveway were beautiful patches of flowers, fountains, stone and wooden benches, sprawling weeping willows, and here and there a small pond in which ducks floated aimlessly, looking more like the imitation birds she had seen often. Their wings fluttered. They made calls and sang in voices impossible to distinguish from the real thing, but they left no droppings and lived forever in an eternal spring, albeit a false spring.

How much of what she was looking at was real? Even the flowers were too perfect, their colors far too vibrant. She half expected to see a camera crew. This looked more like the set of a film.

The limousine wound around the circular drive and came to a stop in front of a grand, stone-faced, three-story structure. All the windows had elaborately faced, round-topped arches over them and over the porch supports and entrance. There were many windows, but the glass in all of them was recessed and tinted, turning them into a myriad of mirrors that caught the now nearly cloudless blue sky and the surrounding grounds but, more importantly, permitted no view of the rooms inside.

The masonry walls had rough-faced, squared stonework. She saw two round towers with conical roofs. There was a set of three parapeted and gabled wall dormers with eyebrow windows between them.

No signs, no plaques, nothing identified the structure or the grounds. She saw no one, either working on the grounds or enjoying the ponds, fountains, and benches. No one came to the door when they arrived, either. In fact, the building looked deserted. A pocket of cold anxiety formed in the base of her stomach. There was no feeling of maternity here. This didn't look like a place to be born in; it looked like a place to haunt. However, it did have a sense of secrecy about it. It was surely the perfect place to keep yourself out of the prodding and suspicious eyes of the world around you.

She heard a click in the doors of the car and realized that during her entire ride from home, she had been locked in the limousine. The chauffeur came around and opened the door for her.

"Were these doors all locked?" she asked, her tone demanding now.

"For your own safety, Mrs. Ross."

"We may be carrying this precaution a bit too far," she quipped.

He didn't even wince. Was he real?

"I simply follow prescribed procedure, Mrs. Ross."

"Don't we all," she muttered. If he heard it, he didn't show any reaction. She might as well be talking to herself, she thought.

"I'll get your things, Mrs. Ross. You can just go into the house."

"Some house," she said, and started for the stairs. Why wasn't there anyone to greet her? Surely, they knew by now that someone had arrived. Glancing about, she saw the video cameras on the sides of the structure. It wouldn't surprise her to see them attached to some of the trees.

When she was a little more than halfway up the stone steps, the front door finally opened. The ten-foot-high doors looked as if they were made of steel but faced to resemble hickory wood. They had such thickness and width they made the full-figured, bluish-gray-haired woman look diminutive in the entrance. She had bright, friendly aqua eyes set in a round face with soft cheeks but firm, rosy lips. There was a slight dimple in her right cheek. She was dressed in a milk-white uniform and wore what looked like oversized white shoes. Her stockings were only slightly tinted white but went well up under the hem of her skirt.

"Hello, dear," she said, extending her hand as soon as Natalie reached the portico. Her fingers were surprisingly short and muscular, firmly gripping Natalie's palm. Her wrist was also unexpectedly thick. In fact, now that Natalie was only a few inches away, she could see that the softness in her face belied quite manly, powerful-looking shoulders and arms. "I'm Mrs. Jerome," she said. "Welcome."

"Thank you," Natalie said.

The chauffeur's steps behind her turned their attention to him.

"Let me show you right to your room so you can rest and be comfortable," Mrs. Jerome said. "You must be hungry. Was it a long trip for you?"

Natalie looked at the chauffeur. "I don't know. What would you say, driver?"

He stared coldly.

She looked at her watch as if she had outsmarted him.

"Looks like nearly three and a half hours," Natalie told the smiling woman, whom she imagined to be at least sixty despite her remarkably smooth complexion.

"I wish we didn't have to be so off the beaten track," Mrs. Jerome said, turning. "But, for obvious reasons, we have little choice."

"What a big building this is," Natalie remarked now that she had stepped into the circular entryway and could see the height of the ceiling in the vestibule. It rose to the very foot of the first tower. Directly in front of them was a circular staircase with a rich mahogany balustrade.

"Yes. Can you believe that at one time it was owned by one man? Fortunately for us, he donated it."

She leaned toward Natalie, and Natalie caught a whiff of lightly scented rubbing alcohol.

"He was sympathetic to our cause," Mrs. Jerome whispered, her eyes glancing at the chauffeur, who stood back, looking bored and impatient.

The hallway before them ran past the foot of the stairway and deep into the belly of the building. A row of chandeliers lit the way with teardrop bulbs that dripped illumination over the walls and slate floors. Oversized oil paintings of country scenes, lakes with animals, and one that looked like a seascape lined the walls.

"I thought my home was big. I guess I could put three or four of them in here."

"Most likely," Mrs. Jerome said, laughing. "Please, just follow me."

She led the way to the stairs.

"You have the first room on the left. Walking the stairs can only do you a world of good. Exercise is so important now, contrary to what some people believe. There is so much misinformation when it comes to this condition, so much misunderstanding. But, like anything alien to one's experience, it can easily be wrongly depicted."

She glanced back once, and Natalie nodded and smiled at her.

"Absolutely," she said.

The steps were wide and deep. They were covered in a softly woven, dark gray carpet and had a spongy feel beneath her feet. What struck her immediately and continued to impress her, however, was the silence in the house. She wondered how many people were here and where they could possibly be. She felt herself breathing faster, her heart thumping when they reached the second landing and paused. Some of it could be attributed to her anxiety, she thought.

Mrs. Jerome turned to her about ten feet to the left. She opened a door and stood back.

"Your room," she said.

Before Natalie reached it, the chauffeur stepped past and into the room. He was obviously in a hurry to get back, she thought.

It was a big room, even wider and a little longer than her and Preston's own bedroom. The bed, however, was a state-of-the-art hospital bed with voice-recognition controls that would raise or lower it into a sitting position for its inhabitant.

Like a modern hospital room, this one had an otherwise warm decor with its light pink and white wallpaper, its light mauve cotton curtains, and its light maple dresser, vanity table, and armoire. There were a half dozen small framed pictures of fruit, birds on a lake, and a sky of blue with marshmallow-white clouds floating toward a gentle ridge of mountains on the horizon.

Natalie immediately noticed there was no video phone, however.

"The bathroom is right here," Mrs. Jerome said, standing in the doorway.

Natalie joined her and looked in at a bathroom adapted for the disabled with railings around the tub and the toilet.

"We have sound sensors in here as well as around the bed, so if you need anything, you merely have to call out," Mrs. Jerome said. She went to the cabinet above the bathroom sink and opened it.

"Anything you require is in here—soaps, toothpaste, whatever," she said.

"I see there is no phone in the room," Natalie said.

Mrs. Jerome smiled. "Of course not, dear. First, we don't want any of our people disturbed, and, second, we have certain security procedures we must follow."

"But how do I speak with my husband?"

"We'll let you know when he calls you, and you can speak with him in the parlor. Why don't you make yourself comfortable? I'll bring up some hot food, and then, when you're ready, we'll tour the house, if you like. Dr. Prudential won't be here until early this evening."

She leaned toward Natalie to add, "It's really a

voluntary service he provides. He has a regular practice elsewhere, of course. You'll like him. I've seen him in action many times. He has what they used to call good bedside manner."

She went to the closet and took out a hospital gown.

"If you'll just take everything off and put this on for your doctor's examination later," she said, laying the gown over the bed. "There, now. You're all set, dear."

She turned to leave. The chauffeur had long since left the building.

"Am I the only one here at the moment?" Natalie asked. She was still taken with the silence in the house.

"Yes, I'm afraid so," Mrs. Jerome said. "We don't have all that many clients anymore. But don't let that depress you. Think of it this way, all our attention will be focused on little old you," she said, smiled again, and left, closing the door softly behind her.

Natalie stood there a moment, turning slowly to look at the room again. Why did they need a hospital bed in here? If they had put a nice bed in the room, it wouldn't seem so . . . so functional.

She was tired. She had underestimated the emotional drain all this had taken on her body. The suddenness of it, the dreary ride, and this strangely Gothic house with all the prescribed security precautions weighed on her brow like a sky of brooding dark clouds.

She opened her suitcase and started to unpack, putting things in the dresser first. Then she went to the closet to hang up some garments. Turning, she gazed at the aseptic hospital gown spread over the bed. It put a little chill in her. There was no need for a hospital gown, she thought, and realized what it was that bothered her about all this.

She was being treated like someone who was sick . . . hospital bed, rest, hot food, a doctor's visit . . .

I'm not sick, she thought.

I'm pregnant.

These people above any others should realize that I'm in a state of perfect health. My body is doing what it was designed by God to do.

I'm in a sea of paranoia, incarcerated first in a limousine turned into a moving coffin, delivered into a world of security procedures and screened phone calls. There should be laughter and music and real flowers, not silence and rules.

How sad, she thought, and for a moment felt sorrier for everyone else than she did for herself.

At least, through her mother, she had known what full motherhood was like. She had tasted the natural beauty. That, above anything else, sustained her.

I'll be all right, she thought.

They won't be.

She continued to put away her things and then lay down for just a few minutes to rest and fell into a deep sleep. She thought she heard the sound of someone crying and woke abruptly, but all she heard was that same deep silence. Groggy, she ordered the bed into a sitting position before she attempted to stand.

She couldn't believe how wobbly she felt.

There was a knock on her door, and then it opened, and Mrs. Jerome came in with a tray.

"Time for something to eat," she announced. "I was here earlier, but you were sleeping so soundly I couldn't bear to wake you. You can consider this an early dinner. I know you're going to like it. We have a rather good chef. She works at a local gourmet restaurant and helps us on a part-time voluntary basis."

She rolled the serving table toward the bed.

"I felt so weak and tired before and still do," Natalie remarked.

"Of course. All this is quite an undertaking, a very draining experience, my dear."

She uncovered the main dish.

"This is chicken Kiev," she declared, smiling and leaning toward Natalie, "which we know is one of your favorite dishes, correct?"

"Yes, but how did you know?"

"Your husband told us, and we assured him we had it ready for you."

"When?"

Mrs. Jerome held her smile, but it looked like a mask suddenly, a smile without the accompanying warm feeling behind it.

"While you were resting, of course," she replied.

"He called? Preston called?"

"Certainly. He wanted to see if you had arrived all right and how you were doing."

"Why didn't you call me to the phone?"

"Oh, I came to fetch you, but, as I explained, you were in a deep sleep, dear. I didn't have the heart to wake you. He'll call again."

"Or I can call him," she said quickly.

"We'd rather you didn't," Mrs. Jerome said, her face a bit severe.

"What?"

"There's reason to be concerned when someone goes off like you have, despite the good cover story provided. You never know if your phones are tapped. Those damn baby squads. It's better your husband calls you from a safe phone. It's prescribed procedure.

"But don't be concerned about any baby squad while you're here. You have nothing to worry about now. You're safe with us," Mrs. Jerome added. "Enjoy your food. The doctor will be here in an hour or so, and then, if you're up to it, I'll show you the rest of the house. Okay? Don't forget to change into the hospital gown, dear."

Natalie just stared.

"You don't want to let your dinner get cold,

dear. I know how good it is, and I know it tastes so much better warm, don't you?"

She took off the cover and placed it beside the plate, smiled again, and started out.

"Enjoy," she said.

She closed the door.

Natalie gazed at the food. It did look good, and it smelled wonderful.

I suppose she's right, Natalie thought as she lifted the knife and fork and began to cut into the chicken. *I'm safe now, and that is all that matters.*

Eleven

::::::::::::

Stocker moved about Natalie Ross's bedroom like someone in a museum, first studying everything without touching anything, and then, suddenly emboldened by her confidence, she began exploring and experimenting with hands on. She sat at Natalie's vanity table and began to put on her makeup. She rarely had worn much more than lipstick, but she was aware of it all, reading the same style magazines most of the girls in school read.

Like the fable of the fox and the grapes, in which the fox who couldn't reach the grapes decided they were sour anyway, she often mocked the other girls in school for their obsession with their own beauty, style, and clothes. Brave enough to get into anyone's face, she was a coward when it came to experimenting with her own appearance, especially in public. There was no question, however, that deep in her heart, she wanted to be more attractive. There wasn't a boy she knew or cared to know who took a second look at her. It was almost as if she weren't there.

Mrs. Ross was one of the most beautiful women in the community. Being in her bedroom was like being in the boudoir of a princess. Her picture was often on the society pages of the county magazine and in the newspapers. She could easily be a model or a movie star. Stocker gazed into Mrs. Ross's vanity mirror as if the glass possessed magical powers, a result of reflecting so beautiful a face for so long. It would show her how to make herself more attractive. Maybe it was child's make-believe, but she couldn't help it.

She tested a different base, put on eye shadow and tints, changed lipstick a half dozen times before concluding the mirror had worked. She was actually taken with her own face. *I do have good qualities. I can be beautiful,* she thought. Heartened by what she saw as her successful attempt to improve her appearance, she went to Natalie's closet and found her wigs.

With her face now fully made up, she tried on different styles and settled on the wing-bone-length blond wig. Amused at herself, she decided to try on one of the dresses, even though she was not even close to the same size as Natalie Ross. Her arms and shoulders were too big, and her waist was too thick, not to mention that she was at least two inches shorter than the woman. Nevertheless, she found one of Natalie's gowns that she could squeeze into if she didn't zip up the back. The bodice was low cut, and her puffy little breasts looked quite seductive, she thought, when she turned and postured in the full-length mirrors that took up most of the south wall. She powdered her cleavage and tried to force her feet into a pair of Natalie's high-heeled shoes. One pair actually tore apart, but another gave way enough for her to parade around the bedroom.

She really did look good, she thought. She decided she had been foolish to neglect herself, especially out of fear of being mocked by the mannequins, for that's all they were: mindless, dressed-up bodies parading through the hallways and giggling in one note. Why couldn't she compete with them?

Once she had money of her own, she would buy herself more glamorous clothing. She might even buy a wig, or maybe . . . maybe she would just take this one. Why not? Why not take anything she wanted? She scurried about, filling one of the carry-on bags she located in the walk-in closet. She shoved in some beautiful cashmere sweaters, makeup, gobs of costume jewelry, the wig, luxurious bubble baths and oils, and expensive skin creams.

Feeling like a child in a candy store with carte blanche, she even scooped up the small gold-plated cuckoo clock on the nightstand. Then she turned around and around in the room, consider-

ing everything else in it. Maybe she had enough. It
was going to be hard enough to explain what she
had to her parents, although she had no doubt
she could fabricate whatever story needed to be
created. Like any child, especially a modern-day
teenager, she knew that her parents wanted to believe her. What parent wanted to suspect his or
her own child of evildoing? It was like admitting
their own failure, and with review boards scrutinizing their abilities to parent a child, it was not
good to admit to even the smallest failures.

Growing a bit impatient now, she carried the
bag and the flashlight downstairs. She wanted to
get this over with and be gone. Still dressed in Natalie's wig and clothes and still overly made up,
she located a box of imported English toffee, let
herself sink down on the settee in front of the television set, and flipped through the satellite channels until she found a very gross pornographic station coming from eastern Europe. What she saw
was disgusting even to her—sex with animals,
women peeing on each other, scooping ejaculated
semen into ice cream cones.

"Ugh," she cried, but then laughed and continued to watch. The parade of male genitals eventually did arouse her. She decided to masturbate and
slipped her hand under the skirt of the dress. She
was so engrossed in it, in fact, that she didn't hear
the front door open and close. Her own moans
drowned out the sound of footsteps.

The light flowing through the windows high up in the walls to catch the late-afternoon and early-evening dwindling sun suddenly threw a shadow over the cabinet containing the wide-screen digital television. It gave Stocker some pause, and she started to sit up and turn when the plastic bag was dropped over her face. The rope around the base of it was tightened with such power and speed it nearly snapped her neck. What it did was pull her back against the small settee and with such force kept her from moving forward. She was soon gasping.

She reached up to claw it away from her neck, but she couldn't get her fingers under the rope, and the plastic was too thick to tear. It distorted and clouded her vision as well. All she saw was the silhouette of someone leaning over her, holding her up like a puppet on a string. She tried to scream, but her voice was instantly muffled, and when she opened her mouth, the plastic rushed in under her teeth, making her gag as well.

She fought as hard as she could. The rope continued to tighten and tighten. She wet herself and brought such pain to her stomach her legs seemed to fall away from the rest of her body. She made a final attempt to grasp at the wrists and pull the hands apart, but that was like moving steel bars. Her strength diminished, her effort barely anything now. The darkness came rushing in like water, like the time she had tripped down at the beach in Atlantic City and gotten picked up by a wave. She remembered how impossible it was to claw her way back to shore and raise her head from the water. She had to close her eyes and wait, and finally, finally, she felt some solid ground beneath her and was able to stand, gasping, crying, rushing up the beach to her mother and father, who were talking with friends. They hadn't noticed anything.

She stood there crying until they looked at her.

"What's wrong?" her mother asked.

"I nearly drowned!" she shouted at them as if it was their fault.

Her father looked annoyed. "Well, you didn't, did you?" he charged, as if she had made a mistake surviving. "Now, go play, or I'll take you back to the room and leave you there," he threatened.

"I couldn't breathe!" she cried, the tears streaming down her face, indistinguishable from the salt water streaking out of her hair. She had sand in her ears, too.

"Well, you're breathing now," her father said.

She stopped gasping.

I should have died, she thought. *That would have taught them a good lesson.*

That's what they'll learn now, she concluded as the darkness thickened and completely took over her eyes.

They'll be sorry.

Even standing on death's doorstep, she could

think only how someone else would suffer more. She was happy about that.

Her last breath gave her the strength for that last thought, that last tidbit of self-satisfaction.

It died on her smothered lips like the remnants of foam from her favorite frozen mocha drink, tiny bubbles popping along her descent through some seemingly endless tunnel to a place outside herself.

She slumped forward, but, because of how much she had perspired, she still wore the bag which seemed stuck on her face, a grotesque mask of death.

"How long have you been working for Mr. and Mrs. Ross?" Ryan asked Esther Robinson. He came directly to the point the moment they all had taken seats in her living room.

The stout woman looked at McCalester as if she needed his permission to answer. It wasn't a gesture lost on Ryan.

"As you know, Mrs. Robinson, and as Chief Mc-Calester can verify, this is a state investigation now. Anyone withholding evidence or information will be charged with stage one felonies," Ryan emphasized.

"Shouldn't I have an attorney present?" she fired back. Her eyes were wide and inflamed with great concern and anxiety. "I mean, I don't want to say anything about anyone that I shouldn't say and get myself into any trouble."

"You are not a target of my investigation, Mrs. Robinson. I have no intention of seeking to arrest you or your husband, for that matter."

Ryan deliberately left out her daughter, something that she didn't miss.

"Where is Stocker?" she asked, almost in a rhetorical tone. She gazed at the clock on the mantel and then at McCalester.

"We've got a full-blown search under way, Esther. She'll turn up."

"How long have you worked for the Rosses?" Ryan repeated more firmly.

"Six years or nearly that much."

"Is Mrs. Ross there when you are working in her house?" Ryan continued.

"Sometimes. Most times, no," Esther said. "They trust me, and I have given them no reason to do otherwise. Most of my clients leave me in their homes."

"Some provide you with a key or access to one?" Ryan followed.

"Yes."

"The Rosses do, correct?"

Once again, she looked at McCalester. He stared at her without indicating his pleasure or displeasure in her responses.

"I don't know that it's anyone's business if they do or not," she replied.

"I'm not an insurance investigator, Mrs. Robinson, seeking to place blame on them for lack of security. I'm a criminal investigator investigating a murder in your community. Should you refuse to answer a question I ask and I find out later that you did indeed know the answer, I will have you charged with impeding a murder investigation. Then you will become a target of this investigation," he threatened.

She looked away a moment and then at Ryan.

"Yes, they've told me where I can find a key to their home when they are not there at the time I arrive. I haven't told a soul about it and certainly not where it is located."

"The last time you worked at the Rosses' house was six days ago. Is that true?" Ryan asked.

"Yes."

"You're due to go back tomorrow?"

"I am. What does this have to do with the murder of that poor girl?" she cried in frustration. "And what does it have to do with my daughter's disappearing from school?"

Ryan stared at her. She didn't know anything about her daughter's clandestine activities, he concluded.

"How often did your daughter accompany you when you worked in the Rosses' home?" he asked.

"How often? Hardly ever," Esther replied quickly.

"When was the last time?"

"I don't know."

"Could it have been as recently as last week?"

"Last week? I . . . yes, I believe she did. They

had the day off at school. It was some teachers' conference or something. Right, Henry?" she asked the chief. It was as if she thought she was exposing something illegal.

"I guess. I don't recall the reason, Esther."

"Well, that's what Stocker told us. Was she lying?"

"I'm not concerned about that for the moment, Mrs. Robinson," Ryan said, almost showing his frustration at the way the woman danced around in her responses. It really wasn't all that uncommon, however. In every investigation, he encountered the same sort of mistrust. So much for the wonder of the new freedoms science had bestowed on humanity.

"When you went to the Ross house, your daughter saw you fetch the spare key, is that right?" he continued.

"I suppose so." The suspicion and fear jumped into her face immediately. "Did she do something in that house? Is that why you're here? Is that why she ran away from school today?"

"Can you tell me if your daughter and Mrs. Ross spoke to each other, perhaps when you were in another room? Any time, ever?" Ryan asked, ignoring her questions.

Esther puffed out her cheeks and shook her head. "I don't know. I don't think so. If they did, it wasn't more than some small talk. Why?"

Ryan held his gaze. He looked as inscrutable as

he was expected to look. "Can you tell me anything about Mrs. Ross that she might not want anyone else to know, something your daughter might have told you about her, perhaps, if you don't know for yourself, as a result of your own firsthand knowledge?"

Esther practically leaped out of her chair. The front door opened and closed at the same time. "I knew it! I knew it! I won't answer another question unless I have an attorney," she fired down at Ryan Lee. Chief McCalester pressed his fingers together and continued to slouch in the easy chair. "And it's not because I'm afraid of being called a criminal. People expect me to keep their homes sacred, their personal business out of the cackle of the gossiping hens around here, and I do. What do you think would happen to me if I didn't? Would anyone hire me again? No. And the other people I work for . . . you can be sure they'd find someone to replace me like that," she said, snapping her fingers.

"What the hell is going on here?" Mickey Robinson demanded from the living-room doorway.

"Just routine questioning, Mickey," McCalester said, turning to him slowly. He turned back to raise his eyebrows at Ryan.

"Well, why? What brings you back here?"

"You know your daughter is missing from school?" McCalester asked in reply.

"What? What the hell are you talking about?"

"She left without permission earlier today, and

we haven't yet located her, Mickey. Any idea where she might be?"

"Jesus. That little . . . no, I didn't know," he said with twisted lips. "But when she walks in here, she'll have trouble walking out again. I can tell you that."

"All right," Ryan said, nodding at McCalester. The two rose. He glanced at Esther. The look on her face, a glitter in her eyes, suggested to him that she did know something. "Anyone who penalized you for helping your community would themselves suffer dire consequences," he recited. He hated the concept and almost choked on the words, but it was his responsibility to emphasize it.

"Sure," Esther said, her lips dipping at the corners. "Everyone would take our side against the rich and influential people employing me. I'm confident of that," she added.

Ryan came the closest to blushing that he had in a long time.

McCalester was smirking at him, and Mickey Robinson, his hands on his hips, was glaring at him angrily.

"Let's go," he practically whispered, and headed for the doorway. He was on an angle enough to catch McCalester's smile and nod at Esther.

Despite the expectations the state had of its citizenry, there were still strong local loyalties, especially when it came to any questions or revelations that could endanger its subsidies. He really couldn't blame them. Their livelihoods, their whole economic history and well-being, were at stake. The truth had little to recommend it when it came face to face with those consequences, he concluded.

"What next?" McCalester asked him when they stepped out.

"I'll go back to pick up my vehicle."

"You're going to visit Mr. and Mrs. Ross, aren't you?"

Ryan got into the police car and waited for McCalester to start the engine. "Don't worry. I'm not taking you along," he finally replied. "You won't be part of anything that could endanger your standing in the community."

"Jeez, you know how to hurt a guy," McCalester said with feigned indignation. Then he smiled. "You know, you're making me feel more idealistic than I have in a helluva long time. I think I'd like to go along. I'll drive you to their home," he added. "I'm either a law enforcement officer or a lackey."

Ryan raised his eyebrows.

Strong words, full of defiance and courage.

Or was it something else? Some other motive that made him want to be a part of all this?

"All right. Drive on, then," Ryan said.

McCalester whipped a right and sped up. "Where are you from, Ryan?" he asked.

"I was brought up in a community on Long Island, Hicksville," Ryan replied. People didn't reply to that question with an answer that included the words "I was born in," anymore. Fetuses were created in national laboratories and could come from any of four locations. An Abnormal could almost be trapped into revelation by answering otherwise. Ryan had no suspicions about McCalester. The man was merely making small talk.

"Nice area, wealthy area. Your parents well-to-do?"

"My father was a physician. He's retired now. My mother was a college professor. Taught higher mathematics. She, too, is retired."

"Any siblings?"

"No," Ryan said. "They barely had time for me."

"I'll bet."

"What made you want to go into law enforcement?" McCalester asked.

Ryan looked at him. Was it a serious question? "I was directed to, my aptitude testing."

"Oh, right, right." McCalester smiled to himself. "Those tests weren't quite as perfected when I was a young man. We didn't rely on them as much as people do these days."

"Then you might be in the wrong profession," Ryan said. It was just about his best attempt at a quip.

McCalester glanced at him and laughed. "I don't know as I'm built to be anything else."

"We'll never know unless you take a test," Ryan said.

"Now? A bit too late, don't you think?"

"To do anything about it but not to know," Ryan replied. It was a good scientific answer.

"Who wants to know he's not right for what he's doing? What good would that do me? Sometimes," McCalester said, "you can have too much knowledge."

Ryan was silent. He agreed, but he would never reveal it. McCalester took the silence to mean Ryan disagreed.

"You CID guys, all business and science," he said.

Ryan didn't disagree.

As they drove up to the Rosses' home, Ryan could see McCalester was watching for his reaction to the house. Ryan could sense that his blasé expression actually annoyed McCalester at this moment. He was expecting him to show a little appreciation.

"Bet you didn't expect to see a house like this out here," McCalester said.

Ryan grunted.

"This may look like the boondocks, but there's some very sophisticated housing here. The Rosses' house is one of the most impressive in the whole county, actually, and Sandburg is a community that takes pride in its citizens' successes."

"That's very nice," Ryan said without much enthusiasm.

McCalester rattled on about Preston Ross as if he were his younger brother.

"He was editor of the *Law Review*, graduated in the top three of his class, and took a position with Cauthers, Myerson, and Boswell immediately on graduation. He passed the bar exams that summer, and we understand he had the highest score in the group taking it.

"He had lots of offers from big-city firms, even a Washington, D.C., firm with a pipeline to the White House, but Preston's real people. His parents brought him up in this community, and he wanted to come back here and make a name for himself on their front lawn, so to speak.

"They were unfortunately killed in that terrible train crash on the New York O and W, the bullet train that went off the track four years ago. Maybe you remember that."

"Yes," Ryan said, finally showing some sign of life.

"One of our biggest funerals. You can imagine . . . burying both your parents . . . he had to have a lot of grit to bear it and continue and be the success he is. Now, he's a partner and a full partner at that. The house was designed by a well-known New York City architect."

He paused as if he were deciding whether or not it would be proper actually to pull into the Rosses' driveway. Preston's Black Widow Spider sports car was parked outside the garage with the driver's door still open as if he couldn't wait to get out and into the house.

McCalester drove in but alongside the vehicle.

"That's a quarter-of-a-million-dollar car. Has the anti-collision system," McCalester said, nodding at the Black Widow.

Ryan said nothing. He opened his door and stepped out. McCalester smirked, shut off his engine, and followed Ryan to the front door, gazing back at the sports car. Before Ryan could press the door buzzer, the door was opened, and Preston Ross stood there, his tie loose at his neck, his hair somewhat disheveled.

He slid his gaze off Ryan's face so quickly one would have thought the detective's visage was made of ice.

"What's up, Henry?"

"This is Ryan Lee from the state CID, Preston. He wants to ask you some questions, if that's all right."

"I was just on my way back to the office," Preston said.

"What brought you home in such a rush?" Ryan asked without skipping a beat.

"What makes you think it was in a rush?" Preston retorted.

Ryan stepped back and nodded at the sports car. Preston glanced at it and laughed.

"Oh, I see. The door . . . a clue. Charlie Chan's number one son," he quipped.

Ryan Lee reddened but only around his eyes. His

lips quivered, and then he, too, smiled. "You didn't answer the question, Mr. Ross," he said.

"Is that what brought you up here?" Preston asked, turning to McCalester, who now looked very uncomfortable.

"No," Ryan said softly, answering for him.

"Well, I was in a rush when I drove up. I thought I had left an important file at home, but as it turns out, I put it under a stack of new files in the office. My secretary just located it and called, so I'm heading back to the office. If that is a satisfactory reply, can we return to what brings you here in the first place?"

Henry McCalester looked down as if he were ashamed of Preston's reaction. Ryan caught it out of the corner of his eyes and imagined the community policeman was hardly expecting Preston Ross to be testy and even a bit nasty. McCalester was probably expecting Ross to be cool, polite, very cooperative, and responsive, which, Ryan assumed, would make him look foolish for asking these questions.

"I'm investigating the murder of a teenage girl, Lois Marlowe," Ryan said in his most officious tone of voice. "The investigation has led me to inquire about another teenage girl, Stocker Robinson, who we have learned this morning has run away from school."

"And?" Preston asked. "I'm sorry to be so curt,

but I really do have some important work to complete today."

"And Stocker Robinson's mother works for you."

"Right, and?" Preston said, making a small circle with his right hand as if he were trying to coax out replies.

"And Stocker Robinson was seen sneaking into your garage with what looked like a flashlight and then emerging without it the other night," Ryan replied. "It resembled the flashlight that was used as the lethal weapon in the Lois Marlowe murder."

"What?" McCalester muttered. He looked at Preston and shook his head. He actually looked terrified. "It's the first I've heard of this, Mr. Ross."

"Who saw her do such a thing?" Preston demanded, ignoring him.

"I did," Ryan said. "I followed her here."

Preston's shoulders slumped a bit.

"You knew nothing about this?"

"Of course not."

"Perhaps your wife does. May we speak with Mrs. Ross, please?" Ryan asked.

Preston shook his head and then looked up. "She's not home. She's away," he said quickly.

"When will she return?"

"I'm not sure. She's doing research on a project. It might be some time," he replied.

"Have you seen Stocker Robinson about your property today?" Ryan asked him.

Preston shook his head slowly. "I'm not even sure I'd recognize her. I don't know if I've seen her with her mother or whatever," he said, tossing a gesture off right.

"I'd like to search your garage," Ryan said.

Preston looked at McCalester.

"Like I said, Mr. Ross, this is the first I've heard of this incident."

"Searching property is a serious thing," Preston said. "That's why we require warrants."

"It is my belief that Stocker Robinson hid or planted some incriminating evidence on your property, Mr. Ross."

"Which is more reason for us to do it all by the book," Preston said. He stood firm and began to tighten his tie and brush back his hair as if he were about to enter a courtroom.

"Do you have any idea why Stocker Robinson would have done such a thing?" Ryan followed. If Preston's authority and firmness bothered him, Ryan didn't show it.

"No. It all sounds quite fantastical to me, if you must know. Maybe you're mistaken."

"No," Ryan said so sharply even Preston's eyes widened with surprise. "But the best way to determine that is for me to search the garage. It's in your best interest."

Preston started to smile.

"And certainly in the community's," Ryan added.

The smile wilted on Preston's face. He glanced

at McCalester and then turned back to Ryan Lee.

"I must return to my office ASAP. Follow the proper guidelines and come back."

He stepped out, forcing Ryan to step back, and then closed his door behind him.

"Can I reach Mrs. Ross on the phone?" Ryan called to Preston, who headed for the sports car.

"No," he said without turning back. He got into the vehicle and reached for the door handle, looking at McCalester mainly, his expression one of great displeasure.

"Let's go," McCalester said softly. "I'll take you to see Judge Mason. We'll call you, Mr. Ross," he told Preston. "You can meet us here when we return."

"If you return," Preston said, slamming the door. He started the car and backed around McCalester's police vehicle.

"Methinks the lady doth protest too much," Ryan muttered.

"What's that mean?" McCalester asked.

"Something one of the first detectives in drama thought."

"Huh?"

"Let's go see your judge," Ryan said. "And have one of your deputies park himself up here until we return."

"You really think that's necessary?"

"Would I have told you to do so if it were not?" Ryan asked him.

McCalester shook his head. "I'm beginning to appreciate my looming retirement," he said.

Ryan laughed.

It was the closest he and McCalester had come to even the semblance of any warm friendship.

William Scranton lumbered into his home, his head down. It was his early day, with mainly morning appointments and some bookkeeping in the afternoon. He was losing the enthusiasm for his work that he had once enjoyed. He could feel it leaking out of him, a little more each day. Soon he would be high and dry, and he would just come to a screeching halt like some mechanical thing that had not been properly lubricated.

Money was no longer an issue for him and Hattie. He could actually opt for an early retirement. She would be more upset about it than his patients, he thought. He could just hear her shouting, "What do you expect to do with the rest of your life? Spend day in and day out watching television?"

How about the traveling he had wanted to do? He could claim that, couldn't he? If they got themselves out in the world more and experienced different cultures, sights, sounds, tastes, maybe she wouldn't be so obsessed with what she did in this community. Her life would be fuller, too. Why couldn't she see that? Why didn't she want that as much as, if not more than, he did?

The truth was, his wife was the biggest puzzle in his life. Perhaps he was simply incapable of ever understanding her. Sometimes she seemed like a body without any soul, a hollow façade of a human being. She had no internal organs, especially no heart. He hated looking too deeply into her eyes, despite his professional interest. It was like looking into a dark tunnel. Sometimes, and he wouldn't dare tell this to anyone, it even frightened him.

How did he ever hope to enjoy a relationship anymore? Retirement wasn't going to be like some magician waving a wand over them, he feared. Spending more time together might be even more disturbing.

He had nightmares about her, too. She was draining the life out of him, a little every day. He was actually afraid to kiss her now, afraid she might suck out his very soul and leave him as hollow and as vacant-eyed as she was. Then they would be like two dark shadows living together, fleeing the sunlight, hovering in the darkest corners, waiting anxiously for the end of the day.

He was tired of it. The turmoil raging inside him assured him he was coming to a major decision. Regardless of how she would take it, he wanted to make some dramatic change. If he didn't, he would die. His heart would simply stop ticking, and he would sink to the earth, where he would melt into a cold pool of some inky substance and be absorbed into the very ground in front of their home. She would walk over him and not even know it, and certainly, she would have no trouble forgetting him.

After he entered the house, he listened for any sounds of her. She wasn't rattling on and on over the video phone with one of her squad members as usual. He didn't hear her moving about in the kitchen, either, and there was no one in the living room or the downstairs bathroom, but he saw that her car was in the garage. She was here. Maybe she was in the bathroom upstairs or lying down, he thought, and went up the stairs to look.

Their bedroom was empty, and she wasn't in the bathroom.

"Hattie?" he called.

He listened but heard no response.

"Hattie, I'm home."

He waited for even a grunt of acknowledgment, but there was nothing, not a sound in the house.

However, he did hear some strange noise, some sound coming from the rear of the house, a thumping. Curious, he walked quickly to the bedroom window that looked out on their yard, where they had a pool she rarely used, a patch of elm and hickory trees bordering their property, and the lawn of Kentucky blue. He took some pride in the grass and the hedges and, from time to time, experimented with different flowers and plants. She had no interest whatsoever in their property and, unlike other women he knew, made few suggestions for any improvements in their home, whether it be their furnishings or simply their decor. What was here when they first married was essentially still here.

But there she was with a shovel in her hand. She apparently had just dug a hole and was finishing filling it and smoothing the earth around it. Hattie? Planting? It brought a smile to his lips. What was it?

He hurried out of the bedroom, down the stairway, and to the rear door, opening it just as she was returning with the shovel.

"Hi," he called. "What have you been doing?"

"Fixing something," she said sharply.

"Fixing? What?"

"A gopher or something made a hole. I thought someone was sure to step in it one day and maybe break an ankle," she explained, and walked past him.

He closed the door and followed. "Who would do that? We hardly ever have people over to use the pool anymore, and . . ."

"Someone!" she snapped. "Maybe the pool man. Did you ever think of that? Then what? Then we get sued or something. Why can't you ever see the most obvious things? Do you know how ironic it is for you to be blind?" she asked, a sardonic smile on her lips. "Really, William. Open your eyes," she said, and walked on to return the shovel to its place in their garage.

He stood there watching her.

I am blind, he thought. *And it is to the most obvious truth of all, Hattie. You and I, we don't belong together, regardless of whatever the computers and the genealogists say.*

Soon, he thought. *Soon, I'll open my eyes wide. And then I'll be out of here.*

Buoyed by the thought, he went back upstairs to change his clothes, shower, and enjoy the rest of his free afternoon.

Twelve

::::::::::::

Natalie had fallen asleep again. She didn't know exactly when, but as soon as she opened her eyes, she realized her food tray was gone. She recalled how tiring the chewing of her rather delicious chicken Kiev had been, how she had paused a number of times to rest and then, having another surge of appetite and energy, continued. Did she finish it all? It was as if her eating had been a dream, an illusion.

Suddenly, she realized she was wearing the hospital gown, too. She couldn't remember taking off all her clothing and putting it on. When did this occur?

Just as she started to sit up, the door opened, and a dark-haired man with a well-trimmed goatee of the same ebony hair stepped into the room. He had a shiny, almost metallic complexion of light rust with lips somewhat on the orange side. His eyes were nearly lime green and very friendly and gentle, she thought. They warmed and brightened his smile.

"Hello there, Mrs. Ross. I'm Dr. Prudential."

He extended his long-fingered, rather soft hand to her.

"Hello?" she said.

He placed his bag on the bed and looked at her so intently, she felt uneasy.

"You've been sleeping a lot since you arrived, and you're concerned about that," he said as if he were more of a mind reader than a physician.

"Yes."

"Mrs. Jerome told me. You shouldn't be concerned. This is a rather emotional experience, and emotional experiences are often more draining than physical ones, especially for someone in your condition."

He had a soft, pleasant voice, soothing and reassuring. She smiled back at him and felt the tension easing in her back and legs.

"Tomorrow you'll feel a great deal better, stronger. You will be able to go out and enjoy the grounds. Beautiful place," he continued, opening his bag. "I especially appreciate the lake this time of year. Ducks and geese make it a significant rest stop on their way farther north. I'm actually from Canada," he continued, "and miss some of that."

He put the digital blood pressure cuff around her arm and slipped on his stethoscope.

"Please excuse the old-fashioned instruments," he said. "I'm kind of an old-fashioned guy."

She smiled. "I remember this," she said. "When I

was a little girl. The doctor in the underground . . ."

"Just relax," he instructed. She looked up at him as he pumped the cuff and listened.

There was a nearly indistinguishable patch of silvery freckles along the ridges of his eyebrows. His nose was thin and a bit long but perfectly straight. Those orange-tinted lips were thin, nearly disappearing when he pressed them together. She estimated he was at least forty years old and close to six feet tall. Slimly built with long arms, he had a feminine fragility about him.

"Not bad," he said. "Were you having any problems of any sort up until now?"

She shook her head. "I've been taking prenatal vitamins, watching my diet, avoiding too much alcohol. Of course, I don't smoke. Neither does my husband."

"Terrific. You've done some good reading on natural childbirth, then, have you?"

"No. My mother was . . . gave birth naturally," she said.

"Of course. May I?" he continued, moving to lift her hospital gown.

"Yes."

"Just lie back, Mrs. Ross. Continue to relax."

She felt the cool head of the stethoscope on her abdomen. He smiled as he listened. "Strong heartbeat. My guess is it's a boy."

She smiled. "Never thought I'd say I hope so, but I hope so."

"Understandable. Well, then," he said, stepping back and folding his arms. "First, let me assure you that everything we need is right here. Mrs. Jerome will show you to the delivery room tomorrow. You'll see we have state-of-the-art facilities for such a procedure. Not easy to get together nowadays, either, but we manage," he added proudly. "Mrs. Jerome is herself a qualified midwife. You know what that is?"

"Yes."

"We'll keep you well monitored, make sure you eat and exercise correctly, and I'll stop by once a week to make sure we're right on track. Let's talk dates, and then I'll examine you and let you know how accurate that all could be," he said.

"I figure I'm starting the sixth month," Natalie said, "despite my size."

"Yes, that seems very possible," he said. "Funny the misinformation that has been circulated about natural pregnancy. I have patients who think once you conceive, you blow right up like a balloon."

She laughed and then grew serious. "I don't want to do anything to speed things up," Natalie insisted. "I have heard of that, and I don't want that to be the case."

"I understand, and from what I have been told, there is no reason in your particular case to worry about your being away for nearly a three-month period."

"No, I can justify it," she said.

He shrugged. "Then there's no pressure on us, no worry. We're going to do fine," he said.

Mrs. Jerome came into the room. "Sorry," she said. "I had something that needed my immediate attention."

"No problem. We're just getting acquainted," Dr. Prudential said. "I'm about to examine Mrs. Ross just to confirm her stage of pregnancy. She's doing fine otherwise, and the fetus sounds very healthy. Been on prenatal vitamins, you know."

"No, I didn't. That's very good," Mrs. Jerome said.

Natalie felt a bit like a schoolgirl being complimented on her work.

"When did you take off my clothing and dress me in this gown?" she asked Mrs. Jerome. "I don't recall a thing. How could I be that deeply asleep?"

Mrs. Jerome exchanged a strange look with Dr. Prudential and then looked back at her, shaking her head as she did so.

"What?" Natalie asked.

"I didn't take off your clothing and dress you in the hospital gown, Mrs. Ross. You must have done that yourself," she said, and smiled.

Natalie stared.

"What's the difference?" Dr. Prudential said quickly. "No harm done. Just lie back again, Mrs. Ross. I'll only be a little while longer."

Was she so tired that her memory suffered? Natalie pondered.

The long delay for the doctor to speak after his physical examination heightened Natalie's concern about herself. She lifted herself up on her elbows and looked at him and Mrs. Jerome. They seemed to have been whispering.

"Anything wrong?" she asked quickly.

"Oh, no, nothing wrong. I just think you're a little more advanced than you estimate, Mrs. Ross. Actually, could be a good thing. The baby's in perfect position, too."

"How can I be more advanced than I thought? I don't understand."

"It's not an exact science, old-fashioned birthing," Mrs. Jerome answered before Natalie could finish her thought. "Nature is unpredictable."

"Which is what brought about our whole new world," Dr. Prudential pointed out. He turned back to Natalie and smiled. "But we appreciate spontaneity, unpredictability, don't we, Mrs. Ross? After all," he said, widening his thin lips until they looked as if they might snap, "the beauty and the mystery of all that is what brought you here in the first place."

Mrs. Jerome nodded. "It's what has brought us all here," she said. "Rest some more, my dear," she instructed. "We can tour the facilities in the morning after I've brought you your breakfast."

"Can't I go down for breakfast? I don't like being treated like an invalid."

They held their smiles, but the warmth, real or imposed, evaporated.

"Nor will you be," Mrs. Jerome said.

"Hardly," Dr. Prudential agreed.

"Of course, you can come down for breakfast. That was what I meant, my dear. Come down as soon as you are up. I'm usually up and about by six-thirty."

Dr. Prudential laughed. "Now, if it were I in that bed, I'd probably take advantage of our Mrs. Jerome," he said.

"Thank goodness you're not, then," Mrs. Jerome said, moving toward the door.

Dr. Prudential closed his bag and followed. They both looked back at her.

"Remember, if there's anything you need, anything at all, just speak up, and I'll hear. Any time," Mrs. Jerome added.

"See you soon, Mrs. Ross," Dr. Prudential said and walked out ahead of Mrs. Jerome, who glanced back once and then closed the door after her.

The silence seemed to rush in under the door and under the closed windows.

Natalie felt that wave of fatigue wash over her again. She closed her eyes and lay back.

She tried to fight off sleep. She didn't want to sleep, but it was as relentless as the tide, sending wave after wave of drowsiness over her.

Her eyes shut.

She moaned and drifted.

Somewhere off in the distance, there was that sound again, the sound of someone crying. She

THE BABY SQUAD   257

fought to open her eyes and listen harder, maybe
to get up and see what that was about. Maybe she
was crying herself.

But her efforts were futile. It was as if a curtain
of lead had been drawn over her body. The weight
of it all was too much.

She stopped hearing the crying. She stopped
hearing her own thoughts.

She was like the dead.

Judge Mason looked like a man with a fire burning
inside him. He had a head of thick, almost lumi-
nescent white hair that was in stark contrast to his
coal-black African-American complexion. There
was a wild look in his hazel eyes that widened so
dramatically when Ryan explained what he wanted
they threatened to pop like overcooked eggs.

"Preston Ross?" He insisted on hearing it repeated.

"Yes, your honor," Ryan said without the slightest hesitation. "As I said, I have good reason to believe the murder weapon is on his property."

Mason sat back in his desk chair. He was at
least six feet four in his stocking feet. At the moment, he was wearing a pair of leather slippers, a
hastily put-on pair of dark trousers, and a white
shirt and tie. The office in his home appeared to
be mostly for show. The volumes on the shelves
looked untouched. There was just a long yellow
pad on his oversized dark walnut desk and no

other sign of work in the room. Scattered over the two available walls were plaques and pictures.

Judge Mason looked at McCalester. When Ryan glanced at him as well, McCalester's eyes shifted quickly toward a plaque.

"Why would anyone plant a murder weapon in Preston Ross's home? Especially a murder weapon used to kill a teenage girl."

Ryan simply stared for a good two to three seconds of silence. McCalester shifted his weight from his right to his left leg and glanced at Ryan, his eyes asking him if he was so arrogant as to piss off the judge and not bother replying.

"I'm working on answering that as quickly as I can, your honor. Once I retrieve the weapon, I'll be able to do that faster," Ryan said, unable to keep his tone from being condescending. If Mason could blush, he would have, but he was more the type of a man who narrowed his eyes and tightened the muscles in his face. Anger flushed through it with an electric pulse.

"What is the alleged weapon we're looking for, Detective Lee?" Judge Mason asked.

"It's a specific flashlight, a Raydox, one of their longer models," Ryan replied.

"I see."

"This isn't a fishing expedition, sir. I'm certain of that. As I told you . . . I saw her leave it in there myself. If I am able to get into the garage, I will be able to ascertain whether it was used as a murder weapon. I can do it in a matter of seconds with the bloodhound," he added.

Mason was acquainted with most of the modern technology utilized by the CID and the FBI, so he knew that Ryan was not talking about a real dog. He didn't need any sort of lecture about the capabilities of the equipment, either.

"I take my search warrants very, very seriously when it comes to members of my community," he said.

Ryan nodded. "I never ask for one until I'm sure I need it, your honor."

"I'm old-fashioned enough to believe a man's home is his castle."

Ryan just stared.

Judge Mason looked at McCalester again. "You going along on this search, Henry?"

"I intend to, yes, your honor."

"I am not requesting him to do so," Ryan said sharply.

"I am," Judge Mason snapped back. He opened a drawer and took out a search warrant. "I'm granting the warrant for the garage only," he said.

"But I can't be sure she didn't get into the house. There is a door into the house from the garage, your honor," Ryan said.

"We'll take it a step at a time. Garage only."

"But your honor . . ."

Judge Mason looked up at him. The fire intensified behind those eyes.

"If I don't find what I'm looking for in the garage, I'll come right back to you, sir."

"Fine. Come right back," Judge Mason said, and signed the document. "If you go into any other part of this property without permission, you'll compromise your investigation, detective."

"I understand, your honor," Ryan said.

"Good," Mason replied. "Good." He held out the warrant, and Ryan took it.

"We're on the same side, your honor," Ryan said.

Judge Mason smiled. "We should be, but that's not always been true, detective, especially with you gung-ho CID officers."

Ryan said nothing more. Now it was his turn to feel the blood rush up his neck. He turned and walked out of the office. McCalester followed a moment later, but he didn't speak until they were out of the judge's home and back in McCalester's vehicle.

"I warned you he's a hardass," McCalester said.

Ryan chose not to reply. He had seen the wagons circle before in communities like Sandburg, and in similar circumstances, too. They liked to take care of their own problems and keep them as quiet as possible for obvious reasons. It was why the baby squads were so popular and, in many instances, so powerful.

Ryan wasn't surprised, therefore, to see Preston Ross's car back in the driveway before they returned from the judge's home to get the warrant. McCalester's deputy stepped out to greet them.

"He just arrived, maybe two minutes at the most," he reported.

"Okay, thanks," McCalester said. "You can go back to the station."

The moment they got out of the vehicle, Preston Ross stepped out of his house.

"I had the impression you had some sort of an emergency at your office," Ryan told him when he walked toward them.

"Seems I have one here as well. Let's see the warrant."

Ryan handed it to him but had no doubts the attorney already knew what was in it. He handed it back.

"I'll open the garage door for you," he said, and went to his car to activate the opener.

Ryan, carrying his bag, walked in as soon as the door went up. He stood for a few moments looking around and then turned back to Preston.

"Is this your wife's vehicle?"

"It's our second vehicle, yes," Preston said.

"Then is she home?"

"No. She had another means of transport," Preston said.

Ryan said nothing. He placed his bag on the table to the right and opened it to pluck out his search tool.

"This is a bloodhound," he explained. "It has already been programed with Lois Marlowe's blood."

It began to tick slowly, resembling a Geiger counter. McCalester and Preston followed slowly behind Ryan Lee as he began to criss-cross the garage to form the investigative X. Midway, the bloodhound's clicking grew more intense and faster. Ryan turned slightly to the right. It diminished. He turned harder to the left, and it returned to its rapid beating. He glanced at Preston, who remained quite cool, almost disinterested, and then he walked toward a tool cabinet.

The bloodhound was raging. Ryan touched the second drawer, and it began to brighten and beep. He opened the drawer and gazed into it. McCalester was at his side, Preston a few feet behind them. The drawer was empty. Ryan and McCalester looked at each other, and then Ryan turned to Preston.

"The weapon was in this drawer, Mr. Ross, but it's not here now."

"I haven't the slightest idea what you're talking about, detective."

"The bloodhound has sensed and recorded the presence of Lois Marlowe's blood in this drawer. The instrument that had been placed in here left it. That instrument is no longer here."

Preston shook his head. "Instrument?"

"Flashlight," Ryan said through tight lips.

"I'm afraid I still can't help you," Preston said.

"The results of a bloodhound have long been

held to be acceptable evidence in court, Mr. Ross," Ryan said as he returned the investigative tool to his bag.

"So?"

"So, what we have here in courtroom parlance is incriminating evidence linking you or your wife to the murder of Lois Marlowe," Ryan recited. "Now, it's missing. It's enough for me to have you arrested or your wife arrested and brought in for formal questioning."

"But you claim you saw someone else put this . . . this . . . instrument, as you referred to it, in here. Perhaps this person has returned and retrieved it. Maybe she just left it here on a temporary basis."

He turned to McCalester.

"We all know we're talking about this Stocker Robinson, and you told me earlier she ran away from school. She could have come here and taken the weapon, instrument, whatever," he muttered, turning back to Ryan.

"Why would she do that?"

"That's your problem, detective, isn't it? The how, what, and why of all this?"

"Being it was on your property, it's now your problem as well. I insist on speaking with your wife."

Preston just stared at him coldly.

"One way or another, Mr. Ross, that's going to happen. Now, if I'm forced to do it, I'll have a warrant issued for her arrest as a potential material witness in a murder case. It's entirely your call."

Ryan held his gaze on him, his eyes like two small flashlights themselves.

"All right," Preston said, relenting. "I'll have her call you. Where can she reach you?" he asked.

"It would be better if you told me how to get in touch with her."

"I have to prepare her for this," Preston said in a softer, more cooperative tone of voice. "My wife is somewhat nervous these days. She's a writer, and sometimes difficulty with a story or with editors puts her on edge. What difference does it make, anyway, as long as you get what you want?"

"It's not what I want. It's what the state wants," Ryan replied sharply, meeting harsh tone for harsh tone. "It's important to me to be face to face with my witnesses," he added, "in the flesh and not on some video phone."

Preston stood firm, his eyes now cold and dark. "What are you, a mind reader, too?"

"I'm a trained observer," Ryan said. "The state spent a great deal of money enabling me to be that, and I see no reason not to investigate this crime under the best possible circumstances. I'm sorry your wife is having some difficulties, but the Marlowe family is having some difficulties, too, at the moment, and I think you would agree that their difficulties are far more severe that what you've described."

McCalester held his breath throughout the exchange. His eyes moved from Preston to Ryan as if he were watching a tennis match. The silences between their statements were so deep he held his breath.

"Give me a little time and I'll make the arrangements for an interview you'll find satisfactory," Preston said. It was more of a demand than a concession or a request.

McCalester looked at Ryan to see how he would react.

"That door leads into your home, does it not?" he asked instead of replying.

"Yes."

"I'd like your permission to take the bloodhound in there right now."

"The warrant says . . ."

"You've seen technical evidence proving beyond a doubt that the weapon was on your property. Why would you not want me to clear the house?" Ryan asked. "The instrument is programmed for only Lois Marlowe's blood sample. You couldn't ask for a more concise search. I can go back and ask the judge to expand the warrant, of course, but if you will sign this paper permitting me to expand the search for this one specific reason, you'll save the state some time and expense and help get the matter out of your face. And I'll wait until morning to arrange to meet your wife and interview her," he added with a definite tone of concession.

McCalester's face was actually red with his subconscious effort to keep from breathing too loudly.

Preston took the paper from Ryan's hands and put it on the table. He scribbled his permission on the document and stepped back. Ryan read it, folded it, put it in his inside jacket pocket, and opened his bag to take out the bloodhound again. He scooped up his bag with his other hand and nodded at Preston, who moved to the door.

The bloodhound began its steady, low clicking, literally sounding like the canine after which it had been named, sniffing its way. The three men, with Preston in the lead, moved into the kitchen. Ryan made his sweep, and they moved through the dining room, into the hallway, pausing at the door of the great room where the Rosses had their entertainment center. The clicking began to increase a bit.

He stood by the settee and gazed at the instrument.

"Something?" McCalester asked.

"No," Ryan said, but he continued to study the room as if he had microscope lenses in his eyes. Occasionally, he glanced at Preston. The lawyer still looked more annoyed than worried. Ryan turned and walked out of the room. They followed the hallway to the formal living room and then went to the stairs after he had opened and closed the doors of the two closets and inspected the laundry room.

McCalester and Preston walked behind in a strange parade of silence, the continuous clicking of the bloodhound the only real noise now in the house. Ryan checked the two guest bedrooms, the bathrooms, and the closets and then entered the master bedroom. He didn't need any state-of-the-art criminologist's device to conclude that someone had left this house in a hurry. Drawers in the closet were half open, some of their contents dangling over the edges. There were drawers still open in the armoire, as well, and garments tossed about, over chairs, some dresses even on the floor of the closet.

"Housekeeper's day off?" he asked Ryan.

"I was supposed to see to all this today, but I've been unexpectedly distracted," he returned.

Ryan's eyebrows rising were the only indication he didn't believe Preston Ross. It was enough for McCalester, who looked down and then at the disheveled room. The bloodhound clicked the way it had in the den, but Ryan said nothing.

"Well?" Preston asked with impatience. "I have some important business to tend to today."

"Okay," Ryan said.

The phone rang. Everyone looked at the receiver by the bed.

"Excuse me," Preston said, leaving the room to take the call in the room next to the master bedroom.

"Seems like Esther Robinson should be called

in a day earlier to clean up, don't you think?"
Ryan asked McCalester.

The burly policeman shook his head and
shrugged. They met Preston in the hallway emerging from one of the guest bedrooms.

"Where can you be reached?" he asked Ryan.

"I'm at the Sandburg Creek Inn, but you can
call Chief McCalester as well," Ryan said. "If I
have to do any significant traveling, I'd like to hear
before eight P.M."

"Understood," Preston said.

They all descended the stairs and parted company at the front entrance. Preston remained inside the house. As McCalester and Ryan got into
their vehicle, the garage door began to close. Ryan
watched it a moment and then got into Mc-
Calester's car.

"What do you think?" McCalester asked him.

"I haven't put it all together yet," Ryan replied.
It was as good as saying, *None of your business.*

His tone seemed to button McCalester's lips.
They barely passed any small talk between them
all the way back to Ryan's hotel.

"I'll call you if he calls me," McCalester said
when Ryan stepped out with his bag.

"Right," he said.

He walked quickly to the hotel. McCalester lingered a moment until he was gone and then drove
off.

As soon as Ryan stepped into his room, he put

the bag on his bed and opened it. He stared at the results on the bloodhound.

What he had seen before and what he saw now made him pause.

This community was on the verge of an earthquake, and whether he wanted to or not, he would be the one causing it.

"What the hell's with that dog now?" Mickey Ross screamed from the living room. Esther had tried to keep herself busy making dinner and not to think about Stocker. Nevertheless, every time she glanced at the phone, she expected it would ring and the police would be calling to say they had picked her up walking on the road or she had been located hanging out at some video parlor.

"I don't know," she called back.

"It's that damn cat. You had to keep it around here. I swear, I'll put a bullet in both their heads!"

She slammed down the pan of chicken cutlets and wiped her hands on her apron.

"She's just been tied up all day is all," Esther said, walking through the living room.

Mickey glared at her. She knew how irritated he was sitting there just waiting as she was. *I do pity that girl when she walks through the front door,* she thought, and walked out and around to where Kasey-Lady was chained.

The dog was barking wildly and leaping against the limits and restrictions of her chain. She practically dangled in the air at times, stepping forward on her rear legs, falling to all fours, and whimpering.

"Quiet!" Esther screamed at the golden retriever. Usually obedient, the dog just barked louder and worked harder at getting itself free.

"What the hell's the matter with you?" she cried. She looked about for signs of the cat, who she imagined enjoyed tormenting the dog, but didn't see him anywhere, which she readily admitted to herself didn't mean the cat wasn't snuggled in some nearby opening, waiting for her to walk into the house.

The dog actually took a few steps back and then charged forward, lunging at the air and flinging her own body back so violently Esther winced. What could make that animal so crazy?

"All right, all right," she said, walking toward the golden retriever. "I know you need a little breathing room."

She did feel sorry for the animal chained up most of the day or at least usually until she or Chester returned from work. With all that had been happening today, neither of them remembered the animal.

That was another thing that riled Mickey. Stocker was supposed to walk the dog every day. It was supposed to be part of her daily chores, but it was obvious she rarely did it, no matter how much she swore up and down that she did.

Kasey-Lady whimpered, pleading with her body and her eyes for Esther to unhook her collar.

"Never should have taken on the responsibility for you in the first place," Esther muttered. "I should have known what Stocker would be like when it came to doing what she promised when we first saw you in the pet shop. 'Please, Mommy, please. I promise. Please.' Anyone who believes in the word of a ten-year-old deserves what she gets," she concluded, speaking to the animal as if she believed the dog understood every single word. She certainly looked attentive, even nodding at the right moment.

Esther laughed. "Go on, run around the house like you do, and then I'll let you in to follow me around the kitchen, hoping for me to drop a scrap of this or that," she told the dog.

The moment she unfastened her collar, she did just as Esther had suggested and charged toward the rear of the house. Esther stood, gazed around looking for the cat again, shook her head, and started for the front door when she heard the dog barking even louder and harder. She wasn't going around the house as Esther had expected. The way she ran sometimes, it was a miracle she didn't smash head-on into the building.

"What is it now?" Esther called. The dog continued to yap. "I need this today." She shook her head. Mickey would be out here in a New York minute if she didn't get the animal quieted. She trudged to the rear of the house.

"Kasey," she snapped, and looked up. The animal was sitting and whimpering, its tail flogging the ground.

Esther let her eyes follow the animal's gaze. For a long moment, it was like a dream, an illusion, something that you could wipe away with your hand or blink away and then laugh about afterward, but it wasn't. It was real.

Stocker dangled from the railing that ran along the rear porch. Her feet were turned down and just off the bottom railing. It looked as though she had been standing there and simply stepped forward into death. The rope around her neck looked embedded in her skin. Her mouth was slightly open, the faded, purplish tip of her tongue hanging over her bottom teeth. Her eyes were two glass marbles. Although her arms dangled at her sides, her hands were closed, the fingers locked like claws.

Esther couldn't swallow, couldn't speak. She stumbled backward and then turned and ran from the sight. Kasey-Lady immediately started her barking again. Esther's legs gave out on her after she reached the front door. She managed to open it and fall forward into the hallway. Still, her voice wouldn't serve her. She could barely manage a loud gasp which was followed by an unearthly, throaty cry.

Mickey Robinson slammed his opened hand on the arm of his chair so hard it stung his palm.

"Damn it to hell!" he screamed. "I'll kill that dog. I'll kill it."

He rose and stepped into the hallway. The moment he saw her, he stopped, his mouth dropping open. She was reaching up for him like someone drowning.

"What the hell . . . what?"

With all the strength she could muster, she took a deep breath and screamed.

"Stocker!"

Then she collapsed into unconsciousness, her face hitting the floor so hard Mickey Robinson winced in sympathetic pain. He stepped over her and walked out and around the house, every cell in his body already aware that he was about to view the most horrible thing he could imagine.

Thirteen

Ryan had just stepped out of the shower when his phone rang. He stared at it. He didn't expect the call to come this soon and thought it was probably Lieutenant Childs checking up on his investigation. He tied the towel around his waist and pushed the receiver button. McCalester appeared on the six-inch screen.

"Sorry to bother you so quickly," he said.

"What's up?"

"We found the Robinson girl."

"Where was she?"

"Hanging around her house," McCalester said.

"I'll be right there. Get dressed."

The screen went dark.

McCalester was there in ten. Ryan was still buttoning his shirt when he called up for him. Ryan grabbed his bag and charged out of the room. On the way to the Robinsons', McCalester described the phone call he had received from Mickey Robinson. They reached the house before the ambulance. Mickey was sitting on the front stoop, his head in his hands. Kasey-Lady was sprawled at his feet, finally quiet, actually exhausted from her hysterical alarms. McCalester and Ryan stepped out of the car and walked slowly toward Mickey Robinson. He raised his head as if it weighed fifty pounds.

"Around back" was all he could manage.

"Jesus," McCalester said when they turned the corner of the house. They both stood there gazing up at the gently swaying body of the teenage girl. "There hasn't been a teenage suicide in this state for more than twenty-five years."

Ryan looked at him.

"I'm just thinking about the press and what will be made of it," McCalester feebly explained.

Ryan said nothing. He climbed up on the railing to get closer to the corpse and began to study the rope, first around her neck and then where it was tied over the beam.

"She knew it was just a matter of time before you came to get her," McCalester rattled on. "You know what else I'm thinking now? This girl was pregnant. We should have followed up on that."

Ryan looked down at him. "Do me a favor," he said.

"What?"

"Fetch my EB."

"What?"

"My evidence bag," he said, and began a detailed survey of Stocker Robinson's face, gently exploring her lips, nose, and temples with the tips of his fingers.

McCalester shook his head. "Never could get close to a dead person," he muttered, and hurried back to the vehicle as the ambulance came tearing up the street.

He and the two paramedics returned to the scene. They stood back in awe. Neither of the two had ever seen a suicide. The sight of someone so young who had taken her own life stunned the seasoned veterans of all sorts of accidents, and gruesome ones at that.

Ryan hopped off the railing and opened the bag as soon as McCalester handed it to him.

"What do you have?" McCalester asked him.

"A dead girl," Ryan said dryly. He took out what looked like an ordinary penlight and climbed back on the railing. The three watched him examine the beam. He turned to the paramedics and McCalester. "One of you lift her," he said.

The two paramedics looked at each other.

"Grab her legs and lift her!"

McCalester stepped forward and did it.

"Just hold her a minute," Ryan said. He slid the rope along the beam. "Okay," he said, dropping himself off the railing to fetch something else out of the evidence bag.

McCalester looked at the waiting paramedics and shrugged. Ryan returned to the railing. He had put on what looked like a metallic glove and slowly began to run it over the beam from left to right until he reached Stocker, and then he stepped behind her to continue running his hand along the beam.

"What is that?" one of the paramedics asked.

"Fingerprint detector. It's lifting the prints and recording them."

Ryan ran the gloved hand over Stocker Robinson's corpse. From the prospective of the paramedics, it looked like some perverted sexual act performed on a dead girl. They grimaced as he cupped under her breasts and moved over her rear end and between her legs. He paused for a few moments at her left rear jeans pocket. With his uncovered hand, he slipped his fingers into the pocket. For the moment, he decided not to reveal what he had found.

He stepped down and carefully slipped off the FD.

"You think this was a murder?" McCalester finally blurted.

"Let's just say I have my doubts," Ryan replied, "which is what I'm trained to have," he added. "You'd better cordon off the area."

"What about her?" McCalester asked.

"She stays awhile."

"You want to leave her dangling here like that?"

"Until the ME arrives. It's an unattended death, isn't it?"

"Yeah, but . . ."

"Just keep everyone away. Extend the perimeter," Ryan ordered.

"What do we do?" one of the paramedics asked him.

"Nothing for a while. The ME will be the one who will tell you to remove the body from the scene and take it to the lab for an autopsy."

They nodded, still quite wide-eyed.

"A lot of nasty stuff in a community so peaceful someone would think he had stepped into God's backyard," McCalester muttered. "The Garden of Eden itself," he added.

Ryan glanced back at Stocker Robinson's corpse still swinging slightly from his examination.

"Looks like we have a snake in paradise," he said.

After McCalester called the ME, he watched Ryan videotape everything and begin a systematic examination of the immediate area. It was behind the railing on the porch floor that he lit up with some emotional reaction. McCalester had been off to the side watching him work and saw the added excitement in Ryan's movements, including his practically lunging for something in his EB.

"What do you have?" he called to him, keeping his six feet of distance from the detective.

"A footprint."

"So?"

"It's not hers," Ryan said.

"So?"

Ryan glanced at him.

"So, it's relatively recent, and it's the print of someone with a larger foot, and it's behind the corpse. Use your imagination," Ryan suggested.

McCalester shook his head. "It's probably Mickey's."

"Maybe. Maybe not," Ryan said, and continued to work the scene until he told McCalester it was time to speak to the Robinsons. They found the two of them hovering side by side on the settee in the living room. Esther had a cold wet cloth over her forehead and eyes. Mickey sat beside her, his body turned and twisted in the wake of his agonizing.

"I need to ask a few questions," Ryan said. Esther didn't move. Mickey straightened up and sat forward. He glared at Ryan, and Ryan thought, *In this father's mind, we're all responsible. Maybe he's right.*

"After we left today, you heard nothing from your daughter?"

"No. If we had, we would have called McCalester."

"And you heard no one in the house, no one back there, no sounds?"

"I had the television on most of the time, trying to keep myself occupied. Esther was preparing dinner. The dog was barking, but she's always barking. We've got this cat that enjoys teasing her."

"Did your daughter ever threaten to do something like this?"

"No," Esther said, ripping the cloth from her head.

Ryan nodded. "I'm just asking what we call routine questions in situations like this, ma'am."

"Routine," Mickey muttered. "Can't imagine something like this being someone's routine."

Ryan glanced at Esther. She looked as if she were on the verge of spontaneous combustion.

"Mr. Robinson," he said softly. "Can I see you privately for a moment?"

Esther began to rock back and forth. Mickey looked at her and then got up and walked with Ryan into the vestibule.

"I don't know how long a look you were able to take back there, but the rope . . ."

"What about it?"

"Was it something you had here?"

"I don't know. Yeah, I guess we have rope here. In the garage. What difference does it make?"

"I have to . . ."

"Routine questions, I know. Anything else?"

"Tell me what you did after you saw your daughter."

"Whaddya mean?"

"How close did you get to her? Did you go around her, try to take her down, what? I'm sorry. I need to ask."

"The moment I saw her, it felt like my heart

dropped into my stomach. I guess I got very dizzy and nauseous and sank to my knees for a few moments. Then I got up and stepped in front of her, looked into her face, and knew she was gone. I hurried into the house and called McCalester."

"You're sure you didn't step behind her on the porch or try to move that rope, take her down, anything?"

"It was pretty obvious that it was too late," Mickey said.

Ryan shook his head. "I'm sorry," he muttered.

"Everyone was on her," Mickey Robinson continued, looking at Ryan but really looking past him. "Me, too. But she never had friends. I know she was trying. That's what got her in trouble in the first place, I'm sure. Kids can be cruel to each other, you know." His eyes brightened and focused on Ryan now. "Kids can be the cruelest. They drove her to this. The whole damn community drove her."

Ryan nodded, remembering his own youth, the discrimination, the hard times he had experienced. "Okay. I'm sorry for your troubles," he said. "I truly am, Mr. Robinson."

Nothing he had said up to this point was as rife with feeling. Mickey Robinson softened a bit, nodded, and walked back to the living room.

Ryan opened the door and stepped out. He saw all the vehicles in the road.

"A little circus," McCalester muttered, waiting for him on the stoop.

Word of mouth was still one of the fastest means of spreading news, Ryan thought, as people living nearby and many from the community continued arriving to witness what was happening. They grouped on the street and waited to hear every little detail. Friends of the Robinsons arrived to give comfort, including some of the people for whom Esther worked as well as Mickey's fellow county highway employees.

After the ME, Dr. Gordon Howard, a man in his mid-fifties, completed his preliminary examination, Stocker Robinson was taken down and covered on a stretcher which was then brought to the ambulance. It quieted down the onlookers, who stood transfixed on the white sheet until the stretcher was loaded and the ambulance drove away.

Ryan joined Dr. Howard at Howard's vehicle.

"What do you think?" he asked him.

"Seems pretty cut and dried to me," Howard replied. Ryan noticed he avoided looking directly at him when he responded.

"I was able to ascertain the depth of the trauma under the ropes. The line is a little too straight. I think there's some possibility she was strangled first, don't you?"

"I'll see, but I don't think the difference is enough to reach any conclusion like that."

"The indentation in the beam is not deep enough for someone of her weight to have stepped off that railing and dropped herself," Ryan added. "People, even those who do it willingly, can't help but struggle. The body insists. I didn't see evidence of that rope burning into the beam. That suggests strongly that she was already gone when she was attached."

Dr. Howard looked at him askance. "I'll do what I do as best I can," he replied. "The rest is your problem."

He got into his vehicle and followed the ambulance.

"Well?" McCalester said, coming up beside Ryan. "Looks like your time here is nearly finished, I guess. You've got your killer and all."

"I don't know," Ryan said.

"You're not going forward with your insistence to interview Mrs. Ross now, are you?"

"Used to be a saying years ago," Ryan replied, walking to the police vehicle.

"Here we go again. What saying?"

"It ain't over until the fat lady sings, and I haven't heard her singing yet."

McCalester clamped his lips together and drove in silence back to the hotel.

"Call me when Preston Ross calls you," Ryan told him as he got out.

"What makes you think he'll call me? You told him where you were staying," McCalester said.

Ryan smiled. "Really, chief, you don't have to be a trained CID agent to know that he'll call you before he'll call me to see if this is all over, right?"

McCalester grunted and drove off.

As soon as Ryan got into his room, he began to hook up his forensic devices. He started by running the prints he had lifted from the railing and from Stocker Robinson's body. Results were just coming back when the phone rang.

He smiled to himself. He had handled this well. He had cornered the big shots and played it all well. He was even feeling a bit arrogant about it.

He hit the receiver button and was surprised to see Lieutenant Childs calling from state headquarters instead of McCalester.

"Ryan, I expected to hear from you after what's just come through regarding the situation down there."

"How did you get that information so fast, Lieutenant?"

He had the sense that he was being watched, evaluated, his every move in this investigation being monitored.

"It came directly from our people in the county district attorney's office. It should have come from you."

"I have one more important interview to conduct before I could give you a significant preliminary report, sir," he replied.

"Why is that necessary?"

"The results are not conclusive on today's discovery, Lieutenant."

"Um . . . this murder case . . . it involves an Abnormal . . . a potential natural childbirth?"

"I believe it does, sir."

"I see. Well, someone cracked your file, Ryan."

"What do you mean, Lieutenant?"

"They know about your natural birth," he replied, avoiding calling him an Abnormal.

"Oh?"

"You know I tried to keep that discreet, and I wanted you to have this case," he added.

"Yes, sir, I appreciate that."

"Well, it's compromised you."

"What?"

"I've been given orders from the adjunct general's office to replace you, Ryan. I'm sorry. I have Detective Sacks on his way to Sandburg. He's coming from another case he's just concluded and should be there in two hours. Please greet him at the airport and fill him in on what you have."

"I don't understand. Why am I compromised?"

"We don't want there to be any suggestion of prejudice, Ryan. If there is an Abnormal involved . . ."

"That's not fair, sir. I haven't done anything to indicate any prejudice. I've been extremely objective."

"I'm sure you have been, but believe me, Ryan, this is for your benefit as much as for the benefit of the investigation."

"Well, can I remain and assist? I still have some work in progress here," he added, looking at his fingerprint report as it continued to come through on his printer.

"I think it's better if you give Sacks what you have and simply return to headquarters, Ryan. I have something else I'd like you to get into right away. This doesn't reflect on your work, Ryan. It's not going to influence considering you for a promotion. In fact, your ability to see the wisdom of all this can only help toward that goal. And faster than you'd expect," he added.

He was being bribed to walk away from the case.

It brought his blood to a boil.

When would this prejudice end? Would it ever end? Was he only fooling himself believing he could achieve any success in the CID? To hold his birth against him! It was as primitive as some twentieth-century prejudice that forced a good black detective off a case involving the investigation of an important white man.

He could hear McCalester's "I told you so." What were some of his exact words? "Your questioning someone as important and influential as Mr. Ross and his wife might be politically incorrect," he had said. "It'll get around, and just questioning someone can taint him or her. Bertram Cauthers, the senior partner in Ross's firm, is very connected. I'd be extra sure before I tapped on those doors."

Well, he had tapped, and it had been heard as far away as Central Headquarters.

"Very good, sir," he said, unable to keep out his

tone of defeat and disappointment, and he was sure Childs saw it in his face as well.

"I knew I could count on you to do the right thing, Ryan. You're going to go far. Trust me."

Far, he thought, but in what direction?

He sat thinking after he hung up. He could feel the steam flowing out of his ears. Anger was broiling his brain.

He ripped the fingerprint findings out of the jaws of his printer and perused them.

For crying out Christ, he thought. *If I turn this over to Sacks, it will be buried for sure.*

An idea came to him. It was defiance, but technically he still had two hours on this case, didn't he? Why waste them sitting around a hotel room?

Without hesitation, he seized his bag and charged out of the hotel room. Minutes later, he was on the road to the Ross residence.

Fourteen

:::::::::::::

A sharp pain that felt as if a string of barbed wire had been dragged through her stomach and out her vagina woke Natalie with a spasmodic jerk that caused her to sit up and cry out. The pain was gone as quickly as it had come. Nevertheless, she pressed her hands to her lower abdomen and continued to sit up, catching her breath. Sweat beads were all along her temples and down her neck. She could feel the trickle over her breasts and onto her stomach. It produced a quick chill and made her shudder.

For a long moment, she couldn't remember where she was. Her memory was that fogged over. The moonlight gave the room a yellow glow, bouncing off the mirror and creating long, rubbery, unfamiliar silhouettes over the walls. It put her in a small panic until her orientation returned and she began to breathe easier. However, now her throat felt so dry she thought she would rip it apart swallowing. She reached over to switch on the light on the nightstand and then turned to get out of bed and go to the bathroom.

Her legs felt as if she had been running for days. The moment she moved them, deep aches radiated up from her calves, over her knees, and into her thighs. She groaned and reached around to rub her lower back.

"My God," she muttered, "I feel like I'm a hundred and ten years old."

What time was it? She looked to her wrist, surprised to discover her watch was gone. When did she remove that, and why? She looked at the nightstand, but it wasn't there. Where had she put it? Why was she having so much trouble with her memory?

When she concentrated on remembering, audio images passed through her mind, seemingly unrelated, voices, someone crying through the walls, a shrill scream, and then soft murmuring, loud whispers, doors closing. What did it all mean?

She stood, feeling wobbly, so wobbly, in fact, she had to sit and get her equilibrium back before she attempted to stand again. It took so long for the room to stop spinning she grew more and more frightened.

"I need help!" she cried at the walls. Supposedly, somewhere embedded in them, she recalled, were microphones designed to carry her voice to Mrs. Jerome. She waited but heard nothing, no steps outside her door, no voice returning to tell her that some assistance was on its way. "Hello? Anyone there?"

Suddenly, she felt quite silly talking to walls. Why wasn't there just an ordinary intercom in this room? Frustrated, she was on her feet again. She used the nightstand to steady herself and then took some steps forward and reached for the wall. She paused to catch her breath and wait until her heart stopped pounding. She was right by the window now and could see how clear the night sky was. There wasn't even the wisp of a cloud against the dark blue. The full moon looked positively immense. It looked as if it had been drawn at least halfway closer to the earth. In fact, the illumination flowing from it made the lights on the driveway and on the poles over the grounds look insignificant, drowned out. The driveway itself resembled a sheet of glass. For a few moments, she was mesmerized the way a moth might be hypnotized by candlelight. She stared down at the front of the building.

Remembering why she had risen in the first place, she started to turn from the window, when a dark figure appeared at the base of the front steps below. She could see it was a woman. There was something vaguely familiar about the shape of her head, her shoulders, that entire posture and demeanor. Moments later, Mrs. Jerome appeared beside her. The two stood conversing for a minute or so before they were joined by a man, who spoke briefly and then headed for a vehicle. When he turned, his face was caught in the moonlight, and she remembered it was her doctor, Dr. Prudential.

Mrs. Jerome and the woman beside her watched him start his car and drive away. They spoke a few moments longer, and then the woman walked around another vehicle and opened the door. The light from inside the car plus the moonlight was as effective as a small spotlight on her face. She even turned and looked up at Natalie's window, making it that much easier to recognize her.

It was as if a shaft of glass had flown up from her face and pierced Natalie's heart.

Standing below was Hattie Scranton. There was no mistaking that visage. What was she doing here? Of all people, Hattie Scranton!

Natalie watched her drive off and saw Mrs. Jerome turn back to the building. Once again, all was quiet and very deserted below. What did this mean? Her throat was screaming in pain. She could barely swallow. She took a deep breath and continued toward the bathroom. When she got there, she flipped on the light and gazed at herself in the mirror over the sink. She looked like a madwoman, her hair disheveled, her face flushed. As quickly as she could, she splashed cold water on her face and poured a glass of it to drink. She had what seemed to be an unquenchable thirst. It took another full glass of water to satisfy her, and now that she had gulped it so quickly, she felt very nauseated. The dizziness was returning, too.

She started back toward the bed, moaning and calling as she worked her way across the room, practically falling over the bed when she reached it. For a while, she lay there on her stomach and then turned herself onto her back and looked up at the ceiling. She felt so different. This lightness in her head, these aches in her body, told her something very serious was wrong with her. Why hadn't they noticed? They were supposed to be so attentive, so concerned.

Gathering her strength again, she got to her feet and went to the closet. She wanted to dress and go downstairs. She needed to have answers. Why was Hattie Scranton here? Had she found out about her and tracked her to this place? Did they deny her access or tell Hattie she wasn't here? What was going on?

More important, why did she feel this way? Why hadn't anyone come to see what she needed? Where was her watch?

The sight of an empty closet revived the panic that had just swirled within her chest and stomach. Spinning about, she searched the room for signs of any of her things. There was none. All she had to wear was this ridiculous hospital gown, and she didn't even have any slippers.

She went to the door and turned the knob. Nothing happened. The door looked cemented shut. The idea that she would be locked in a room was so alien and ridiculous to her that she actually had a small laugh over it. It couldn't be so. Why would they lock her in the room? That made no sense, no sense at all. She turned the handle again and pulled as hard as she could, but the door did not budge. Yes, it was indeed locked.

She stood back a moment and contemplated it, and then, with all the might she could muster, she attacked it, pounding with her small fists until her wrists stung. She shouted at the top of her lungs at the same time. The drain of energy was instantaneous as soon as she stepped back again. The room spun, and she felt herself go so soft she thought she might be melting, sinking into a pool of herself as she floated downward. In her mind, it took a very long time, but in truth, she hit the floor in a split second, and then all went dark.

Ryan pulled to the curb about a thousand yards from the Rosses' driveway. He punched up the Rosses' phone number on his cell phone and waited. It rang and rang, and then the answering machine came on. It was good no one was at home, but he was confident he could get done what he wanted to get done undetected, anyway.

He stepped out of his vehicle, his VFR in hand, and closed the door softly. Then, under the cover of some deep shadows cast by an amazingly full and bright moon, he hurried along the embankment onto the Rosses' property and made his way to the garage door, reached into his pocket for a key, opened it, and entered. He didn't have to put on any light. The window on the west end was practically on fire with the moonlight. He knew where the phone was located, anyway, and went directly to it, quickly removing the brain cover and inserting the VFR. He read the numbers of the last dozen outgoing and incoming calls with their dates, quickly replaced the brain cover, and left the garage.

He drove some distance away before he pulled over to trace the phone numbers and get names and addresses. Only one interested him, because it was the only one made to a location out of the area, and it had a protective shield. He had to go through the central office tracing mechanisms to break through. The call had been made to a property located just outside Rochester and owned by a foundation simply called the Rescue Foundation. What did they rescue? Why did they have an unlisted number with a high-security block?

He went to his pocket computer and ran a search but came up with zilch. There wasn't even a nonprofit filing for the organization. He checked his watch. He had to be at the airport in less than an hour now. It made him feel like someone watching a time bomb tick away. What to do?

Sometimes the simplest and most obvious things serve best, he thought, and punched out the telephone number on his cellular. It rang twice be-

fore a female voice answered with a simple "Hello"
and not "This is the Rescue Foundation" or anything like it.

"I'd like to speak with Mrs. Ross, please," he
said.

There was a very long pause.

"Hello?" he said.

"Who is this?"

"It is very important that I speak with Mrs. Ross
immediately. It could be a life-or-death matter," he
said, testing to see what over-the-top dramatics
would bring. It was already interesting that the
woman hadn't immediately said that there was no
one there by that name.

"Who is this?" she repeated.

"This is the New York State Criminal Investigative Division, Officer Lee. To whom am I speaking?" he fired back.

There was a click.

"Hello?"

He hit redial, and the phone rang and rang.
This time, after five rings, an answering machine
picked up.

"This is the Rescue Foundation. At the sound of
the beep, please leave your name and number and
the time of your call. Thank you."

He heard the beep and hung up, satisfied that
he had reached the necessary conclusion to keep
him on the case.

* * *

Natalie woke on the bed, the blanket drawn up to the base of her chin. The lights were on brightly, and she could see the door to her room was now wide open. Mrs. Jerome was taking her pulse. She smiled down at her.

"How are you, dear?"

"What happened to me?"

"You had a fainting spell. Not unusual for someone in your condition. Right, Dr. Stanley?" she asked someone standing at the foot of Natalie's bed.

"Right," she heard, and then saw a rather short man, no more than five feet four, with bushy, reddish brown hair, strands brushed hastily to one side. He stepped up to the bed. He was wearing a dark brown suit and a cream-colored tie. He had a sickly, pale complexion with watery, dull, dark brown eyes and a long nose that thickened around the nostrils. He seemed to smear a smile over his face, his lips widening and flattening with his effort to bring them back in the corners. "Disorientation, memory loss, a crisis of identity, even, all characteristic," he recited.

"Of what?" Natalie practically screamed. Or at least she thought she had. She didn't seem to have the strength to raise her voice loudly. Her chest actually ached with her effort to speak.

"I'm Dr. Stanley," he said, instead of replying to her question. Maybe she hadn't actually voiced it but only thought it.

"Where are my clothes? Why was the door locked?"

"Your door wasn't locked, dear," Mrs. Jerome said. "And your things are right here," she added, stepping toward the closet and indicating her garments. They were all hanging there.

"They weren't there before," Natalie insisted.

"Of course they were," Mrs. Jerome said. She smiled at Dr. Stanley. "Why wouldn't they be? We don't play musical chairs with clothing here."

Dr. Stanley laughed.

They're making me feel foolish, Natalie thought angrily.

"Where's my watch?" she demanded more forcefully.

"Your watch? Why, you're wearing it, my dear."

Natalie looked at her wrist. She was right. It was there.

"But . . ."

"The mind plays tricks," Dr. Stanley told Mrs. Jerome, who nodded and smiled.

They were both smiling at her now, making her feel so ridiculous.

"I saw Hattie Scranton," Natalie insisted, this time with real intensity. She started to lift herself from the pillow. This they couldn't deny. She wasn't confused about this. "I looked out my window and saw her with you below, on the steps. And I'm not mistaken. I know her well."

"Who?"

"Hattie Scranton. From my hometown. The leader of the baby squad. Hattie Scranton!"

"Oh, dear," Mrs. Jerome said. "Doctor?"

"Not unusual," he said, nodding with that same calmness. "Paranoia is a sister to it all, and hallucinations are common, especially at this stage."

"I saw her," Natalie insisted.

"Yes, you did," Dr. Stanley said. "You certainly did. No one is going to deny it. But what you have to do is think of it as you would think of a psychosomatic pain. You actually feel the pain even though there is no physical reason for the pain. In fact, you can be treated for the pain."

"What? What are you saying?" she asked, grimacing.

"Dr. Stanley is an expert in your condition, dear," Mrs. Jerome said.

Natalie glanced at her and then at him. "Where is my other doctor, Dr. Prudential?"

"He's no longer needed, my dear," Mrs. Jerome said. "Dr. Stanley is the doctor who is needed. He will help you. He's an expert when it comes to your condition."

"You keep saying that. What is my condition?"

"Doctor?" Mrs. Jerome said, stepping back as if she had introduced a performer who would now take the stage.

"Well, Mrs. Ross, we call it false or imaginary pregnancy."

"What?"

Dr. Stanley sat on the bed and reached for Natalie's hand. She watched him take it as if it weren't her hand, as if she were observing him holding hands with someone else. He smiled at her.

"Not many people know, but it's more common now than it ever was," he said. "You know, what's interesting . . . there are some dogs that are not bred but develop behavior related to giving birth, especially after they've had intercourse with a neutered male dog. It's as if their bodies are telling them, 'This is what you're programmed by nature to do, and so do it.' I've known rabbits to build nests for their imaginary offspring to come."

He widened his smile. His teeth were rather small, Natalie thought, almost as small as a child's.

She shook her head. "I don't know what you're talking about."

"No, I don't suppose you do, Mrs. Ross. Even you would be most unlikely to hear about such things."

He leaned toward her.

"It's considered very unwise to let the general population know that women experience this. Some women, I should say. Not all, not all, by no means."

"Experience what? What are you saying?" she demanded in a more frantic tone.

"Why, a false pregnancy, Mrs. Ross. That's what we've been talking about. That's why I'm here."

Natalie stared at him and then looked at Mrs. Jerome, who was staring at her and smiling.

"Dr. Stanley is an expert," she said. "Listen carefully to what he's telling you, my dear."

Natalie shook her head. "I don't care about his expertise. This isn't a false pregnancy. I'm not imagining it. I've had all the symptoms. I've missed my period, and I haven't had another. I've had morning sickness. I've had and still have sensitive breasts, and I've had food cravings. No," she said, "this isn't imaginary." She smiled. "I don't understand why you are talking like this to me. Where's my other doctor? What's going on here?"

"Dr. Prudential examined you, my dear. Remember?"

"Yes, yes, I remember. I remember him saying I was farther along than I had thought and the baby was in good position. And don't say I imagined that!"

"No. They were said, but we decided to say those things so as not to upset you, my dear. Once Dr. Prudential realized what was happening, we wanted you to hear everything from Dr. Stanley instead. He's the expert."

"What kind of expert? I'm pregnant! I need an old-fashioned obstetrician!"

"Now, now, dear. Please try to stay calm. Dr. Stanley is here to help."

She shook her head, trying to deny everything

she heard. Dr. Stanley continued to smile warmly at her.

"You see, Mrs. Ross, you did go through all the motions. Just like the rabbit, you mated and you believed you conceived. Your body reacted to the power of your positive thinking. The mind has so much more control over the body than people think. Did you know that it has been shown with empirical certainty that people have the mental capacity to heal themselves?"

Natalie continued to shake her head.

"As I understand it, you reinforced your thinking with prenatal vitamins, a strict diet regimen that a pregnant woman should follow, all giving support to your own false conclusions about yourself."

"No," Natalie said, tears coming to her eyes. "It's not so. It's not false. It's not!"

"Did you ever have an examination by a real doctor before this, Mrs. Ross?" he asked her, his smile lifting off his face quickly.

She stared at him.

"Well?"

"A woman doesn't need a real examination to know she's pregnant," she insisted.

"Yes, yes, there was a time when that was somewhat so, but not now, Mrs. Ross. You're not aware of it, perhaps, but there are additives put in our food that reinforce NL1."

"People get pregnant. Women still get pregnant," Natalie said.

"Yes, some do slip through, but not you, Mrs. Ross."

"I took a pregnancy test," Natalie said, even though she hadn't. "At home."

"You mean, you acquired one of those primitive self-tests from some underground source?"

"Yes."

"Very unreliable, Mrs. Ross. There are too many factors today that could produce a false positive, anyway. Some of those additives I just mentioned, for example."

"No," Natalie said, shaking her head. "I'm pregnant."

"You're not pregnant, Mrs. Ross. You need to rest. We'll help you. It should take only a few days. I'll spend as much time with you as necessary to get you to see what's happened."

"My body," Natalie said, losing some confidence. She pressed her breasts. "Sensitive, bloated . . ."

"You won't believe this, I know, Mrs. Ross, but I've seen women who are so convinced they are pregnant, so convinced, that their abdomens actually become swollen to the point of an eighth-month gestation. Really. Why, they even experience labor pains, pains that are very real to them. Some even go through the exquisite agony of birthing, convinced a fetus has emerged. It's quite bizarre, I assure you, but nevertheless a psychological phenomenon. Fortunately for you, we have caught your condition early enough to help you. You'll be fine in a few days."

The tears that were streaming down Natalie's cheeks felt as if they had been boiled inside her first.

"I'm pregnant," she said. "It's not my imagination. I want my husband. I want to speak with him."

"Of course. As a matter of fact," Dr. Stanley said, rising, "I have asked him to come here. I believe he will be here soon."

"I want to get dressed," Natalie said, trying to sit up. Her head felt so heavy. The room took a spin. Both Dr. Stanley and Mrs. Jerome stood next to each other, watching her struggle and then fall back to her pillow. "What's wrong with me?"

"Emotional exhaustion," Dr. Stanley said. "Very common, very characteristic."

"Dr. Stanley is an expert when it comes to treating women in your condition," Mrs. Jerome said. It was as if something he did or something Natalie did triggered an automatic recitation in her.

"I want to get dressed," she emphasized. "I want to get dressed."

"Just rest for a while," Dr. Stanley said. He seized her shoulders gently but forced her back. "Take it easy."

"I want my husband," Natalie said, but with her eyes closed, her lips barely moving. "I need my husband. Please. Let me get dressed."

Her words began to slip over her lips, her tongue barely moving.

"He's on his way, dear. I'll send him right up as soon as he arrives. Rest," she said, fixing the blanket.

"I'm pregnant," Natalie managed to mutter firmly once more.

It was the last thing she said before drifting off again. She didn't hear them leave. The sound of someone crying rode over it.

Who's crying? she wondered.

She was terrified the sobs she heard might be her own.

Fifteen

::::::::::::

Ryan reached the airport only minutes before the agency plane touched down and taxied to the gate. He wasn't surprised to see McCalester already there talking to a flight attendant at the desk.

"Where you been? I called you as soon as they called me, but you had already left the hotel," McCalester said as soon as Ryan approached.

"I had an errand to run," Ryan replied.

"I don't understand. They're replacing you just as you're about to wrap this up? What's going on?" the local policeman asked.

"What do you think?" Ryan asked as if he were really confused himself.

McCalester shook his head and then shrugged. "Well, I told you about knocking on the wrong doors, going at it head-on like that. I guess someone made a call," he replied with an unexpected frankness.

Ryan stared coldly and nodded. "Yes, someone."

"Hey, you don't think it was me, do you?"

"It doesn't matter," Ryan replied.

"It matters to me," McCalester said. "I'm a cooperative member of my community, but I don't compromise my police work."

"Not even to get ahead?"

"I'm not going anywhere else, except to a retirement community where I can perfect my golf."

"That's still somewhere," Ryan told him.

He looked at the plane. The door was opening. A moment later, Hilton Sacks emerged and hurried down the steps to the tarmac. The six-feet-four-inch, two-hundred-twenty-pound, blond, blue-eyed first-class detective was a prime example of what genetic engineering and the natal laboratory could produce. Not only was he physically impressive, but his IQ went off the charts, and he had that Superman arrogance Ryan detested. The confident, condescending smirk was already on his face the moment he touched ground and set eyes on him. It was written all over Hilton's face: he was here to save the day and fix the political mess Ryan had made.

"Henry McCalester," McCalester said, stepping forward to extend his hand.

Sacks considered it as if he wanted to be sure it was clean enough to touch. The short pause brought some redness to McCalester's face. Sacks seized his hand and shook it firmly. Then he turned to Ryan. "Hello, Ryan," he said. "In a bit over your head?"

"If you're speaking of bullshit, yes," Ryan responded.

Sacks laughed and then shut the laugh off the way someone might shut down a television set by pulling its plug. "Where are your data to date?" he demanded, seeing Ryan carried nothing.

"In my vehicle," Ryan said. "I thought we'd take some time to review my findings."

"You mean in *my* vehicle, don't you, Detective Lee?" he asked with that infuriating smile. "If you're going to return on the agency plane, Ryan, you have only about twenty minutes. So we had better make it fast."

Someone's in quite a hurry to get me out of here, Ryan thought.

Sacks turned to Henry. "McCalester, where can someone get a halfway decent cup of coffee around here?"

"It's late," McCalester said. "Just about everything's closed in town. If you don't eat here, you'll have to go to the hotel snack bar."

Sacks shook his head. "I hate these jobs in the boonies. Probably can't even get a decent vodka martini anywhere. You owe me one, Ryan."

"I'm sure you won't be here long, Hilton," Ryan said as they walked to the parking lot.

"Not a minute longer than I have to be."

The three stopped at Ryan's vehicle. Ryan reached in for the folder containing all his printouts and handed it to Sacks.

"Okay," Sacks said. "Let's hear what you have. As I said, we don't have that much time."

"It should be worth all the time it needs," Ryan said.

"Some of us can grasp the important things faster than others," Sacks replied.

Ryan glanced at McCalester, who looked at Sacks with an expression of disgust and then turned to Ryan with an expression that said, *I'm better off with you.*

"A teenage girl, Lois Marlowe, was killed with two blows to the cranium, the second blow shattering her skull," Ryan began. "The ME concluded she expired almost instantly. The murder occurred just outside the village near a lake and a deserted old hotel called the Lakehouse."

"This is the girl the baby squad had questioned and had insisted be examined for pregnancy?" Sacks asked, looking more to McCalester, who nodded.

"Yes."

"And as I understand it, she was going to reveal the source of the pills the following day."

"I think we pretty much confirmed that she acquired the prenatal vitamins from another teenager, one Stocker Robinson. We questioned the girl, and she claimed she traded a pornographic VRG movie instead, but I never believed that," Ryan said.

"Because?"

"Stocker Robinson's mother cleans and cares for the home of Mr. and Mrs. Preston Ross, an attorney of some standing . . . great standing, apparently," Ryan corrected. "I followed Stocker one night and observed her fetching a secreted spare key to the Rosses' residence. She entered the garage and planted the weapon that killed Lois Marlowe. The bloodhound confirms that. You can read the results on the report in the folder.

"With great difficulty," Ryan continued, shifting his eyes to McCalester and back to Sacks, "I acquired a warrant to search the garage. Mr. Ross consented to my searching the house itself after he saw the bloodhound's report."

"And?"

"We didn't find the weapon in the house, but I believe . . ."

"Stick only to the evidence, Ryan. I don't want to hear any more theories. This Stocker Robinson committed suicide today, correct?"

"That's not conclusive. I have good reason to question it, and I think the ME will have as well, if he bothers looking. The ME should not treat this as a fait accompli, Hilton."

"All right, I'll speak with him."

"How did you know it was a he?" Ryan asked quickly.

Sacks smiled. "I took a wild stab at it. What the hell's the difference, Ryan? Are you having some kind of a breakdown under all this respon-

sibility for the first time? You can't trust any-
body?"

"There's more to do here, Hilton," Ryan insisted.
"I was about to be permitted to question Mrs. Ross
when your expertise was suddenly and quickly required," he added coldly.

"That's it?"

Ryan nodded. It was all he wanted to reveal.
There was enough in the reports to give an agent
of Sacks's expertise reason to continue the investigation anyway.

"This Stocker Robinson ran away from school
today, is that correct?" Sacks asked in the tone of
a prosecutor.

"Yes," McCalester volunteered.

"Well, after you track her, was this girl ever
checked for pregnancy?" Sacks asked Ryan.

"No, but . . ."

Sacks shrugged. "You don't have to be too brilliant to figure this out, Ryan. Even you could do
it. This other girl found out about her, got the prenatal vitamins from her, blackmailed her, and she
killed her," Sacks said. "How's that for a theory,
since you're hot on theories?"

"I don't think that's all that's happened here,"
Ryan said. "And I don't think you will, either."

Sacks turned to McCalester.

"She should have been brought in, interrogated,
examined. We wouldn't have this mess!" Sacks
cried, his hands up.

McCalester started to shake his head.

"I'm not blaming you. You're just the local law, but my colleague here should have done so."

"There's more to this, Hilton," Ryan insisted.

"If there is, Ryan, I think I'm capable of discovering that."

Ryan stared, pondering whether he should bother continuing. "Why would Stocker Robinson try to implicate the Rosses in the murder of Lois Marlowe?" Ryan posed. "She would have to have some reason. Know something that would make the Rosses suspects in the murder of Lois Marlowe, perhaps."

"Like what?"

Ryan glanced at McCalester. "Maybe Stocker Robinson stole the prenatal vitamins from Mrs. Ross and traded them with Lois Marlowe, and maybe Lois Marlowe knew where she had gotten them or Stocker would say she did."

"Oh, so the Ross woman is the pregnant one? That's who you suspect would have killed her and made it look like a suicide, is that it?"

"It's possible."

"And all this is possible in your mind because she hid the weapon in their garage, which was available to her because she knew how to get in safely."

"Maybe."

"Maybe she was just looking for a place to hide the weapon in question away from her own home and thought of that," Sacks said. "You might be reading too much into it, ascribing any other motive, Ryan. You had a kid in a panic. She did a bad thing. You paid her a visit. She was afraid you'd be coming around any moment to arrest her and everything would be revealed. She couldn't live with it, so, being high strung and all, she did herself in. That's all."

"She could have simply thrown the thing into the lake," Ryan said dryly but firmly.

"But she didn't, and she panicked."

"I thought you were only interested in evidence, Hilton. That sounds like a manufactured theory created to end all these questions quickly and conveniently. If you really read my reports and findings there, you won't be so quick to make that sort of judgment."

Sacks stared at him and then turned to McCalester. "Lead the way, will you? I'm hungry enough even to eat something in a boondocks hotel snack shop. The keys in the car, Ryan?"

Ryan handed them to him, and Sacks got in.

"Your bag, doctor," he said, handing Ryan his device bag. "And your suitcase."

Ryan took it out.

"Lucky you," Hilton Sacks said before he closed the door. "They've got some milk run for you when you get back."

"Something tells me you'll wrap things up here and be back before me," Ryan retorted.

Sacks laughed. "Probably," he said. "It's about the ratio of achievement time between a Natal and a Natural these days."

He closed the door and started the car.

McCalester looked at Ryan, and from the expression on his face, Ryan thought it was possible he didn't know.

"For what it's worth," McCalester said, crossing to his own vehicle, "it was interesting working with you. Good luck with your career."

Ryan watched him get into his car and start off. Sacks shot a slick grin at him and followed McCalester. The two cars exited the airport parking lot. For a moment, he stood there in their wake, watching their taillights grow smaller and disappear in the darkness. Then he turned toward the airport.

The pilot and the copilot of the agency jet were standing near the stairway. They turned as he approached.

"Ready, detective?"

Ryan stood there. It was as if he could see his whole life projected before him. Would he ever get an opportunity like this again? Would he always be burdened by his birth and never rise above being someone else's assistant? Eventually, he would be relegated to a desk job, probably. In the twentieth century, women complained about hitting the glass ceiling. It was nothing like the glass ceiling he would find hovering above him forever and ever, he thought.

"Detective Lee?"

"Oh. No. There's been a change. That's what I was coming out here to tell you," Ryan told the pilot.

"Change?"

"I'm not going back with you. You're free to take off any time you like."

Surprised, the pilot looked from the copilot to him. "But . . . we received no message from the central office."

"I did directly," Ryan said. "Nothing to concern yourselves about. Thanks," he added, and left them.

He went directly to the charter counter and hired a flight to Rochester.

Less than an hour later, he was in a rental vehicle and following the GPS system to a place he knew only as the Rescue Foundation. He wasn't sure what he would find, but he was sure that whatever it was, it was important to this case and maybe more important to his career, to the rest of his life.

It was especially important to his opportunity to wipe that self-satisfied grin off Hilton Sacks's arrogant face.

Sometime during the night, Natalie woke and realized someone really was crying through the walls. It was not her imagination. It was not part of some dream, some nightmare. She lay there with her eyes open, staring at the wall across from her and listening. This last sleep session had left her feeling a little better. Her legs still ached a bit, but at least when she sat up slowly, she didn't lose her equilibrium. The room did not spin. Her breathing was less labored, too. For a few moments, she sat there thinking about the visit she had with this new doctor and the wild things that he and Mrs. Jerome had said. She shook her head as if to rid her memory of it all and then stood up. She was still doing fine.

She remembered seeing her clothing hanging in the closet. When she opened it, it was all there this time. No illusion, no dream. As quickly as she could, she took off the hospital gown and got into her own clothes. Just doing that made her feel much better.

I've got to get out of here. I've got to speak with Preston, she thought, *and tell him this is the wrong place. These people can't help us.*

She went to the door and opened it slowly. It was nearly ten-thirty. The hall was lit, but all the illumination was reduced so that it had an ethereal, unreal look. The walls looked as if they were undulating, the floor buckling. She started toward the stairway, but when she reached it, she heard the sobbing again. She stood there and listened, drawn by the sounds as much as by the sight of the stairway before her.

Who was crying? It was definitely a female. Why was she crying? Was it Mrs. Jerome?

She went to the door and leaned against it, placing her ear to it. The sobs sounded like small chokes.

"Hello?" she called. "Are you all right in there?"

The sobbing stopped. And then, after a moment, it started again.

Natalie looked back at the stairway. No one else was in the hall, nor did she hear anyone below. She contemplated the door knob and then turned it and heard the small click. The door began to open.

"Hello?" she said, and looked into the room. It was dark, but the moonlight bathed the bed and revealed a figure on her stomach, her head submerged in the pillow, her long, reddish-brown hair spread over her shoulders and down her back. Like a mane, she remembered. Those had been Preston's words. Like a horse's mane, rich, thick, flowing.

The woman wore a hospital gown exactly like the one Natalie had been wearing.

"Miss?" Natalie said. "Are you all right?"

She stopped sobbing and started to turn. Natalie drew closer. When she was nearly to the bed, she saw her face and stopped, her whole body freezing over, all the blood draining to her feet. She couldn't speak. She couldn't swallow. She couldn't move.

The woman in the bed was an exact replica of her.

She stared at the ceiling as if Natalie weren't nearby.

"They took my baby," she said. "They took it from me, and then they came to me and told me my pregnancy was all in my imagination. They took my baby."

Natalie finally had the strength to back up. The woman continued to chant: "They took my baby."

She reached back for the door knob and, instead, found her hand in someone else's hand.

Spinning, she turned to face Mrs. Jerome.

"Why, Mrs. Ross, why are you up and dressed? Where are you going at this hour of the night?"

She flicked on the light.

"Who is that in the bed?" Natalie screamed at her.

Mrs. Jerome's soft smile didn't change, but her eyebrows dipped with the deepening of the folds in her forehead.

"Who is who in what bed?" she asked.

"That!" Natalie cried, and turned, pointing at the bed.

Her hand seemed to evaporate in midair. She stared in disbelief.

There was no one in the bed. All that was there was the hospital gown she had been wearing.

She gazed slowly around the room.

It was the room she had been in. She had merely returned to it.

"Please, Mrs. Ross, let me help you back into

bed. You're just a little confused. It will be all right. Everything will be fine."

She took her arm. Natalie shook her off.

"No," she said, the horrific realization soaking into her brain like blood into a sponge. She turned to her slowly. "You took my baby. That's what you did. That's why Hattie Scranton was here. You took my baby. You lied to me. You're all lying to me. You and that doctor. I'm not having any false pregnancy. You lied."

"Mrs. Ross, really. This sort of paranoia is becoming tiresome, even though Dr. Stanley explained it was part of your condition. You must make an effort. We can't help you if you don't make an effort, my dear," she warned. "You don't want to have to stay here any longer than necessary, now, do you? And if we can't help you here, we have to transfer you to a place for people who are having difficulty readjusting. Some of them are there for years and years, and some of them are there forever, my dear. You don't want that, now, do you? Come along," she said, reaching for Natalie's arm again. "Let me help you get out of your clothes and back to bed. I'll give you something to help you sleep, and in the morning, your husband will be here, and you'll be on your way to a fine recovery. Doesn't that sound wonderful?"

Natalie let herself be turned and guided toward the bed.

"That's a good girl. We're all going to be fine.

Everything is going to be as wonderful as it was. You'll see. As wonderful as it was."

She began to slip the light-blue leather jacket off Natalie's shoulders.

Natalie gazed at the bed.

She could see herself again, see herself looking up at the ceiling.

She could hear the chant: *They took my baby. My baby is gone. They took my baby.*

The jacket was nearly down her upper arm when she spun around and caught Mrs. Jerome on the bridge of her nose with her right elbow. The blow was surprising enough and sharp enough to stun her. She stumbled back a step.

"You took my baby!" Natalie screamed at her, and hit her again, this time with the base of the palm of her left hand, just the way she had been taught in a self-defense class. She struck her on the right cheekbone, and the collision sent a vibrating shock down her arm, through her elbow, and into her shoulder. Mrs. Jerome's head whipped to the right. She lost balance, put her left foot over her right to catch herself, and tripped, falling forward, stunned and nearly unconscious.

Natalie fled the room but ran directly into Hattie Scranton, who stood so hard and firm it was like running into a wall. She actually bounced back. Hattie barely winced. The sight of her put enough fear into Natalie's heart to weaken her legs. She gasped and tottered.

"Where do you think you're going, Mrs. Ross?" Hattie asked.

Mrs. Jerome came to the doorway, her right hand over her bruised face, a small trickle of blood coming from both her nostrils.

"What have you done?" Hattie asked Natalie.

"She's gone mad," Mrs. Jerome said.

Hattie smiled and nodded. "Not a surprise to me, her being an Abnormal." Her eyes grew small when she turned back to Natalie.

"Don't you know what a terrible embarrassment you are to our community? What damage you could have done? Don't you know how you nearly ruined your husband's life? How can you dare? Get back into that room where you belong until we decide you can return, if we even decide you can. Go on," she ordered, pointing her long arm at the door of the room.

"Come back, dear," Mrs. Jerome urged softly. "Come on. Everything will be fine now. Everything will be all right."

Natalie, who had been staring at Hattie the way she might stare at a nightmare come alive, shook her head and backed up a few steps.

"Go on, do what you're told!" Hattie screamed. "Do you think you're the first one, the only one we've brought here? We know exactly how to handle you, what to do with you. If you're cooperative, you'll go home. If not . . . you'll end up on the funny farm with a few of the other failures. Get in there!" she bellowed, charging at Natalie.

Natalie cowered. Mrs. Jerome took her arm, keeping a safe distance this time, and, with Hattie poking Natalie from behind, brought her back into the room.

"Get her in bed, and give her something. I'm going downstairs to call Mr. Cauthers."

"Cauthers?" Natalie asked, turning.

Hattie smiled. "Yes, Mrs. Ross, that's right. Mr. Cauthers. I'll have to tell him about your behavior, and he'll decide whether we return you or not."

"My husband . . ." Natalie started to say.

"Yes, your husband," Hattie remarked with a smirk. "Is there any doubt men are dumber?"

She glanced at Mrs. Jerome and left the room.

Natalie started to cry. She was too weak to resist Mrs. Jerome's rush to strip off her clothing. She let her body be twisted and turned rather roughly until she was naked. Mrs. Jerome put the hospital gown on her and got her back under the blanket.

"It was not very nice, your striking me like that, dear. It doesn't tickle."

Natalie gazed up at her.

"You had better just lie there quietly now until I return. Another outburst like this, and Mr. Cauthers won't have much of a problem deciding what to do with you. No one will," she threatened, and left the room.

Natalie wanted to cry, but her face was hardened into a mask. She felt as if she were sinking inside herself. It no longer mattered what they did to the outside of her body, the shell. She would be safe if she didn't let any of their words get in and didn't see them or whatever they did. She would curl up into a ball, like a caterpillar, and they would never, never bother her again.

Sixteen

::::::::::::

Ryan Lee slowed down when he reached the tall
hedges bordering the property. He brought the car
to a complete stop at the sight of the gate. Entering the property without a search warrant would
compromise any investigation, but at this stage, he
had been pulled from the case anyway, he
thought. He was here because, despite his training, this had become personal. A natural pregnancy was being kept secret, and if a murder had
to be covered up to do so, that was all right with
the powers that be. Well, it wasn't all right with
him. Inherently, he felt as if they were telling him
in the strongest possible way that he, like the
other Naturals, was so much of an embarrassment
that even murder was justified to keep the Naturals nonexistent in the eyes of the community.

*Lieutenant Childs was right. I was the wrong
person for the job they wanted done,* he thought,
but he wondered just how far up this conspiracy
actually reached. He considered himself a fairly

good judge of men, and Lieutenant Childs always struck him as a fair-minded, decent man who would not tolerate anything remotely like this. However, it could easily have been beyond his power to do anything about it, either.

Ryan stepped out of the car and searched the front of the property, noting that there was some space between the branches of the tall hedges about a dozen yards from the gate. It really wasn't wide enough for him to slip through, but he went for it anyway, pushing and tearing at the branches to widen the opening. He scratched his neck and his legs, tore the bottom of his trousers, caught the sleeve of his jacket on a branch, and had to tear that, too, in order to pass through the hedges and get inside the property.

Once that was accomplished, he paused to study the driveway leading to the building. He looked for security cameras and saw them on the poles. Everything depended on how well they were being monitored, he thought, but that was taking too much of a chance. There was always the possibility of laser alarms as well, which when broken would arouse a sleeping security guard.

He gazed over the expanse of lawn and took out his pocket reader. Besides searching for explosives, it could detect a variety of security systems. He directed it at the lawn and quickly saw that the whole property was covered in a laser grid, and, as he had suspected, it stretched over the driveway as well. Just taking a few steps forward on this lawn would set off alarms. It was good that he had stopped and kept himself close to the hedges.

However, such a security system in a rural area like this would have to take into account small field animals, or there would be endless false alarms. A quick check showed him the system was set at least two to three feet high, making allowances for ground hogs, rabbits, squirrels, and the like. It was sophisticated enough to differentiate between birds and land animals.

He put away his reader and went down on all fours, moving on his forearms to go lower. Every ten yards or so, he paused and checked the area with his pocket reader. He crawled on. Heavy humidity brought out the sweet smell of earth and freshly cut grass, filling his nostrils with the aromas. Above him, the increasingly overcast sky drowned out the splatter of stars that had been visible. The lit windows in the grand house seemed to brighten, but he saw no movement, nobody silhouetted behind the glass and curtains.

It was some distance to the building, but he was in terrific shape and was able to crawl rather quickly and relatively effortlessly until he reached the curb of the driveway directly across from the front steps. He saw the roving video cameras sweeping the driveway and kept himself down in the shadows. Now what?

He could rush the door, but it had to be locked,

and he would break one of the beams in his attempt. He could try to breach one of the windows on the first floor, but the chances that they were armed to prevent intrusion were too great. He studied the scene before him some more and had turned to fall back into the shadows when he heard the gate opening and saw a vehicle start up the driveway. An authorized arrival automatically shut down the laser beams. Here was an opportunity.

The car pulled into a parking space, and Preston Ross emerged. He was alone. For a long moment, he just stared at the front door of the building as if he really didn't want to go inside.

Ryan waited for him to take his first steps before coming up behind him and putting his pistol against his back. Preston started to spin around.

"What the . . ."

"Easy, counselor. Don't make any foolish moves on me."

"Detective Lee." He glanced at the front door and then back to Ryan. "What the hell are you doing here?"

"When you didn't call as you promised, I thought I would take some initiative," Ryan replied, smiling.

"I was told they had replaced you. I thought the case was solved and it wasn't necessary for me to call anyone. Actually, I thought you had already left Sandburg. Why are you here?"

"That's quite a bit of thinking, Mr. Ross, but no

harm done," Ryan said, directing his pistol at the front door. "I can speak with your wife right now, can't I? This is where she is, right?"

"How did you find out?" Preston asked, a little too calmly for Ryan. What gave the man such confidence? Ryan wondered. He should be nervous. Ryan quickly glanced from side to side and then undid the safety on his pistol with an obviousness designed for its dramatic impact. Preston's eyes did widen.

"Professional secret, I'm afraid. Shall we go in?"

"This isn't right. You don't have a right to be here and search this property," Preston warned him.

"How do you know that I don't have a proper search warrant, Mr. Ross?"

Preston smiled. "You didn't just walk up and knock on the door. Even knowing you as short a time as I have, I don't doubt that's what you would do."

"Maybe I was just waiting for you," Ryan told him.

Preston lost his smile. "You're out of bounds, Lee. You're only going to get yourself in serious trouble."

"You mean I'm not already? That's a relief. Go on," Ryan ordered.

"This isn't a good time. You don't understand what's happening here," Preston said without moving.

"I understand exactly what's happening here.

You and your powerful allies made some phone calls to get rid of me because you realized I know."

"That's not . . ."

"There are now two dead teenage girls in your community, Mr. Ross, and I'm convinced that they were both murdered. The key to ending all this might be waiting in that house. Now, either you walk in under your own power, or I'll drag you in behind me," Ryan threatened.

Whatever Preston saw in Ryan's eyes convinced him instantly that it wasn't a bluff. He turned and walked up the steps. Just as they reached the door, it opened, and Mrs. Jerome stood there looking out at him and Ryan. She carried a small tray in her right hand. It had a syringe on it.

"Mrs. Jerome? I'm Preston Ross," he told her.

"Of course. We've been expecting you, Mr. Ross," she replied, and looked at Ryan. "However, there was no mention of an additional visitor."

"This is Detective Ryan Lee of the New York State CID. I did not know he was coming here tonight. It's as much of a surprise to me as it is to you."

"Why is he here?" she asked.

"He wants to speak with my wife. In fact, he insists on speaking to her."

"Speaking to her? But . . ." Mrs. Jerome looked at Ryan and then at Preston. "Haven't you told him how she is, described her current condition?"

"I wasn't given that opportunity, Mrs. Jerome. Perhaps you will do it for me."

She turned to Ryan and brought her shoulders up and back as if she were about to begin to address a roomful of premedical students.

"Mrs. Ross is in the midst of serious emotional and psychological trauma. She can't see anyone but her husband, much less answer questions intelligently. I'm afraid I can't permit it," she concluded firmly. "I would certainly have to confer with the doctor in any case."

Ryan brought his pistol into view, and her eyes widened. "As you can see, we have special permission," he said. "You don't have to trouble yourself with any of that bureaucratic stuff, going through channels and the like."

"But . . ."

"Lead us to her immediately," he commanded.

She looked at Preston.

"You'd better do as he asks, Mrs. Jerome."

"This is utterly ridiculous. I mean to make a complaint," she muttered.

"Get in line," Ryan said. "Let's go." He waved the pistol at her.

"I don't understand why you have a gun pointing at me. It makes me very uncomfortable."

"Consider it pointing at Mr. Ross," Ryan said. "And this model has been known to go off accidentally, almost as if it has a mind of its own," he added.

"Please, just do as he asks," Preston urged.

She turned and started up the stairway, Preston and Ryan right behind her.

"I can't imagine what could be so important not to wait for the woman to be coherent. What good is it going to do you to speak to her now, anyway?" she asked, turning at the top of the stairs. "What is this about?"

"It's about murder and cover-ups and all the good things that make our lives complicated," Ryan told her. "There's a real sense of urgency, too, otherwise I would chitchat all night with you. Where is she?"

Mrs. Jerome's face tightened, her lips pressed so hard together she looked as if she would choke herself.

"How did you get that vicious black-and-blue on your cheek?" Ryan asked her now that she was directly under the hall light.

"I walked into a door," she snapped back, turned, and headed into Natalie's room.

She flipped on the overhead light, and Natalie, who was staring up at the ceiling, brought her arm over her eyes and uttered a small cry.

"Baby," Preston said, hurrying to her side. "How are you doing?"

He seized her hand, sat on the bed, and leaned over to kiss her on the cheek. Natalie immediately began to cry.

"Hey, don't worry. I'm here," Preston said, embracing her. He stroked back strands of her hair and kissed her forehead lovingly. "I came as soon as they called me. You'll be fine. Everything's going to be all right, Nat. You'll have the best doctors, everything."

She shook her head vigorously and pulled herself from Preston's embrace.

Ryan moved up beside Mrs. Jerome, who stood off to the right.

"They took our baby," Natalie sobbed. "They stole our baby, Preston."

"Now, take it easy, honey. That's not what happened. I've been briefed on it all."

He smiled at her.

"You were suffering a condition that's a lot more common than people know. No problem. You're going to be fine. We'll apply for our child the right way, and we will start our family. Just like the Normans," he added. "Can't you just see you and Judy pushing baby carriages together? It's all going to happen, just the way you hoped."

"No, Preston. I didn't imagine it. No. They took our child!"

"Nat," he said, moving to embrace her again.

"No," she cried louder, and swung her arms about wildly.

Preston seized her wrists "Easy, Nat, easy," he urged.

"Do you see?" Mrs. Jerome asked Ryan. "You see how utterly ridiculous it would be for you to ask her questions now? Please leave."

"What is she saying? What does she mean, you took her child?" Ryan demanded instead of replying.

"She is suffering a condition known as false pregnancy. She was under the psychological misapprehension that she was pregnant. She's not, and when that was explained to her by our resident psychiatrist who is an expert in the matter, she had a nervous breakdown. It's not unexpected. It will pass. She will improve in time, but there is nothing you can do at the moment except leave these people be," Mrs. Jerome lectured. "Now, please go before you cause more trouble and do her more harm than she's already done to herself."

Preston turned, his face no longer rigid with defiance or arrogance. His eyes were teary. "Satisfied?" he asked Ryan. "That's what I was trying to tell you outside."

"I'm not imagining it, Preston," Natalie insisted in a loud whisper.

Ryan stepped closer to the bed. "My name is Ryan Lee, Mrs. Preston," he said. "I'm a special investigator with the state CID. What do you believe has happened to you?"

"I was aborted," she said with absolute firmness.

Ryan stared at her. To him, she didn't look like a woman who was rambling out of her mind.

"She's hallucinating," Mrs. Jerome said.

"I'm not," Natalie insisted, and turned to Preston. "Hattie Scranton was here. She made them do it. They took our child."

"Hattie Scranton?" Ryan repeated.

"It's all part of the hallucinations," Mrs. Jerome said when Preston turned to her. "The doctor said so and will explain it further to you as well, Mr. Ross."

"Where is the doctor? I thought he was going to be here when I arrived," Preston asked.

"He'll be here soon. For now, I had better give your wife her shot so she can get some rest."

"Not yet," Ryan ordered, waving her back from the bed. He stepped closer and turned to Preston. "You sent her here to give birth, correct?"

"Yes."

"You were going to have a natural child?"

"It's none of your business, but yes. I thought she was pregnant. I took her word for it. She didn't look very pregnant, but I understand women can be as late as she is and not show that much. I'm no expert on it, so I believed her."

"I was pregnant!" Natalie screamed, sitting up on her elbows now. "Aren't you listening to me? I had all the symptoms, physical symptoms. I still have evidence of it. They performed an abortion!"

Ryan looked at Mrs. Jerome, his eyes narrowing.

"People who suffer her delusion actually do experience physical symptoms. It has been explained to her, and it will be understood in time."

"Why is she saying she was aborted?" Ryan demanded.

"It's part of the condition, what happens when they realize they're not pregnant. The mind creates the explanation, an explanation that will satisfy them. Abortion," she continued. "How utterly ridiculous. We're here to help people who require natural birthing. That's why the foundation was established. This isn't some underground abortion clinic."

Ryan turned back to Preston. "It shouldn't be hard to determine what went on here and what didn't, Mr. Ross. We'll take her to a doctor who can examine her and determine if an abortion was indeed performed on her recently. Even the newest techniques will be detectable. Let's get your wife dressed and out of here."

"That would be very foolish," Mrs. Jerome said. "The doctor is on his way here, and he'll explain why. She could suffer irreparable damage and never recover from this psychological phenomenon. We have seen it before with cases such as Mrs. Ross's, and the aftermath for some has not been good."

"In a word, bullshit," Ryan told her. "Where are her clothes?"

She didn't move; she didn't speak.

"Where are they?" he shouted, stepping toward her. "Talk fast if you don't want to walk into another door."

"In the closet, of course," she replied. Despite his fury, she remained coldly defiant.

He walked to it and opened the door. The clothing was there. "Why don't you help her get dressed, Mr. Ross, and we'll get to the bottom of it all tonight?" Ryan said, turning back to Preston.

Preston's eyes nearly popped out of his skull. Ryan grimaced with confusion.

"What?"

"Watch out!" Preston screamed.

Ryan turned just as Hattie Scranton, like some animated scarecrow, emerged from inside the closet, a pair of long surgical scissors clutched in her right hand. She lunged at him and brought the scissors down with a forcefully determined motion, but Ryan was able to sidestep a few inches, and the blade just missed his neck. He seized her around the waist and spun her around with such force she slammed into the wall and sank to the floor, stunned.

However, the moment he threw off Hattie Scranton, Mrs. Jerome stepped forward and drove her syringe into the back of Ryan's neck, plunging the sedative into him. The pain surprised and confused him for a moment. He swiped back at her, driving her away from him, but it was too late. He saw the room start to spin.

Natalie screamed and screamed.

Preston stood up.

Ryan heard an audible groan and turned back toward Hattie Scranton, who recovered, rose to her feet, and started toward him, the scissors up. He put all of his concentration into remaining conscious just long enough to get off one round. The bullet practically lifted her off her feet, tore through her chest, driving her heart out through a twelve-inch-diameter hole between her shoulder blades. Blood was flowing so fast she hovered a few moments and then fell back into a pool of it and died seconds before Ryan collapsed to the floor, the darkness closing in around him like those clouds that drowned out the stars.

Seventeen

Hilton Sacks took Ryan Lee's suitcase and evidence bag from the back of the rental car and closed the door. He waved to the driver, who then started away. For a moment, Sacks watched the vehicle until the rear lights disappeared, and then he walked slowly back to the front gate of the Rescue Foundation. It was opened. Preston Ross was driving out and slowed down as he approached the entrance. He came to a stop and rolled down his window.

"How's she doing?" Sacks asked him, nodding at Natalie, who was sprawled on the rear seat, her head on a pillow, a blanket over her, and her eyes closed.

"Resting comfortably," Preston said.

"Good. Sorry about all this, Mr. Ross. If there is anything more we can do to help . . ."

Preston glanced at his rear-view mirror and saw Natalie's eyes shut tight, her lips opened just a tad. Her face still looked quite flushed.

"We'll be fine," Preston said. He leaned farther out of his window so he could speak *sotto voce*. "You can't put too much blame on Mrs. Jerome here. She had no idea who he was, and he didn't exactly employ the best bedside manner. He was quite threatening, and she was frightened, I'm sure, despite the brave front she put up."

"Don't give any of it a second thought, Mr. Ross," Sacks said, smiling.

"Hattie Scranton . . ."

"It's all been taken care of, sir. Have a safe trip home, and good luck," Sacks said, and patted the roof of the car.

"Thank you," Preston said, rolled up his window, and drove out of the complex.

Hilton Sacks continued to trudge up the driveway, carrying Ryan Lee's suitcase and bag. A CID trainee stood in the doorway. Tall, wide-shouldered, with a chiseled face, he looked like a Roman palace guard, even in his dark suit and tie. He had a small receiver in his right ear but no wires around the lobe.

"Bring the ambulance up, and then you and Hansen come up to get him," Sacks ordered.

"Very good, sir," the trainee said, and moved quickly down the stairs.

"Hold on," Sacks said. "You might as well take this and put it in the vehicle now."

"Yes, sir," the trainee responded. He hurried

back up, took the suitcase and evidence bag, and walked quickly down the stairs and around the side of the building.

Sacks moved slowly, almost as if he were very tired. As he climbed the stairs, the soft smile lay in his face like a permanently implanted mask. He shook his head, laughed softly, and stepped onto the landing, moving down to the room past what had been Natalie Ross's room.

Mrs. Jerome stood just inside the doorway, her arms folded under her bosom, glaring at Ryan Lee on the bed.

"How are you doing?" Sacks asked her.

"After the day I've had, I'll be happy to go to sleep," she replied dryly.

He laughed. "That makes two of us. The director wants me to issue you a formal apology and to assure you that this sort of behavior is unprecedented for a member of the CID."

Mrs. Jerome raised her eyebrows. "I'm not the one who should be receiving any assurances or apologies," she said. "I'm just an employee here."

"Understood," Sacks replied.

They both turned as the two CID trainees came up the stairway carrying a stretcher. They unfolded it and rolled it toward the room.

"Is there anything further I can do?" Mrs. Jerome asked as they approached.

"No, ma'am. Thank you," Sacks said.

"That poor woman," Mrs. Jerome said.

"Which one are you referring to?" he asked with a smile.

"Figure it out," Mrs. Jerome snapped at him, and walked away and down the stairs.

He shook his head after her and nodded at the two trainees, who moved quickly into the room. They lifted Ryan Lee off the bed and placed him on the stretcher.

"Let's get the hell out of here," Sacks told them. He walked ahead of them, bouncing down the stairs. Outside, he stood on the steps and looked over the beautifully manicured grounds. He nodded appreciatively.

The two trainees carried Ryan Lee past him and brought him to the rear of the ambulance. One opened the doors, and they loaded him in and started to close the doors.

"Hold up," Sacks said. He approached them. "He's having too easy a time of it for what he did," he said, and climbed into the ambulance.

They watched from the rear as he sifted through a medical bag and produced a syringe. He took a bottle out of his pocket, inserted the syringe, and drew out the medicine. Then he held it up and squirted it in the air, smiling at the trainees.

"Six months as a paramedic. You guys should not look down your noses at that training. It is sure to come in handy sometime, if not a few times, during your careers."

"Yes, sir," Hansen said.

Sacks injected Ryan Lee in the neck.

"I gave a guy electro-cardiac treatment with a taser gun once. Saved his life. I ever tell you that story, Hansen?"

"No, sir."

"It's a good story. Happened after we arrived at a hostage situation in Yonkers. Ever been to Yonkers, Hansen?" he asked, keeping his eyes on Ryan's face.

"No, sir. I mean, I've driven through it, I think."

"Yeah. That's what happens with a lot of communities these days . . . people drive through them."

Ryan's eyelids fluttered.

"And the princess kissed the frog, and behold," Sacks cried, his hands extended toward Ryan Lee.

Ryan's eyes opened wide and remained open for a moment. He flickered his eyelids and then turned slowly and looked up at Sacks.

"Hello, Detective Lee. Have a good nap, did you? Glad it wasn't on company time."

The confusion on Lee's face brought a wide smile to Hilton Sacks. He looked at the trainees.

"Doesn't know where the hell he is. I bet you thought you landed in hell, huh, Lee?"

"What . . . the fuck . . . is going on, Sacks?"

"Well, let's see. For one, Lieutenant Childs has taken a rather big hit from the director, thanks to you. His position, his rank, is actually in grave danger for assigning you to this case in the first place.

"Two, you disobeyed a direct order to remove yourself from the present case and return to headquarters and, on your own, a loose cannon, proceeded to create a rather embarrassing situation for the agency. Fortunately, I was able to get onto the scene in time to clean up the mess before our good friends from the media got wind of any of it."

"Stocker Robinson was murdered," Ryan said, "and I'm pretty sure I know who murdered her."

"Uh-huh. Well, good. You can put it into your memoirs. Of course, no one will publish them, but you'll have the satisfaction of knowing you served your country well."

Ryan started to sit up.

"Oh, no, no, no," Sacks said, forcing him back. "You don't have any idea how weak you are. That was a good dose of sedative she gave you. I had the antidote to bring you out of it faster, but you'll have a very severe headache if you don't keep your head down. The fluid in your spinal cord is raging. You remember the stuff . . . $Qx2$."

"What about Mrs. Ross?"

"She'll be fine. She's on her way home. After a while, this will all seem like a nightmare to her, I'm sure. It's not our concern, anyway, Ryan. We weren't sent here for any of that, and you shouldn't have tracked her down. There was no point."

"I was right about her. She was pregnant. She

was the one with the pills. Stocker Robinson got the pills from her house, stealing them when she accompanied her mother one day. She traded them to Lois Marlowe, and Lois Marlowe wanted her to confess. Stocker killed her in a rage and then decided to make it seem as if the Rosses were involved. I suspect she was either planning to or had already begun blackmailing them."

"You're exhausting yourself, Ryan. None of that matters anymore. She killed someone and killed herself."

"But she didn't . . ."

"Goodbye, Ryan. You're going home and then, probably, to traffic direction school. Where," he added at the door of the ambulance, "a Natural belongs, anyway. Hansen, take him home."

Hansen got into the ambulance.

The other trainee went around to the driver's side and got in.

Sacks closed the doors and stepped back. The ambulance was started up and a moment later was off. Following in the direction of the other vehicles, it disappeared under the cloak of a continually deepening darkness.

William Scranton stared at the miniature grandfather's clock on the fireplace mantel. He wasn't staying up and waiting for Hattie out of some deep emotional concern for her welfare so much as he was tired of the way she treated him when it came to her activities as head of the community's baby squad. She never let him even have the illusion that he was more important than her work, much less at least as important. If her work kept her from making their dinner, he had to fend for himself. If there was an event, an invitation they had accepted, and she was busy, the event was sacrificed, even if it was something that had to do with his work or one of his more prestigious patients.

Lately, she had become even more fanatical. It used to be that she would call to tell him she wasn't coming home or that he should cancel whatever arrangements they had made. He appreciated that, even though when she called, she let him know through her tone of voice that it was an inconvenience to bother with him. He should have no doubts that her work was more significant than anything he did. Listening to her, he imagined she was speaking to him in front of her followers, showing them how she treated him, how far down the totem pole he was, and how he would accept and be grateful for the bone she had thrown his way.

Now he didn't even have that bone. He had silence. When she returned, he could ask her where she had been, and she would reply, "Doing work for the community." If he complained, she would chastise him for thinking more of himself than he did of the community's needs.

"How would that look?" she challenged. "My own husband, self-centered? Just think what it would do to your practice here."

She was actually threatening him the way she would threaten other poor slobs in the community, he thought. As the evening wore on, he became more irate. It all festered in him, growing like a cancerous tumor, spreading through his thoughts to the point where he couldn't read, couldn't watch any television, couldn't sleep.

He knew that calling around in search of her would enrage her. She was not incapable of phoning from wherever she was and in front of whoever was with her, chastising him as a parent would chastise a child.

His anger made him frenetic. He paced through the house, straightened up whatever looked messy, went into the garage, and actually began reorganizing things to make more space. While he did so, he focused on the spade he had seen her using the other day to fill in a so-called gopher hole.

He stared at it a moment. How unlike her it was to care, despite what she had said about the potential for some lawsuit if someone stepped into the hole. He couldn't help thinking there was some other reason. Hattie was so secretive about the things she did in the name of the baby squad, making it seem as if she were performing some highly sensitive government spy missions. He was always the last to know what the baby squad did, even though people in the community thought otherwise. Sometimes he pretended he knew just so he wouldn't look foolish or let them know just how little she thought of him.

He lifted the spade and turned it around, thinking about it, and then he charged out the side door of the garage and around to the backyard. He flipped on the floodlights that illuminated the pool, their few trees and bushes, and slowly perused the grounds until he found where she had filled in the hole. It had created a small bald spot in the lawn. He hesitated, looked back at the house, and then, impulsively, angrily, shoved the spoon of the spade into the ground and began to dig up the earth she had so carefully packed.

He wasn't at it two minutes when he heard and felt the spade hit something hard. He dropped the shovel and got down on his knees to claw away the rest of the soil until he saw what looked like something in a plastic bag. Carefully, he dug around it until he could extract it easily and hold it up against the light.

It was a long black flashlight. Why the hell would she bury such a thing? He turned it around for a closer inspection. He couldn't make any sense of it. He started to unzip the bag to take it out and stopped. Maybe he shouldn't touch it, he thought. It was obviously placed in the bag to protect it for a reason. It was evidence of some sort. Why was she burying evidence?

He was torn between putting it back and not, and in the end he decided he would not. He replaced the earth, trying to make it look as close as he could to the way it had looked before, and then he carried the flashlight in the plastic bag back into the garage.

He placed it on his work table and turned on more direct and intense light. Cleaning off the bag, he was able to look more closely at the flashlight. He thought the lens of it looked stained, but he could see no other clue to why his wife would have hidden such a thing. Still, he felt as if he had something over her. When she returned tonight and he questioned her about her whereabouts and complained about how she had left him stranded again, in the dark about where she was and when she would be home, and she started to attack him for having the audacity to question her like some common criminal, he would mention this and see just what sort of reaction he got. He felt certain she would come down from her high horse, and maybe, maybe, she would show him some respect.

He hid the plastic bag and flashlight in the bottom of his tool cabinet and put the shovel back. Then he went inside, cleaned up, and poured himself a stiff scotch and water. He took it to his easy chair and sat waiting, his eyes back on the clock and then shifting toward the front door.

"Come on home, Hattie. Come on home," he

muttered. He felt really good and couldn't remember when he had enjoyed a drink as much. He enjoyed it so much, in fact, that he went and poured himself another, just as stiff, and returned to his chair. The clock ticked on. He anticipated the sound of her vehicle pulling into their driveway, but it didn't come.

Silence stole away his moments of satisfaction and his great anticipation. An hour later, he was sullen again, sullen and tired. He dozed off and woke and dozed off. When he woke again and saw how late it was and realized she was still not home, he dug his fingers into the arms of the leather chair like a convicted murderer being electrocuted. His mouth stretched, his nostrils widened, and his eyes were wide and protruding like those of someone with a terrible thyroid condition.

"Hattie!" he screamed. "Where the hell are you?"

She would drive him mad.

She would drive him into an early grave, he thought.

If he let her . . . if he let her.

But he wasn't going to let her. There was someone he had made promises to sometime ago, promises he was always afraid to fulfill. Tonight he would, he thought, and went to the video phone. He held the flashlight in the bag in front of the camera.

"Hattie buried this in our backyard," he said. "I thought you should know."

The screen went blank almost immediately, and less than ten minutes later, he heard a vehicle in his driveway. He rose and went to the door. Almost as soon as he opened it, the bullet lifted the top of his skull off in a shattering of skin and bone. It was a gruesome death, the sort of assassination carried out by someone driven by hate more than idealism.

From the expression on his face, one would assume his last thought was, *why didn't I just leave well enough alone?*

Close to a half hour after they had left the foundation grounds, CID trainee Hansen closed his eyes and sat back on the seat in the ambulance. The vehicle was practically hovering over the road like a small helicopter, its engine droning along. Ryan could feel the speed. He was being vacuumed out of here, scooped away and deposited in some heap of inconsequence in which he would spend the rest of his professional life. Hilton Sack's smile lingered on his retina like a flash of light that would not dissipate. It was a smile full of ridicule and contempt as well as arrogance. It made Ryan close his eyes and try to swallow down the ugly taste it all left in his mouth. He felt his body harden. He was recuperating a great deal faster than Hilton had assumed he would.

In an instant, he made a decision that he knew could turn him into a fugitive himself and give them all a good excuse to hunt him down and silence him forever, but he suddenly felt trapped. He felt as if he were being squeezed into a box far too small for him and made to bend and twist into something he wasn't, something he would be forever. It wasn't going to happen. He wasn't going to let it happen.

He groaned and seized his stomach, turning on his side as he did so. Hansen's eyes popped open, and he looked down at him curiously.

"What the fuck's wrong with you now?"

"Pain," Ryan said. "Terrible."

"You're not supposed to have any pain."

Ryan squeezed his eyes to grimace with agony and then opened them and looked at his hand. "Blood," he claimed.

"Blood?"

Hansen leaned closer, and Ryan spun on the stretcher so that his left fist came up and caught Hansen smack on his Adam's apple. The blow stunned him. Ryan brought up his legs and caught Hansen's legs behind the knees, dropping him to the floor of the ambulance. Before he could react, Ryan struck him between the legs with his closed right fist. Hansen cringed in real agony, and Ryan struck him behind the head with an open scissor blow that rendered him unconscious. He fell back.

Quickly getting to his feet, Ryan took Hansen's weapon and rapped on the closed window. The trainee driving opened it. With his back to the window, Ryan shouted, "Stop the ambulance and get back here! Hurry!"

"What?"

"Hurry!"

The driver slowed down and pulled over to a stop. The moment he did so, Ryan opened the rear doors and jumped out. As the driver was opening his door, Ryan came up on him and struck him sharply behind the head with the butt of his pistol. The trainee started to sink to the road. Ryan caught him and dragged him to the side. Then he went back into the ambulance and pulled Hansen out, placing him side by side with the driver.

"Sorry, boys. I know this isn't going to go over well for you with Hilton Sacks, but it couldn't be helped. Nothing personal. No hard feelings."

He got into the ambulance and started away. A half hour later, he pulled into the University of Rochester Medical Center. He knew that in a short time, there would be an alert for this ambulance, and driving it on main highways would make it easily discernible. Parking it here on the hospital grounds was the most inconspicuous way to leave it. It would be some time before it was noticed, he was sure.

He hopped out and went around to the rear,

opened the doors, and reached in for his suitcase and his bag. He opened it and quickly located the fingerprint gloves. Hilton had not bothered going through his things. Good. He closed the ambulance door and made his way to the main entrance of the hospital. Less then ten minutes later, he got into a taxi and was on his way to the airport.

This wasn't over. Not by a long shot, he told himself. This wasn't over.

With Natalie still under the effects of a sedative, Preston thought it would be simple and best if he just drove them home, despite the length of the trip. She slept all the way and was still deeply under by the time he arrived at the house. He pulled into the garage and carried her up to their bedroom. She moaned, but her eyes didn't open or even flutter after he put her to bed and brought in her things. That done, he went downstairs and poured himself a double scotch on the rocks and sat at his bar. He was physically tired but still on an emotional roller coaster. The ride back had let him down some, but now that he was relaxed and at home, the whole series of events came tumbling back at him, raging like water over a falls.

He lowered his head to his folded arms on the marble bar. How did all this happen? How did it happen? He couldn't help feeling like someone who had wandered into the path of a hurricane.

For the longest time, all the years of their marriage, perhaps, he was deluded by the calm of the eye of the storm. It was just lying in wait out there, threatening to destroy him and everything he had built. Now it was over, and he was thankful.

It would take time, he thought. Natalie would have to make a significant recovery from all this. Perhaps she never would. No matter how well he explained it, she would never understand, and she would never forgive.

He lifted his head and sipped the remainder of the whiskey, thinking now he might be able to get some sleep.

"She was killed in this house, wasn't she?" he heard, and turned to see Ryan Lee standing in the doorway.

For a moment, Preston blinked and shook his head as if he were seeing a ghost.

"Lee! How the hell did you get here? I thought . . . how did you get here?"

It was as if Detective Lee's physical accomplishment was the most important thing of all.

"I made a necessary detour. You didn't answer my question," he continued, drawing closer to the bar. "She died in this house, correct?"

"Who?"

"I think we both know who, Mr. Ross, but if you want me to say it, I will. Stocker Robinson. In fact," he continued, gazing around the room, "from the way my bloodhound reacted, I would safely consider the scene of the crime to be possibly right here. Well?"

"I don't know what the hell you're talking about, and after all the commotion you caused at the foundation, I would have thought your superiors would have assigned you to lower Slobovia or someplace."

Ryan smiled and took the corner stool. He looked relaxed and cool, which made Preston's anger simmer.

"How did you get into my house?"

"In a moment," Ryan said. "You threw me back there when you warned me about Hattie Scranton coming out of the closet. Actually, however, I think you were surprised about that yourself."

"I was, for Christ's sake."

Ryan nodded, staring at him, infuriating him with his confident smile. "Maybe you were. Maybe murder wasn't ever part of the scenario you envisioned, but it became part of it, and, I repeat, it happened right in this house, correct?"

Preston shook his head. "I don't know what you're talking about, and I don't think I'm going to answer any questions."

"Without the proper procedure, I know. We've been through all that." Ryan reached into his pocket and held up a key.

"What's that?"

"You should recognize it, Mr. Ross. It's the key to your house. How did you think I got in here?

Were you worried that someone gave me your lock code?"

Preston raised his eyebrows. "You found out where our spare key was hidden?"

"Oh, a while back. I followed Stocker Robinson here and saw her put the flashlight into your garage, remember? I saw her fetch the key from under the fake rock, where your wife left it for her mother to have so she could get into your home to do her domestic engineering."

"So?"

"So, I didn't find it under the fake rock. It wasn't there anymore. Do you know why, Mr. Ross?"

"I expect you'll tell me."

"It wasn't there because I found it in the back pocket of Stocker Robinson's jeans when I examined her at the scene of her alleged suicide. Then, when the bloodhound indicated a tracing in this room, I concluded she was in here and with the flashlight, correct? Some cells of Lois Marlowe's blood must have flaked off. The instrument is so sensitive it doesn't take much at all, microscopic, in fact."

It was Preston's turn now to stare, and he did so. Ryan could almost see his mind working, wondering if he should admit to anything, reveal anything.

"I don't know about any murder in this house," he finally said.

Ryan smiled. "That's possible. It's possible you were only told what they wanted you to know," he agreed. The way he did so convinced Preston Ross that he knew more, a great deal more.

"Stocker Robinson tried to blackmail you, didn't she? My guess is the day she ran away from school, she came here to see your wife. No one answered the door, so she got the key and entered. I could check the video phone brain here and in seconds know if a call was made to your office from this location on that afternoon. Was it?"

"I didn't kill that girl," Preston insisted.

"Maybe not, but if you didn't, you called someone after you received the call from Stocker, and that set off the events that brought us together tonight."

Preston started to shake his head.

"Stocker Robinson wasn't the only one blackmailing you, Mr. Ross. She was simply the most obvious and unsophisticated about it. My guess is she wouldn't even have made much of a demand on you, but it was enough that she knew your wife was pregnant and that she was intending to have a Natural. Your whole career, your life here, all that you have, was truly in jeopardy. No, maybe you didn't kill her, but you didn't shed a tear or perhaps even have any regrets about what did happen to her."

"Where are you going with all this?"

"Wherever it takes me," Ryan replied.

"It's going to take you straight to hell, believe me. And I'm not the one threatening you. I don't even have control of the threats or the outcome, even if I wanted it. I'm just as much a pawn in this scenario as you are."

"I'm not anyone's pawn, Mr. Ross. No one's pulling my strings," Ryan said.

"Really?" they both heard, and turned to the doorway.

"It's a regular traffic jam in here tonight," Ryan said.

McCalester smiled. "Boy, you should see the video phones and the laser fax going in my office. You're like one of the ten most wanted or something, Ryan."

"I imagine I am. Actually, I'm surprised it took you so long to get here. I was half expecting to find you in the house with Mr. Ross when I arrived or waiting for me outside."

"Hey, you know this is a helluva job. I don't get enough time off as it is," McCalester complained. He had his right hand resting on his pistol, which was still holstered.

"Yes, you're a busy guy, McCalester. No one could accuse you of resting on your laurels."

McCalester laughed. "I like you, Ryan, I really do. I thought you were just another CID hardass when you arrived, but you have a way of getting under someone's skin."

"I'll take that as a compliment."

"That's the way I mean it, despite the situation."

"Right, the situation," Ryan said. "As chief of police, you have the access code to this house as well as any. Is that how you got in now?"

"Absolutely."

"And that was how you told Hattie Scranton she could get in, too," Ryan said.

Preston turned to McCalester, who just stood there smiling.

"And why would I do that?"

"So she could take care of the problem. Mr. Ross called you as soon as Stocker Robinson called him, I imagine," Ryan said.

"Reaching a bit to save your own rear end, aren't you, Ryan?"

"Don't we all? The night we parted and I staked out the Robinson house, you staked me out, McCalester. You followed me following her and saw her put the flashlight in Mr. Ross's garage. Don't try to deny it. I traced your government-issue tires to the scene."

"I knew I should have let you leave first. I guess I let my discovery get the best of me, the excitement and all," McCalester said.

"Once you saw that, you knew what I suspected was true. You knew Mrs. Ross was pregnant, and you confronted Mr. Ross immediately."

"Is that so?"

"Everyone thinks the baby squad here was run by Hattie Scranton, but you're the one who really runs it," Ryan said. "Oh, I don't think you do it all on your own. I think you take orders, maybe from the rich and the powerful, like your new partner, Mr. Ross," Ryan said, turning back to Preston, "Mr. Cauthers.

"I like to think you really did send your wife to give birth to a natural child, Mr. Ross. Maybe that was truly your intention, and maybe you were betrayed, too, or forced to comply once Stocker Robinson was done in."

Preston simply stared, his lips looking pasted together.

"I know I'm probably deluding myself, but it's the romantic in me," Ryan said. "I'm like your wife. Perhaps it's a characteristic of Naturals. Makes sense when you think about it. We're imperfect, so we can dream, fantasize, fall in love, and imagine other people doing the same. We love people for their failures, their inadequacies, in short, their humanity."

"Ridiculous," Preston muttered. "To cast aside all the great strides and accomplishments man has made just to cling to some illusions."

"It's those illusions that in the end make it all seem like a great and wonderful journey. To run and never have fallen, to laugh and never have cried, to see the sun and never have seen a cloudy day, denies you the wonderful sense of appreciation that can come with accomplishments. Sift through your files to guarantee the state you'll recommend only the qualified people to become parents and, with a sweep of the pen, deny those who would work a little harder, try a little harder, just so they could have a family."

"Wasted energy and, more importantly, wasted social resources," Preston said.

"I'd love to stand here all night and listen to this," McCalester said, "but there are some important people who would like to talk with you, Ryan. Seems you've been on some sort of a rampage, not only killing Hattie Scranton but her poor bastard husband as well."

"Really? What did he discover? Your involvement?"

"What difference does it make now?"

"I wondered why you were never worried about the prints I would find on Stocker Robinson's body. You never asked about them because you knew if I found any, they would be Hattie Scranton's prints. You were a little worried about the footprint I found on the porch floor. When I determined Mickey Robinson didn't go there, I knew whoever it was helped Hattie because Stocker was far too heavy for even a powerhouse like Hattie Scranton to lift, and besides, it would have taken two people to set up that charade."

McCalester just smiled.

"The shoeprint . . . those damn government-issue shoes of yours."

"So far, it looks like my biggest mistakes are

caused by following departmental regulations when it comes to uniform and vehicles," McCalester said, smiling at Preston.

"From the look on Mr. Ross's face here, it would appear he didn't know the full extent of your involvement, not only in this specific murder but as the baby squad enforcer. Don't you see, Mr. Ross, it makes perfect sense to employ someone with McCalester's credentials. He has police power, and he's been here for years and years. Who better to read the community and to do the bidding of the powers that be?"

"Who better to care about the community and its economic welfare, you mean, Ryan."

"Socking it away for that impending retirement, eh?"

"I do my duty for my community, and if I am rewarded well for it, so be it," McCalester said. "Time's up for all this chatter," he added, and drew his pistol. "Let's go, Ryan."

He pointed the pistol at him. Ryan sat there a moment as if he were really deciding whether to be cooperative or simply permit himself to be shot.

"It won't be hard for Mr. Ross and me to claim a rogue CID detective broke into this home and threatened him. Not after all the other things you've done. I came just in time to save the Rosses," McCalester said.

"You go along with that, another murder in your home, Mr. Ross?" Ryan asked him.

His silence was the answer.

"I guess you're just going to have to do it, then, McCalester. The problem for you is that I have transferred all the forensic material to central headquarters, along with my report. It may not be covered up. Your superior might not have the juice."

"You're bluffing, and anyway, he does have the juice," McCalester said. "But just in case he has some difficulties, you're probably right. It would be better to do away with you here and now."

He started to raise his pistol when an almost unearthly scream was heard from the doorway leading to the hallway and stairs. Natalie Ross was standing there in her nightgown, her hands over her ears as if she anticipated the great report from the pistol. Her piercing howl drew McCalester's attention from Ryan, who dropped off the stool and spun around behind the bar. McCalester shot twice, the bullets taking off a chunk of the marble bar and the splintered remnants shattering the mirror behind it.

Natalie screamed again. Preston leaped from his seat and charged at her, embracing her and pulling her from the doorway and the room. Ryan heaved a bottle of soda over the bar and to his left. It smashed against the wall. McCalester turned to it just as Ryan rose and fired his pistol, leaping backward and onto the bar simultaneously. He threw himself over the side, got into a crouch, and peered at the door.

McCalester wasn't there. In the other doorway, Preston Ross embraced Natalie, who had fainted. He scooped her up, and as best and as quickly as he could, he fled toward the stairway.

"What we have here," McCalester called from outside the room, "is a hostage situation. Fortunately, your compatriot Hilton Sacks is arriving any moment with a full contingent of officers, and he's pretty pissed off. You can have the house to yourself for now, detective. It will help us write the story. You know that old adage: History is written by the victors. Besides, how would it look for a Natural to have outwitted a superior Natal like Hilton Sacks?"

He heard McCalester laugh and then heard him go out the front door.

All was silent. Ryan rose slowly and moved toward the front of the house. He saw the lights of approaching vehicles and backed away from the window. There was just enough time to go out the rear of the house, he thought. McCalester was right. They could make it look as if he was holding the inhabitants hostage. He had to get out.

He spun around to do so and faced Preston Ross, who had come silently down the stairway and stood there with a pistol in his hand.

"Drop your gun, detective. Quickly, or I will shoot you. I don't want to, but you heard McCalester. It would be easy to explain it. Drop it!"

Ryan let the pistol fall from his hands.

"Okay, now march yourself to the front door."

"If I step out there, they'll probably let loose," Ryan said. "McCalester will certainly shoot to cover up, so don't delude yourself into thinking you're somehow going to escape being a murderer, Mr. Ross. You were responsible for Stocker Robinson's death."

"She killed another girl and would have done me great harm. I have no pangs of conscience about her."

"What about your wife, your own child?"

"I did what I had to do, and besides, that's not your business. If you had stuck to the simple case, you wouldn't be in trouble now. You lost your focus. A Natal would have been smarter."

"You don't believe that."

"I do."

"Then I do feel sorrier for you," Ryan said.

"Get out of my house. Go on," Preston urged, extending his arm and the pistol at Ryan.

Ryan turned and started for the front door. Outside, the voices of agents could be heard shouting orders, Hilton Sacks's voice above all. A bright light was turned onto the front of the house. By now, they had it surrounded, Ryan thought sadly.

Maybe it was all too much. Maybe he was like the perennial Dutch boy with his finger in the dyke. How do you swim upstream? How do you do battle with an entire society fixed on its new mores and morality, its fervent shift from what was once human to what was now scientific, carrying with it all the weight of that new certainty and confidence that gave mankind no pause when it challenged the very spiritual soul of life itself?

In a strange way, he almost welcomed what awaited him on the other side of that door. If this was the world he had to tolerate, maybe it was better to evacuate. He smiled to himself.

"What's so funny?" Preston asked.

"I feel like you're doing me a favor," he replied, and reached for the door knob.

Preston pointed the gun at the floor and let off a round. The sound of it put the agents and policemen outside into a frenzy. They crouched, threw themselves behind protection, and directed their weapons at the front door.

Ryan opened the door.

But just as he was about to step out, he heard a loud cry of *"Noooooo!"*

As he turned from the door, Natalie Ross charged Preston, hitting him from behind with her hands up. The blow sent him falling forward through the doorway and into the light. He raised his arms quickly, but he held the pistol.

Ryan lunged for Natalie and drove her out of the light that spilled through the doorway and into the entryway. The two of them hit the floor just as the barrage of bullets tore through Preston Ross and slammed in and around the doorway, ripping out chunks of the walls and shattering the window which sent a rainfall of glass all around Ryan and Natalie. It looked like a deluge of diamonds.

The deep, heavy silence that followed made it seem as if God himself were holding his breath.

Epilogue

::::::::::::::

Ryan was not surprised to see the moving van in front of the Rosses' residence. He had swung around from Monticello, the county seat, where he had met with the district attorney and given her his evidence and detailed information on the investigation. Her name was Carla Stickos, and he quickly learned that those attorneys and law enforcement officers who had nicknamed her "Stickler" were not far off the mark. Of course, he couldn't blame her for being as thorough and as demanding as she was with him. After all, she was supposed to go after some very influential members of the community, as well as a chief of police. He could only imagine the weight of pressure she had to carry and sidestep to do her job.

In the end, he actually found himself liking her. There were times when a perfectionist was not only needed but desired. Privately, she let him know how awful she felt the baby squads were, but she was diplomatic enough to survive in a political arena.

The sweetest irony for Ryan came when Hilton Sacks was brought before the CID review board to explain how it happened that he was so easily manipulated by a local policeman to the extent that he and the men under him shot and killed Preston Ross. His eagerness to prove himself superior turned out to be his hubris. Greek tragedy was alive and well in the modern world, Ryan thought. Arrogance, pride, conceit were all still quite infectious, even for the so-called Natals.

It wasn't as easy to bring down Cauthers. Men like that made sure to protect themselves, never to leave their prints or personal marks on anything, and McCalester wasn't about to turn on him. He would need all the help he could get in the days, months, and years to come serving time in one of the state correctional institutions.

Ryan's great sense of satisfaction was tempered by his feelings of regret and sadness for Natalie Ross. She had literally saved his life, and in a different sort of way, perhaps, he had saved hers, but he knew that none of this was ever on her radar screen. Living with all the revelations had to be difficult, especially in this community.

That was why he had practically expected to see the moving van in front.

He parked off to the side and walked up the driveway. The movers glanced at him with little interest. He could see their eagerness to get this job finished and get on with it. Perhaps this house and everyone ever connected to it had become pariahs. Perhaps they thought the bad luck would rub off. He didn't blame them; he never blamed anyone for his or her fears these days. The perfect world had made people softer in so many ways. Rarely having to contend with displeasure, the old diseases, career and social defeats, they lost the old defenses, no longer had the armor plates woven with rationalizations, excuses, and fantasies.

He knocked on the open door jamb.

"Hello?"

Another pair of moving men came down the stairs carrying a dresser. He got out of their way, but as they passed, he asked them if they had seen Mrs. Ross about.

"In the back," the closer mover said, and nodded toward the rear of the house.

Ryan walked down the corridor. Already quite emptied, the house echoed with his footsteps. Someone was bound to get a great real estate bargain here, he thought, and almost wished it were he.

He paused at the rear door and looked out at Natalie Ross, who sat with her back to the house. She was in a big lawn chair, sitting quite straight and gazing at the small patch of woods off to the right of the property. A pair of sparrows not a yard away from her did a dance of delight on the lawn, pecking at some insect food and then soaring off toward the trees. Every time a bird finds something to eat, its heart must be full, Ryan thought. How simply most everything else in Nature is satisfied. Humans are the only pains in the ass.

"Hello," he said, approaching. He didn't want to pop up beside her and frighten her. He knew what it was like to be in a daze, to soak in wonderful warm thoughts and turn off the world around you.

She smiled. "Hello, Detective Ryan. Somehow, I knew I would see you again before I left."

"I've been at the district attorney's office, helping her prepare her prosecution. Actually, I'm on my way back to Albany."

"This is out of the way, though, is it not?"

"Yes," Ryan said, smiling like a little boy caught in a white lie.

She smiled and looked at the trees again. "I was so in love with this place," she said. "I think I was more in love with it than I was with Preston."

Ryan nodded even though she didn't look his way. He could understand why she would say that.

"Maybe you should stay," he suggested softly and with no real expectation of agreement.

"No, it's gone. This place, my so-called good friends who want nothing to do with me. It's all swept away. It looks more like a dream to me already."

She turned back to him. *What a beautiful woman she is*, Ryan thought. In her sadness, in her soft moments of regret, she seemed to be blossoming. How unfortunate the Natals were, he concluded, never having the wonderful pleasure that came from making an absolute fool of yourself because you're head over heels in love with someone and the mere sight or sound of her sends such ripples through your blood your heart sighs. He laughed at his own thoughts.

"What?" she asked, widening her smile.

"I read one of your novels."

"You did?"

"When I first came here, as a way of getting to know you."

"Really? They're just romantic fantasies, oldtime stories hardly anyone lives anymore," she said.

"Actually, I knew as soon as I had finished the book that you were a Natural. I had this sixth sense about it," he said, laughing at himself.

"Really? I thought a CID detective believed in nothing but tangible and empirical truth."

"I'm not exactly the run-of-the-mill."

"You're a Natural, too, aren't you?"

"Yes. Why, does it show?"

"They used to say it takes one to know one. What gave me away?" she asked.

"After I read your novel, I thought, how could anyone created in a natal lab be so filled with such deep yet imperfect emotions, know what I mean? The longing your characters expressed for each other, all the unrequited love, couldn't be learned in some science class or psychology class. It had to be something from the heart, something untouched, not tampered with and destroyed."

"Very perceptive of you. You are a good detective."

He shrugged. "I can only try."

"We all try. You succeed." She smiled. "Humphrey Bogart says that to Paul Henreid in an old movie . . ."

"*Casablanca.*"

"Yes. You know it?"

"Very well."

"He's telling the leader of the French underground how much he admires him, but he's really expressing regret about himself, regret that he isn't trying anymore, that he's lost the hunger for idealism, for hope."

"Yes."

"A lot like people we know today," she said, her smile fading.

"As long as we have it, some of us still have it, we can keep the candles burning."

She turned to him sharply. "That's . . ."

"The last line in your book . . . whenever you look this way, look in the window, we can keep the candles burning."

"I'm flattered," she said, blanching.

"Good. Where are you going?"

"I found this place farther upstate, near the border, actually, a small town full of the most unso-

THE BABY SQUAD 373

phisticated people you can imagine. It's not as grand as this house, but it has a large pond on it, and from what they tell me, ducks and geese come there in the summer months.

"I suppose it doesn't matter all that much. I intend to do a lot more writing, and a writer takes his or her luggage along anywhere. It's in here," she said, holding her hand over her heart. "In the winter, I'll visit with my parents in California."

"Sounds like a plan," he said.

"And you?"

"Well, I think I'm going to get some more challenging assignments, if that's what you mean. I am . . . redeemed," he cried as if he were on some Shakespearean stage.

She laughed. "You're a nice man, Ryan Lee."

He shrugged. "I'm a man, no more, no less."

"Definitely no less," she said. "As hard as that is for them to swallow."

He laughed. "Thanks for saving my life," he said.

"Thanks for saving mine."

"I've wondered . . . how much of that conversation among Preston, McCalester, and me did you overhear that day?"

"Most of it, although I had the suspicions in my heart. I suppose if you hadn't arrived and Hattie Scranton hadn't appeared again, they all might have had me at least doubting."

"I'm sorry you experienced all that betrayal."

"Thank you." She smiled. "But I'm reborn," she said. "You just can't keep a good naturally born woman down."

He laughed and looked at the house.

"Well," he said, "I'd better get moving. Take care."

"Detective," she said as he started away. He turned back. "Track me down one day when you're between investigations."

"I'd like to," he said.

"Good. I'll send you my next book."

"Looking forward to it."

She watched him go and then turned back to the forest for a few more moments before rising from her chair and following.

"No tears," she whispered. "No more tears."

In the trees, a crow, sounding more like a human baby, called after her.

Its voice was seized by the wind as if it had plucked a jewel out of the woods.

Visit
❖ **Pocket Books** ❖
online at

www.SimonSays.com

Keep up on the latest new
releases from your favorite
authors, as well as author
appearances, news, chats,
special offers and more.